MW01067864

GHOSTS OF THE BUFFALO WHEEL

Book Two of the Sam and Gunny Series

Joe Jennings

Ghosts of the Buffalo Wheel Copyright © 2018 by Joe Jennings. All Rights Reserved.

All rights reserved. No part of this book may be reproduced in any form or by any electronic or mechanical means including information storage and retrieval systems, without permission in writing from the author. The only exception is by a reviewer, who may quote short excerpts in a review.

The cover image was obtained from Pixabay.com and is used in accordance with the Creative Commons CCO.

This book is a work of fiction. Names, characters, places, and incidents either are products of the author's imagination or are used fictitiously. Any resemblance to actual persons, living or dead, events, or locales is entirely coincidental.

Joe Jennings
Visit my website at www.ghostsofiwojima.com

Printed in the United States of America

First Printing: June 2018
Amazon

ISBN-9781980726098

This book is dedicated to Clay, Mara, Maia, and Iben.

ACKNOWLEDGMENTS

AMAZINGLY, the folks who gave me so much help with *Ghosts of Iwo Jima* didn't run and hide when I came looking for help with this book. Thanks to David, Bonnie, George, Nan, Mac, Erika, Katie, and Christian, and my newest reader, Monte. And, of course, Betsy, always Betsy.

AUTHOR'S NOTE

THIS IS THE SECOND BOOK IN A SERIES featuring Sam Webber and his Golden Retriever search dog, Gunny. The first book, *Ghosts of Iwo Jima,* recounted their experiences looking for the remains of five Marines on the island of Iwo Jima. Although the story you are about to read refers to the first book in several places, it isn't necessary to have read that book to enjoy this one. I, of course, hope that you will like this story so much that you will get the first book as soon as you're finished.

Both of these books combine historical or realistic fiction with an element of the paranormal. What do I mean by that? Historical fiction takes something that happened fifty or more years in the past and weaves that into a story along with fictional characters or events. An example would be what I imagine may have happened on John Jarvie's ranch in July of 1889 as told in Chapter Seven.

Realistic fiction tells a story with fictional characters and events in a realistic setting. Most of Chapter Four is about the training of a cadaver search dog, and that story is based almost entirely on actual cadaver dog training that I have observed or participated in over the last ten years or so. By the way, everything that the dogs do in this book is based on the actual capabilities of the remarkable animals we call K9s. Well, except for some of the paranormal stuff.

So, what about the paranormal stuff? I like a good ghost story, and I like it better when it sounds believable or plausible. Stephen King is the king when it comes to this. I don't claim to have Mr. King's talent, but I've read enough of his books that, maybe, some of it has rubbed off.

Chapters Five and Seven also have a fair bit of historical fact in them, and I hope you find this interesting and that you are enticed to learn more about the history of the Old West.

And, as always, I hope you enjoy reading this as much as I enjoyed writing it.

Joe Jennings

Eden, Utah

June, 2018

CONTENTS

Joe Jennings

CHAPTER ONE

Notoniheihii

If we wonder often, knowledge will come

Arapaho saying

Medicine Mountain

Bighorn National Forest, Wyoming

Thursday, 2 November

WINTER COMES EARLY at ninety-six hundred feet in the Bighorn Mountains of Wyoming. The ground was snow-covered, and the pre-dawn air had a sharp bite.

The *hiitheinoonotii*, the medicine man of the Northern Arapaho tribe, pulled the Navajo blanket tighter around himself. Sitting on the ground in the middle of the ancient stone circle, he looked to the East. He knew that it would be more than seven moons before the sun would rise behind the cairn across the wheel from him to begin the longest day of the year, but watching the sun come up from this place always reminded him of his connection to the rest of the universe. Medicine men, shamans, spirit guides, healers and

5

others from all the tribes of this land had been coming here since the First People—those who had no iron or horses but had understood the universe well enough to make a wheel that predicted the seasons.

Yesterday had been hard for a man in his seventies. The trail had been snow-covered, steep, and difficult. He and the others had walked in because the road was closed for the coming winter, and because that was the way the *hiitheinoonotii* had always come to this place. He was grateful for the three young men who had carried the tipi and the other supplies even though they had not come voluntarily. The council had given them a choice, help him in his journey to *notoniheihii* or go to jail for using meth on the rez.

Thinking of that day in the council room brought a brief smile to his face. The young men had not understood what the council was telling them— they didn't know the old words. He had explained to them that he must go to *notoniheihii*, the Buffalo Wheel. The young men still did not understand. They thought that they had been given an easy sentence for their crime. They did not know that the trail to The Buffalo Wheel rose from the valley floor to the top of Medicine Mountain more than three thousand feet above, or that they would be carrying everything so that the *hiitheinoonotii* could just focus on putting one foot in front of the other. The young men had been so tired when they arrived that they had gone to bed as soon as the tipi was up and they had started a fire.

At least they still remembered how to make a fire.

There was a time when I could run up that trail and sit here for three days and nights waiting for a vision and then run back down. That seems like a long time ago. I've only been out here for one night this time, and my old bones are aching.

As he waited for the dawn, he was glad that he was not alone. Just beyond the stones across from him, he could see his spirit brother, *hooxei*, the wolf, pacing anxiously.

The *hiitheinoonotii* was an educated man, a cultural anthropologist, and he knew that *hooxei* was not real. He also knew that when *hooxei* sat next to him on a cold night, he could feel his warmth and smell his wild scent.

Many years ago, when he had come here on his first vision quest, a spirit wolf appeared to him at the darkest part of the long night of his third day of fasting and prayer. The wolf had sat next to him and shared his warmth and calming presence. Later, when he told his father what had happened the old man was happy. "*Hooxei* is now your spirit brother. He is strong, and wise, and brave. He will look after you, and you will learn much from him."

On this night *hooxei* was worried about something, just as the *hiitheinoonotii* himself was.

The Buffalo Wheel had been a sacred and peaceful place for millennia. No matter how bitterly the tribes might be fighting, there was never any anger here. In this place, men who had vowed to kill each other could sit quietly, side-by-side, and, sometimes, that peace continued after they had left. For a little while, anyway.

As the first light of the sun bathed the old man's face, he prayed for that peace, but he was afraid that it had been lost. Since the time his grandfather had been the *hiitheinoonotii* something had been wrong here. Most people could not sense it, but the *hiitheinoonotii* and the others like them knew. There was a disturbance, a slight disquiet that the old man feared.

In these days there were so many things that threatened the Arapaho; the loss of the old ways and the spiritual life, the drugs and whiskey, and the squabbling for money from the casino. And of all the things that the Arapaho had to deal with, there was one constant— the white man, always the white man. Over one hundred and fifty years ago the Arapaho had been forced to move onto the Wind River Reservation to share it with the Shoshone. Then, it had been a dry, barren place that took everything the Arapaho and

Shoshone could do to eke out a bare subsistence. Now, that dry land covered deposits of oil and natural gas that the whites wanted very badly. Even here, in this beautiful and sacred place, he could feel their presence. The sea of tall, old-growth timber around him, now frosted with the early snow, would be worth millions if it could be cut and turned into lumber.

He knew that the answers to his people's problems could not come from without, from the material world. No, the ills of the Arapaho came from within and could only be solved from within, from the spirit. He knew that places like *notoniheihii* would be crucial, and they must not only be preserved, they must be made whole.

He had hoped that this trip would bring him some insight, some idea of what to do, but now he saw that he had been wrong. He thought he knew the problem, but he didn't know how to solve it.

I think I'm going to have to get some help.

◆ ◆ ◆

Cowboy Bar

Riverton, Wyoming

Saturday, 4 November

"… so I stick my head out of the tipi, and it's colder'n well digger's ass, and there's the old man sitting out on that stone circle with just a blanket wrapped around him staring off toward where the sun was comin' up. Crazy as a loon, you ask me."

"And then what'd he do?"

"Well, he sat there for a long time until it was light and then he got up, and he had some kind of stick or rod, and he was walkin' aroun' poking that stick in places."

"What kind of places?"

"Hell, I don't know. Up under rocks and bushes and stuff."

Jake Cooley leaned back in his chair and drained his beer while he thought.

In many ways, Jake Cooley was the perfect meth dealer. He was big, six five, two seventy-five, and nasty, with the meanness of a high-functioning psychopath. He could have been a decent defensive tackle, but he'd never liked to work very much. He preferred to find the easy route and, failing that, he would just bull his way through and if somebody got in his way and got hurt that was just fine with him.

The old man thinks there's somethin' there all right, but what? Could the story be real? Could this be his chance to make a big score, the score he needed to get out of this shithole state and out on the coast where a man like him could live in style? Prob'ly worth trading some merchandise to find out.

"Ok, Tonto, listen up."

"My name ain't Tonto, I keep tellin' ya."

Sliding a sealed, white envelope across the table, Cooley continued, "Yeah, whatever. Here's a little somethin' for you and them other two boys, but goddamn it be careful where you smoke this shit. You get caught agin, and you ain't gonna get off easy like you did the last time."

"Yeah, sure Jake, no problem." the young Arapahoe said, "Thanks."

"You keep an eye on that old man, and you tell me when he does anything unusual. And keep your ears open, too."

"For what?"

"For anything that don't sound right. Any stories, or rumors, especially any of that mystical shit the old man talks about."

"Yeah, sure Jake, we can do that."

"Good, but you listen real close here Tonto. Anybody finds out what I got you boys doin' and the three of you are gonna end up as very good little Indians."

"You mean very dead little Indians."

"Yeah, same thing."

CHAPTER TWO

Gunny

We don't rise to the level of our expectations ... We fall to the level of our training.

Archilochus, Greek Soldier, Poet, 650 BC

Mirror Lake County Courthouse

Leadville, UT

Wednesday, 7 March

MR. WEBBER, JUST WHOSE IDEA was it for you and your dog to conduct the illegal search of my client's property?"

"Objection, Your Honor!"

"Objection sustained. Counselors approach the bench."

11

When the prosecution and defense attorneys stood before him, the judge continued, "Ms. Rosswell this is the third and last time I will warn you about your conduct in my court. I don't know how you do things back in New York City, but you're in Utah now, and you will act according to my rules. If you cross the line one more time, I will hold you in contempt, and your stay in Utah may be longer than you anticipated. Is that clear?"

"Your Honor, I ..."

"Is that clear, Ms. Rosswell?"

With her best bored-teenager look, Janet Rosswell, the attorney for Brian Bridges, standing trial for the murder of his wife, replied, "Yes, Your Honor."

Turning to the jury, Judge Howard Stone said, "Ms. Rosswell misspoke, and you should disregard her comment that the K9 search was illegal. As I have made clear previously, the legality of the K9 search conducted on Mr. Bridges property is not at issue here. That search was conducted under a perfectly legal search warrant. The issue that we are trying to address now is whether the subsequent search, which was based, in part, on the K9 search was also legal. Do any of you have any questions about this issue?"

When he saw no response from the jurors, Judge Stone turned back to the two attorneys, "All right, let's continue and let's stick to the issue at hand."

Both replied, "Yes, Your Honor," with different degrees of sincerity.

"Mr. Webber you told the prosecutor under oath that, and I'm quoting here from the record, 'K9 Gunny showed a change of behavior consistent with sensing the presence of human decomposition odor. He walked along the patio with his nose down on the surface sniffing until he came to the edge of the concrete portion of the patio. He then worked along the edge of the concrete to the north for about ten feet until he came to a point where there was a small hole under the concrete. He pawed the ground by this hole several times sniffing rapidly and then gave his trained alert response to indicate the presence of the odor of human decomposition.' Is that, in fact, an accurate description of what your dog did?"

"Yes, it is."

"And what is your dog's 'trained alert response', as you call it, to the 'presence of the odor of human decomposition'?"

"He sits and barks."

"He sits and barks???" Rosswell replied her voice rising in incredulity as she turned toward the jury. "He sits and barks???"

"Mr. Webber, do I understand that you would have us believe that the State of Utah was justified in conducting an invasive search of my client's property that included digging up a very expensive patio because your dog sat and barked??? Really??? Dogs sit and bark all the time, usually for no reason at all. And even more incredibly, you expect me and the jury to believe that your dog has some special ability to smell a body that has been in the ground for fifteen years and your dog was sitting and barking because of this special ability, not because he's just a dog who likes to sit and bark. Do I understand you correctly Mr. Webber? Remember, that you are under oath."

"Yes, you understand me correctly," Webber replied.

Turning to the judge, she said, "I have no further questions for this witness, Your Honor."

"Mr. Prosecutor, do you want to redirect?"

"Yes, Your Honor, I do."

Organizing the papers on his desk before walking to the front of the court, Ed Burrows thought to himself, *Rosswell did a pretty good job sowing*

13

some doubt in the jury's mind. She may almost be worth whatever astronomical fee Bridges is paying her. She's also done a good job keeping the jury ignorant of the fact that the late Mrs. Bridges body was found five feet under the patio, right where the two dogs said she was. She's smart, but she's only been out here for a week, and she hasn't done all her homework. I just need to stay cool, and this'll be a slam dunk.

"Mr. Webber, you're a retired Marine. Is that correct?" Burrows began.

"Yes, Sir. It is."

"So, are you familiar with Article 107 of the Uniform Code of Military Justice?"

"Yes, Sir, I am." Sam Webber had forgotten most of what he knew about the UCMJ, but he and the prosecutor had rehearsed this little act last night, and now he was playing his role.

"Article 107 of the UCMJ," Sam continued, "Prohibits making false official statements and things like lying under oath."

"And it prescribes some pretty serious penalties for violation of the article, is that correct?"

"Objection, Your Honor, irrelevant."

Judge Stone turned toward Burrows so that Janet Rosswell could not see the small smile on his face, "Let's get to the point, counselor."

"Yes, Your Honor. The defense seems to have some concern that Mr. Webber doesn't understand what it means to be under oath, and I just wanted to remind him that civil courts frown upon lying just as much as the military courts he may be more familiar with."

Ed Burrows was not in the least bit concerned that Sam Webber would lie under oath. This whole charade was being played out because he knew, as Janet Rosswell did not, that Judge Stone's first four years after law school were spent as a Marine Corps lawyer, a fact of which the Judge was very proud.

It's called home field advantage, Janet.

"Mr. Webber, now that we've established that you won't lie under oath let's continue."

"Ms. Rosswell doubted that your dog, Gunny, could detect the odor of a body that had been buried for fifteen years, and, I must admit, that sounds a little hard to believe. Yet, in your testimony, you sounded very confident. Can you tell the jury why?"

"Well, this wasn't our first rodeo, Gunny's done this sort of thing before. Actually, he's done things that were a lot harder."

"Can you give the jury an example of what you mean?"

"About a year and a half ago, Gunny was credited with finding the remains of five Marines and one Japanese officer on the island of Iwo Jima who had been missing since March 1st, 1945."

Burrows waited until the surprised murmuring in the courtroom had subsided.

"That's over seventy years ago. That's amazing. Now, I know we've talked about being truthful under oath, but something like this may be a bit difficult for the jury to believe. Do you have anything to support this claim?"

"Yes, Sir. It's sitting right there on your desk."

As Ed Burrows had hoped, that got a small laugh from everyone. The jury would be sure to remember this testimony.

15

"Your Honor, I would like to introduce as evidence this Letter of Commendation sent to Mr. Webber by the Commandant of the Marine Corps, which fully supports Mr. Webber's statements."

Judge Stone nodded assent and Ed handed the document to the court clerk.

"Now, going back to your experience on Iwo Jima, all of the remains you found were underground, and, in fact, two of the sets of remains were in a cave whose entrance had been filled in by rocks and sand. Is that correct?"

"Yes, Sir."

"But rocks and sand aren't as dense as concrete. Is it possible for a dog to detect the odor from a body buried under concrete?"

"Yes, it's done all the time. At the molecular level, where you would find the chemical compounds that make-up decomposition odor, concrete is quite porous. My colleague, Sharon Adams and her dog, Rascal, and many other dogs have found bodies in concrete in both training and actual searches."

"Was Ms. Adams involved in the search on Mr. Bridges property?"

"Yes, she was."

"And do you have direct knowledge of what her dog found?"

"Not direct knowledge, no. We each worked independently so that we would not influence each other."

"Can you explain why that is important?"

"Yes. Dog's are very observant creatures, and they watch their handlers closely and can pick up on subtle clues that the handler may not even be aware of. If I were to watch Ms. Adams's dog work and saw him indicate at a particular place, I might inadvertently give my dog a clue to indicate at the same spot. Therefore, I didn't watch her, she didn't watch me, and the dogs stayed in their crates out of sight when they weren't working."

This was another scene that Ed and Sam had rehearsed. Ed wanted to make sure that the jury knew that the dog teams were following a prescribed protocol that minimized the chance that a dog might give a false alert. Sharon Adams would be Ed's next witness, and he knew that she would testify that her dog Rascal had alerted in the same place as Gunny. Adams, a retired FBI special agent, was a member of the same K9 Search and Rescue team as Sam, and a very experienced dog handler. Her testimony that her dog, Rascal, had alerted in the exact same spot as Gunny would more than double the odds that the jury would believe Sam's statement.

"All right, so odor can seep through concrete and be detected by a trained dog, but presumably there would be many different things under that patio, dead animals for instance. Can a dog discriminate one type of decomposition odor from another?"

Ed was taking a chance here. Rosswell had not introduced the possibility that the dogs could confuse human and animal decomposition odor, probably because she didn't want to talk about there being anything dead under that patio, but Ed knew the question could come up later, so he wanted to get it out of the way.

"Yes, in fact, one of the tests that we take before a team is certified for cadaver search is to place several human bones in among a scatter of bones from a dead deer or some other animal, and the dog has to alert on the human bones and ignore the animal bones."

"And when you say, 'alert,' you mean the dog must give its trained alert response, which, in Gunny's case is to sit and bark. Is that correct?"

"Yes, Sir, it is."

"So you and Gunny have trained extensively on his response to the odor of human decomposition."

"Yes, Sir, we have."

"Can you tell the jury approximately how many times you and Gunny have successfully trained his alert response?"

"I can tell you exactly. I went through the ten years of training logs I have and counted the number of times Gunny successfully found the odor source and gave his trained response, both in training and on actual searches, and the total was one thousand, four hundred, and forty-two."

"So when Gunny is searching he doesn't just sit and bark for no reason."

"No, Sir, he doesn't."

"So, Mr. Webber, how confident are you that Gunny had successfully detected the odor of human decomposition at the spot on the edge of the defendant's patio where he sat and barked?"

"One hundred percent."

"Thank you, Mr. Webber. No further questions, Your Honor."

◆ ◆ ◆

Ogden Valley, Utah

That Evening

"What did Ms. New York City Lawyer look like when the judge allowed the Sheriff to tell the jury about finding poor Mrs. Bridges under that patio?" Rebecca Webber asked her husband.

"She was fidgeting in her seat until the recess and then she couldn't run fast enough over to Ed Burrows to offer a plea bargain," Sam replied.

"So, that slimeball Bridges is going to get off with a manslaughter charge?"

"Yeah, but he's going to plead guilty and get ten years in prison for killing his wife, and later they'll add on all the other charges they're working on," Sam replied.

"But he killed her because she was going to rat him out on all the child porno she found on his computer! Everyone knows he killed her."

"Sure, but knowing and proving are two different things. Especially proving pre-meditation. Plus, back when she disappeared no one knew anything about his child pornography or those kids he abused, so the cops didn't know he had a motive for her murder, and they didn't get all the evidence they could have."

"What does Sharon think about all this?"

"Well, on a professional level she knows that this was the best outcome and that Bridges will get what's coming to him in the long run. Personally, she's pissed. Before she left the Bureau, she worked a lot of child abuse cases, and she hates those guys."

"What's she gonna do?"

"Well, she's getting a chance to put the guy in a hole. The Sheriff is going to have her and Rascal do a thorough search of the house and grounds. If they find so much as a drop of blood, they're going to tear that place apart."

"Why aren't you and Gunny in on this?"

"Rascal has a lower scent threshold than Gunny. He's good at tiny, trace amounts of material like old, dried blood. Plus, I've learned that when Sharon's angry, it's better to leave her alone."

"Coward!"

"I'd rather face a squad of VC than a pissed off Sharon Adams any day."

"I still don't understand why Bridges could be such an evil idiot," Rebecca said. "He's got more money than god, he's got grown kids, three or four houses all over the country, and he has to get his kicks watching child pornography and abusing innocent children. What could make a person be like that?"

"I have no idea, and, fortunately, that's not my problem. I just help find the evidence, and, with the stuff the FBI is finding now about actual child abuse, I don't think Mr. Bridges is going to see any of his beautiful houses or his money ever again."

"That's two murders you and Gunny have helped solve in the past year, what's next?"

"Well that first one shouldn't count, it was too easy. That idiot dragged his brother's body a hundred yards back into the woods and left a blood trail two feet wide. Gunny couldn't have found him any quicker if the guy had put up a neon sign."

"Sure, but you're avoiding the question. What's next."

They both looked across the room to where Gunny lay sleeping on his mat in front of the fire. In the past year, the white fur around his eyes had spread along his chest and sides. He was almost eleven now, and he still had as much hunt drive as he'd had as a young dog, but these days he tired quicker and spent more time curled up asleep.

"I think I can work him for another year, but I've got to be careful especially if we work any large areas. I think he knows he has to take it slower and pace himself, But I've gotta keep an eye on him and not let him over-do."

"And you're not going to get a new puppy like Sharon, and the rest of the team want you to.?"

"No, for two reasons. First, I just can't imagine going out the door to work with a new dog and leaving Gunny behind. No matter how sick or sore he might be he'd want to go, and it would break his heart to be left behind, and that would break my heart."

Sam paused to wipe his eyes. Rebecca pretended not to see.

"And the second reason?"

"I'm almost seventy-one years old. At this age, it wouldn't take much to put me out of action, and it wouldn't be fair to a high-drive puppy to not be able to work because I'm laid up. That plus the fact that there's a good chance that at my age a young puppy could outlive me. No, it wouldn't be fair."

"We won't get another dog after Gunny's gone?"

"I don't think we should get a puppy. When the time comes, I think we should get in touch with the folks down at Companion Golden Retriever Rescue and get an older dog that needs a home."

"And you'd be OK with that."

"Sure, it's time for me to slow down too."

And go crazy inside of a month, Rebecca thought. *I hope something comes up soon to keep these two occupied or they're gonna drive me nuts.*

While The Man and The Woman had been talking, Gunny had drifted in and out of sleep. Each time he started one of his favorite dreams he would hear his name and come partially awake to see if it was Time to Go to Work. Now, The Man and The Woman had stopped talking, and Gunny could get back to his dream. Dogs experience the world primarily through their noses, and they dream mainly of odors, and since he was a puppy, his favorite dream had been of the scent of the first human hand that had held him the night he was born. But tonight he had been dreaming his new favorite dream. He dreamed of the Good Man he had found, the one they called Robby and who smelled like Old Bone, and the time that he and Luke had been with the Good Man and his dog Rusty, who also smelled like Old Bone. He and Luke and Rusty had run together on the soft, green grass like young puppies until they were exhausted. At some level, Gunny knew that this had been something like a dream too, but it had seemed so real. It didn't matter, just thinking about the Good Man, and Rusty and Luke made him feel peaceful and safe, and he slid into a deeper sleep.

CHAPTER THREE

Luke

*We hold these truths to be self-evident: that all men
are created equal; that they are endowed by their
Creator with certain unalienable rights; that among
these are life, liberty, and the pursuit of happiness.*

Thomas Jefferson

University of Virginia

Charlottesville, Virginia

Friday, 9 March

THIS IS INCIDENT COMMAND to all units. Incident Command to all
units. Standby for RF jammer and K9 deployment."

"Incident Command to all units, RF jammer activation and K9
deployment in five…, four …, three …, two …, one …, Now!"

Steve Haney looked down at the black Lab sitting at his side. Luke was calm despite the hundreds of flashing lights and strange men wearing helmets and flak jackets and carrying a variety of weapons running around behind them. Steve then looked over at the base of the steps leading up to the Rotunda of the University where a box about a foot long in each dimension and wrapped in plain, brown paper sat waiting. That was their target, and it was time to go to work.

Steve looked back over his shoulder to a police van about twenty yards away and got a thumbs-up that indicated the RF jammer was powered up and working. A lot of the Marine units that Steve and Luke had worked with during their eleven months in Afghanistan had used radio frequency jammers to make it harder for the Taliban to use a cell phone or garage door opener to remotely detonate an IED. Steve had managed to talk Lieutenant Price, the commander of the Charlottesville police SWAT team, into buying one and using it in a situation like today's. Of course, it shut down everyone's cell phone in about a quarter mile radius and screwed up garage door openers, but no one had complained—yet.

Steve looked at the flags at the entrance to the Rotunda and saw that the slight breeze was blowing across the face of the building from his right to left so Steve pointed Luke to the left and said, "Luke! Seek!" and sent him downwind to begin checking out the target.

The box had been found just after dawn by one of the early arrivals at the Rotunda. Like the previous two, there was a message scrawled on the top in a childish hand with a black marker, "This is a bomb."

Now there were about a hundred members of various federal, state, and city law enforcement agencies gathered around, but none were as close to the box as Steve and Luke. Their job, just as it been in Afghanistan, was to determine if there were any explosives in the box.

A box with a cubic foot of volume can make a big bang if it's full of dynamite and ammonium nitrate, Steve thought.

Lieutenant Price had wanted Steve to wear a full bomb suit like the EOD guys, but Steve had refused. The bulky suit slowed him down and made it hard to see and impossible to hear what Luke was doing, and watching Luke was Steve's primary job.

Besides, Steve thought, *Luke doesn't have any protection, and he's the one out on the pointy end.*

As a concession, Steve wore a helmet and flak jacket.

Steve worked Luke to a point about twenty yards downwind of the box and then walked him past it, keeping about twenty yards away. This was the first pass and, although Luke had quickly figured out what he was supposed to do, he wasn't showing any particular interest in the box.

On the next pass, Steve got five yards closer and still no interest from Luke, but on the third pass, Steve saw Luke focus intently on the box as his nose started sniffing more rapidly. Steve brought Luke downwind again and watched as Luke slowly moved toward the box. When he was about ten feet away, Luke stopped and slowly sat and looked back over his shoulder at Steve.

This was Luke's final alert indication, but Steve interpreted the look on his face to mean, "Yeah, there's something here, but not much."

Steve called Luke and walked him about halfway back toward the vehicles and had him sit and gave him a couple of jerky treats and praised him for being a "Good boy! Good dog, Go Seek."

Luke liked it better when Steve threw a ball for him to fetch as his reward for a good job, but Steve didn't think it would be good for the hundred or so nervous cops to see the bomb dog running.

When they got back to the IC vehicle Lieutenant Price, Chief Thomas and some guy in a suit who had to be FBI were waiting for him.

"What was that all about?" the FBI agent asked before Thomas or Price could speak. "Does your dog know what he's doing? He doesn't look very smart."

Steve looked down at Luke's broadly grinning face and happily wagging tail. Luke's black coat, which almost matched the color of Steve's skin, was marred along one side by a patch of grayish white fur about eighteen inches long, a souvenir of their last firefight in Afghanistan. When Luke wasn't working, Steve had to admit that he looked like your typical happy-go-lucky, goofy black Lab.

"Sir, if you have any questions about Luke's ability you can ask the Commanding General of the Second Marine Expeditionary Force. He's the one who wrote Luke's commendation for finding over two hundred IEDs and a couple of Taliban ambushes during our tour."

What I want to say is, "Fuck you and the horse you rode in on," but the Chief probably wouldn't appreciate that.

"Agent Johnson, this is still my scene, and it's my call. I have complete confidence in my K9 bomb team. Let's hear what Steve has to say."

"Well, Sir, this is a bit unusual. You know on the first two of these boxes Luke said there were no explosives and he was right. On this one, he's saying there's something there, but not a large amount. I think it's safe to send the robot in and blow it."

"When you say, 'not a large amount,' what are you talkin'," Agent Johnson interjected. "A pound, two pounds, what?"

"Sir, if there were a pound of explosives in that box Luke would have smelled it from back here. No, I doubt there's more than an ounce or two in that box."

"Well, Chief, like you said, it's your call, but I think you should wait for an FBI dog."

"Nope, I'm not going to shut down this University and half of my town waiting for another dog. I trust Luke. Lieutenant Price, send the robot."

"Yes, Sir." Then, yelling across to the SWAT van, "Send Tread Head!"

"Steve," Price continued, "Is it OK to turn off the jammer?

"Yeah, even if something goes, it won't be much."

Price yelled again, "Kill the jammer!" A moment later there was the sound of pings all around as delayed text messages were delivered.

Steve watched as "Tread Head," the Department's remotely operated bomb disposal robot, was readied for action. Mounted, as its name implied, on rubber treads, it was one of the smaller and simpler of the ROVs used for bomb work, but it was sufficient for the job at hand. Tread Head mounted a high definition camera and a twelve-gauge shotgun. Its role was to destroy a suspected bomb without exposing an Explosive Ordnance Disposal officer to unnecessary danger.

Tread Head moved forward trailing a fiber optic cable behind. In a couple of minutes, it was in place with the muzzle of the shotgun about a foot from the front side of the box.

On Lieutenant Price's order, the shotgun was fired, and the box blew apart into a blizzard of shredded paper, just like the other two boxes that had been found on the University grounds in the last two weeks. Steve knew what they would see when they examined the shreds of paper—a hundred or so copies of Thomas Jefferson's masterpiece, *The Declaration of Independence*, but he wondered what it was that had gotten Luke's attention and he wandered over to Tread Head's van where he could look at the video screen.

"What do you see there, Ed?" Steve asked the man who was Tread Head's operator and an EOD expert.

"C'mere and look at this, Steve. Our fake bomber is getting cute."

As Steve leaned in to look over the operator's shoulder, he was joined by Lieutenant Price and Chief Thomas.

"See those three little round balls down there in the bottom of the box?"

"Yeah, Ed," the Chief replied. "What are they?"

"I think they're cherry bombs."

"Cherry bombs? You mean the big firecrackers?"

"Yep, you can buy em most anywhere here around the Fourth of July. They've got enough bang to maybe blow off a finger if they went off in your hand, but that's about it."

"Why would he do this if he's the same guy who did the other two?" Chief Thomas asked.

"I don't know for sure," Ed replied, "But I can tell you what I think."

"Go ahead."

"I think our bomber's been watching what we do here. He's probably watching us right now, and he's watched Luke the past two times, and I think he just wants to mess with our dog."

Steve thought for a moment and said, "Yeah, maybe he's just messin' with Luke, and maybe he's testing Luke's ability."

Lieutenant Price replied, "That's kinda scary."

"Either way," said Chief Thomas, "I still don't understand what he's doing or why he's doing it."

At this point, Agent Johnson, who was standing a few feet away, joined in. "Our folks at Quantico think he's got some kind of grudge against

Thomas Jefferson or the University or both. They think he's trying to make some sort of a point, but without any letters or ultimatums or demands we don't know what it might be."

"I think it's just some kid getting a kick out of jerking us around." Chief Thomas said, "But we have to go on the assumption he's serious, and one of these days there's gonna be a real bomb in one of those packages."

Chief Thomas looked at each of the others who all nodded in agreement.

"Anyway, good work everyone. Steve, buy Luke a steak on the Department. He proved himself again today; he called it exactly right."

"Thank you, sir."

◆ ◆ ◆

University of Virginia

Charlottesville, Virginia

Friday, 9 March

An Hour Later

Steve and Luke hung around until most of the cops had left and the scene was clear except for the crime scene techs gathering evidence. The crowd of onlookers, who had been cordoned off across the street, had mostly dispersed, but a few remained, and these curious ones moved closer once the barriers came down.

Steve headed back to his vehicle with Luke on a leash by his side. Steve was only an auxiliary member of the police force, not a sworn officer. He trained with the SWAT team and was called out for anything related to explosives, but he didn't have a patrol vehicle, and he and Luke just rode in his old Bronco.

As he walked, one of the onlookers, a young man who looked like an undergraduate, approached.

"Hey, great dog! I was just watching you guys. Can I pet him?"

There was something in the man's posture or tone of voice that made the hair on the back of Steve's head stand up. He looked down at Luke and saw his nose sniffing rapidly.

"Sure, he's friendly."

As the man approached, Luke's tail was not wagging, his mouth was shut, and his nose was working hard. When the man reached out his hand, Luke took one sniff and instantly sat and looked back at Steve.

The man immediately realized what had happened and jerking back his hand he turned on his heels and began to run.

"Suspect running, suspect running. Officer needs assistance!" Steve yelled.

Four police officers heard Steve's yell and focused on the running man, but he had a head start and was moving fast. Steve was afraid he'd get away when out of the corner of his eye he caught a flash of black and tan moving at high speed.

Zeke was an eighty-five pound German Shepherd and one of the Department's patrol dogs. He was trained to take down a running suspect, and he was very good at it. In a few seconds the man was down and screaming at the top of his lungs:

"Get him off me! Get him off me! He's hurting me!"

Steve and the other officers arrived just as Zeke's handler was commanding, "Zeke! Raus, Raus!" Zeke released the man but stood over him growling.

The senior officer, a sergeant, turned to Steve. "I hope you know what you're doing or we're all gonna get sued."

"Get the crime scene techs over here. That guy's got explosive residue on him and when Luke alerted he knew what was happening and he took off."

◆ ◆ ◆

West Range, Room 31

University of Virginia

Charlottesville, Virginia

Friday, 9 March

That Evening

Luke was curled up by the fire sleeping peacefully while Steve was trying to get caught up on a work schedule that had been thrown out of whack by the events of the morning. There were stacks of paper and a couple of books on his desk more or less separated into two piles. In one pile were undergraduate history essays he was grading in his role as a teaching assistant to Professor Willard Smyth, in the other were notes for his presentation at this week's Twentieth Century American History graduate seminar. He had been working steadily on both tasks since he got back from police headquarters at around three and still had a couple more hours work to do before he could go to bed.

Steve took a short break for a cup of coffee and to relax. He looked around his room and thought of how he enjoyed it here. The room itself wasn't much, it was a little larger than an undergraduate dorm room but still small and spare. The fireplace was nice, but having to go outside to get to the bathroom wasn't much fun, especially in the winter and more so at night if Steve had taken his prosthesis off and had to use his crutches. It wasn't the physical attributes of his room that Steve liked, it was the history and tradition that it represented.

The Range was part of Thomas Jefferson's original Academical Village. It had been built in 1819 and hadn't changed very much in almost two hundred years. In that time, just a little over one hundred students had lived in room thirty-one, and most of them had gone on to successful careers in academia, business, and public life. The most famous former resident was Woodrow Wilson who had lived in this room for two years. Steve sometimes sat in the room's rocking chair by the fire and thought of sitting in the same chair as the twenty-eighth President. It never failed to inspire him and to make him realize how fortunate he was.

Steve and Luke had returned separately from Afghanistan. On their last day in combat, they had alerted the patrol they were with to a Taliban ambush and had probably saved some lives. Unfortunately, they had been out in front when the fighting started and had been hit by a Taliban rocket-propelled grenade. Steve had lost a leg and been evacuated to Bethesda Naval Hospital while Luke had been sent to the military veterinary hospital at Lackland Air Force Base in Texas with a severe wound in his side. They were both medically retired from the Marine Corps, and Steve had adopted Luke.

Steve and Luke had taken an unusual sabbatical from school to join Sam Webber and Gunny on the search for five Marines still missing from the battle of Iwo Jima. Their job had been to clear unexploded ordnance in the search areas, and Sam credited Luke with saving Gunny's life. To show his gratitude, Sam had commissioned a beautiful portrait of Luke, which was hung proudly above the fireplace.

Before leaving for Iwo Jima, Steve had been accepted into the Ph.D. Program in the Corcoran School of History and had applied for one of the prestigious Range rooms. While he'd been overseas, he hadn't been able to follow up on his application, and he knew that the competition for Range rooms was intense, especially if you were requesting a waiver to have your dog in with you. When they got home, Steve was pleasantly surprised to see that not only had he and Luke been accepted into the Range but into one of the more sought-after rooms.

I guess it pays to have a war-hero dog on your room application, Steve thought when he read the letter from the Range committee.

Because Steve considered himself so fortunate, he had a hard time understanding a young man like Jeff Phillips, the one the news broadcasts were now calling the "Phony Bomber."

After Park's arrest, Steve and Luke had gone with the SWAT team to Parks' apartment off-campus. Luke had alerted at the door, and SWAT had spent two hours sending in Tread Head to search the rooms after first evacuating the entire building and the buildings on both sides. Tread Head had found three suspicious boxes that turned out to each contain a hundred or so cherry bombs, more than enough to allow the FBI to bring charges of domestic terrorism. It was also enough to explain how Luke had smelled explosive residue when the man had tried to pet him and would provide plenty of probable cause to justify the arrest.

Phillips was a kid from the affluent Northern Virginia suburbs of Washington, D.C. He had been handed the perfect life on a platter. He had gone to the best schools and been given the best opportunities to learn and grow. He should have used his time at UVA to prepare himself for some meaningful career. Instead, he had been dismayed to learn that he was expected to work and meet high academic standards. He was also required to adhere scrupulously to Virginia's Honor Code. When he failed to do that and was caught cheating on an exam he was brought before the Honor Court and, when his guilt was established, was given the only possible sentence, immediate dismissal from the University.

Before he left headquarters, Steve had learned through the cop grapevine that Phillips hadn't bothered to tell his parents he had been kicked out of school. Instead, he had spent the last couple of months, and the money his parents continued to send him, drinking, trying various drugs and plotting revenge against both the school in general and Thomas Jefferson in particular. Phillips was one of those people who had to blame someone else for whatever mess they managed to get themselves into. Now he was in the Charlottesville jail waiting for the lawyer his parents were sending, and vowing to sue everyone in the city government for police brutality. Evidently, Mr. Phillips did not believe that his harmless pranks justified being attacked by an angry German Shepherd.

As Steve thought about Phillips, he had no sympathy for him. *I met too many kids Phillips' age in the Marines who had to work their ass off for everything they had and still turned out to be decent, brave men. What the hell happens to cause someone to be like Phillips?*

As usual, whenever he thought about the Marine Corps, his thoughts turned to Sam and Gunny and the rest of the team and what they had done together on Iwo Jima. *What Luke and I did there was one of the highlights of my life so far. I wonder what those guys are doing now. I need to give Sam a call and see how Gunny's doing. I wonder if I can work out some way to get out to Utah and see them. I bet he'll be surprised to see what Luke can do now.*

While Steve had been an undergraduate, he had volunteered with Luke as an explosives detection team with the Charlottesville PD. When they had returned from Iwo Jima, he had been offered a position as an auxiliary member of the SWAT team, which was essentially a paid, part-time job. He and Luke trained with the team and were on call for any actual incidents potentially involving explosives. The problem, or blessing depending on your point of view, was that those types of events didn't come up very often, so Steve looked for something else to do.

Steve contacted the Virginia Search and Rescue Dog Association and asked about getting some additional training. The folks at VSARDA were happy to help, and it didn't take long to train an experienced dog like Luke to work with new target odors. Now Steve and Luke were certified by the National Association for Search and Rescue for cadaver and human remains search.

I think I'll give Sam a call and see what he's doing this summer. I'd love to see him and Gunny again, and I'm curious how Luke will match up to Gunny as a cadaver dog.

CHAPTER FOUR

Iwo

Happiness is a warm puppy.

Charles M. Schultz (Peanuts)

Cordelia Camp Building

Western Carolina University

Cullowhee, North Carolina

Thursday, 15 March

"OK," DOCTOR ALICIA PHILLIPS SAID, "I'm going to show you three last images that I think summarize the points I've been making in the rest of the presentation."

"The first photo is of the area around the north end of the gully that ran along the eastern side of the Amphitheater. The ground here is typical of the terrain in this part of Iwo Jima; rock mixed with dark, volcanic sand with sparse, low vegetation. Looking at this photo, there is no way to tell that below the surface are the remains of three Marines and two Japanese soldiers who died near there on March 1st, 1945."

"The next photo is the same area after Gunny and Luke had done their preliminary search. The red flags outlining the area mark the places where Luke showed interest, probably based on the scent of explosive residue from the ammunition and grenades that the men had carried. Inside the red flags, those green flags showed Gunny's points of interest based on the very faint scent of seventy-three-year-old human remains. You can't see it in this photo, but three of those ten flags are marked with an "X", which indicated that Gunny had gone to his trained final alert at these points."

"This last image is taken from the Ground Penetrating Radar System that we used. It shows what was below the surface directly under one of Gunny's X-marked flags. The image is two feet on a side, and it goes down about four feet. The three articles circled in green are human remains, the long one in the right corner there is a humerus from one of the Japanese. The four items circled in red are .30-06 caliber bullets that would have been carried by the Marines."

"The lesson I take from these images and that I'd like you to take from my presentation is that Gunny and Luke were absolutely essential to the successful accomplishment of our search. If Gunny had not found that human ilium that we later determined was from Corporal Jeff Hanks on our first search day, we probably would have wasted most of the limited time we had wandering around this huge search area just trying to figure out where to look. Without Luke's explosive detection work we would have been exposing ourselves to a significant level of risk."

Looking at the twenty or so future forensic anthropologists filling the classroom Alicia knew that her presentation, "Bringing Home the Heros of Iwo Jima," had gone well. The audience had been attentive throughout, and she could see that several of them were anxious to ask questions.

"Any questions?"

"Doctor Phillips, you said that K9 Gunny got the scent of that first piece of bone, the ilium, from almost seventy yards away, but then indicated that he had to be much closer to find the other remains. Can you explain why that was?"

OK, Alicia thought, *these kids are smart. Gotta be careful here.*

"No, I'm not sure that I can explain that first find because you're right, Gunny should have been much closer to get that scent. He must have just caught something on a puff of wind and followed it to the source. Never forget that sometimes you just need to get lucky, although I'm sure Gunny would have found that bone anyway, as he got closer to it."

Lucky my ass. Gunny found that bone with help from the ghost of Robby Durance, but there's no way I'm going to say that here, or anywhere else for that matter.

"Next question."

"Doctor, did your dog participate in that search?"

Alicia looked over to where Iwo, her not-quite-year-old Golden Retriever, lay quietly on his mat. Iwo had been there throughout Alicia's hour-long presentation with hardly a sound. *Thank you, Sam and Sharon*, she thought.

"No," she replied with a smile, "Iwo hadn't been born then. He was a gift from Gunny's handler, and I'm training him, with a lot of help, to work with me at crime scenes."

After several more questions, Professor Adams, whose class this was, stood up.

"Ladies and gentlemen we've already gone fifteen minutes over our schedule, and I know that some of you have other classes to get to. Doctor Phillips will be here over the weekend attending the cadaver dog workshop, and she has kindly indicated that she would be happy to answer additional questions if you can find her during her free time. Now, let's show Doctor Phillips how much we appreciate her interesting and informative presentation."

After the applause had died down and she had shaken hands with Professor Adams and a few others Alicia walked over to Iwo and, clipping a leash to her collar said, "C'mon, Iwo. Let's get you out for a walk." Although he was well-trained, Iwo was still a puppy, and he responded with a joyful bark and a lot of jumping up, which Alicia tried to discourage without much luck.

A few minutes later after Iwo had run off some of his energy exploring Cullowhee Creek the two continued to walk side-by-side, and Alicia's thoughts turned to the coming weekend.

Starting tomorrow, I'm going to be taking my eleven-month-old, partly-trained dog into a class intended for certified cadaver dogs where he will be introduced to full-body human remains for the first time. What was I thinking?

This is all Sam and Sharon's fault.

♦ ♦ ♦

Ogden Valley, Utah

Friday

The Previous October

After the tenth time or so that Alicia had called Sam with a question about training Iwo, Sam had suggested, with some exasperation Alicia thought, that it would be best if Iwo got some hands-on work with an actual dog trainer.

This idea turned into what Sam was now calling, "Cadaver Dog Boot Camp."

Alicia and Iwo were in a field that was a mix of open and sagebrush-covered areas near Sam's home. Sam had just introduced Alicia to Sharon Adams whom Sam had asked to help get Iwo started with her training. In addition to her years of experience working with cadaver dogs, Sharon was also a certified dog trainer.

Sharon was a tall woman with a solid, athletic build. Her shortish, brown hair was pulled back in a no-nonsense ponytail, and her face was set in a serious look. Alicia knew that Sharon had to be in her mid to late forties because she had retired from the FBI, but she could have passed for thirty-five.

She's a little bit like a larger version of me, Alicia thought.

"So, what will we do first?" Alicia asked.

"First, we're gonna test your dog because I'm not wasting a bunch of time working with a dog that hasn't got what it takes," Sharon Adams replied.

Alicia glanced over at Sam who was looking on with a slight smile.

OK, you're the good cop, and she's the bad cop. Got it.

Alicia was used to being the alpha female, hell, the alpha anything, in just about any situation, but now she knew that she had a worthy competitor. This could be fun.

"Ok, what do you want us to do?"

Sharon looked hard at Alicia, "Let's see if he has any prey drive. Let me have your dog, and give me his favorite toy."

Sharon took Iwo to a spot about twenty yards away and gave him a "Sit." She then showed Iwo his toy, which started him wriggling in anticipation. Sharon then threw the toy about ten yards away, and Iwo ran after it, grabbed it and looked back at Sharon.

Sharon commanded, "Iwo! Come!" and got no response. Again, "Iwo! Come!" with the same result.

"What's the matter with your dog?"

"Uh, he likes to play keep-away."

"Search dogs don't play keep-away. What's his command to release?"

"Drop it."

Turning back to Iwo, Sharon said in a low, even tone, "Iwo! Sit!" Iwo looked confused for a moment and then slowly lowered his butt to the ground.

"Oh, you're going to do that a lot faster before I'm through with you, young man."

Sharon walked forward to a point about five feet from Iwo and in the same tome of voice commanded, "Drop it!"

Iwo gave this new person, who spoke so differently than anyone else, a confused look and then lowered his head and dropped the toy on the ground.

Sharon immediately put a big smile on her face, and her voice went up two octaves, and she said happily, "Good boy, Iwo! Good boy, drop it!"

Iwo still looked a little confused, but now his tail was wagging.

"Ok, puppy, let's try this again."

Iwo learned quickly and, after two or three more tries, was running enthusiastically after the toy, bringing it back and dropping it at Sharon's feet. Sharon kept the exercise going until Iwo had done it ten times and his tongue was beginning to hang out.

"I have a question," Alicia said when Sharon brought Iwo back to her.

"Shoot."

"He picked up on what you wanted him to do after a couple of tries. Why did you keep going like that? Were you reinforcing the behavior?"

Sharon looked at Alicia with a little less hostility than before, "No, he's a smart dog, and he'll learn quickly. You're the one I'll need to work on, but this wasn't about training, this was testing, remember? One way to evaluate prey drive is by throwing a toy repeatedly to see if he chases it as enthusiastically the tenth time as he did the first time. Most dogs will lose interest after the fourth or fifth try, a good dog will go seven or eight. Iwo ran hard for ten out of ten, so the first indication is good."

"Great! What's next."

"I want to do a hunt drive test, and then I'll work him on some uneven surfaces to see how confident he is in an unusual situation. I won't bother with testing sociability. He's a Golden Retriever for god's sake, he couldn't be unsociable if he wanted to. We'll do a few other tests, and I'll know in an hour or so what he'll be able to do. Before we go on, though, give your dog some water."

"I didn't bring any water, I didn't know…"

Sharon cut her off, "Look, you seem like a nice person, and you're obviously smart, but you're starting at level zero as a dog handler. Ninety percent of problems with dogs can be traced back to something the handler did or failed to do. Your dog is watching you every moment, and he'll pick up on every little cue you give him from your body language to your tone of voice to the way you smell. You have to think like an actor who's on stage

42

constantly, and your dog is your audience. I think you may have a good dog here. The question is whether you're willing to do the work you need to do."

"I'll do what it takes to make Iwo successful as a crime scene dog."

"Good. Lesson One, water. Always, always have water for your dog. If Iwo has the kind of drive I think he does, he'll push himself to the limit and beyond when he's working. That means that he's likely to ignore little inconveniences like dehydration and impending heat stroke. It's your job to keep your dog healthy and working. Let's take a break and go over to my vehicle and get him some water."

An hour later Sharon had satisfied herself that Iwo could be, "…maybe as good as Gunny, but not Rascal." Now Sharon and Sam focused on basic commands working Iwo over and over on "Come!" "Sit!" "Down!" and, most difficult of all, "Stay!"

Throughout the training Sharon had Sam focus on Iwo while she worked with Alicia continually coaching her on tone of voice, posture, gestures, eye contact, and a lot of other things that Alicia would have thought were unimportant until she saw how much difference they made in Iwo's behavior.

After two hours it was time to give Iwo a break. That didn't mean that Alicia stopped training. Back at Sam's house, Sharon set up her laptop and started working Alicia through a series of presentations on everything from scent theory to canine nutrition. When she began to talk about crime scene investigation, Alicia interrupted her.

"Wait a minute, Sharon, I think this is something I know more about than you do."

After Alicia spent thirty minutes giving her own presentation based on her years of experience with the Tennessee State Bureau of Investigation Sharon grudgingly admitted that Alicia was right.

After everyone got tired of sitting and looking at computer screens they went outside where Sam and Sharon demonstrated how to train and reinforce a cadaver dog's alert indication.

They went back to work with Iwo that evening. For two hours they trained him for fifteen minutes followed by fifteen minutes of rest and then again to work. Doing this kept Iwo fresh and eager to work.

I'm glad my dog is happy to work because I'm dragging ass, Alicia thought.

◆ ◆ ◆

Ogden Valley, Utah

Two Days Later

It was early Sunday afternoon when Sam and Sharon agreed that they had done as much as they could in two and a half days. Iwo had been introduced to cadaver odor and had been taught to sit and bark when he found it. His response to commands was almost immediate, and he had learned that when his vest went on it was Time to Go To Work. Iwo had a solid foundation for the rest of his training.

Now Alicia and Sharon sat with Sam and Rebecca on their patio enjoying the views of the fall splendor of the Ogden Valley, working on their second bottle of Pinot Grigio, and talking about human post-mortem decomposition.

Why can't I have a nice, normal husband who just likes to watch football on Sundays?

"I thought Iwo did very well when we introduced him to cadaver odor," Sam said.

"Yeah," Sharon replied, "He's a typical Golden, really likes the smell of dead stuff and wants to get his nose right on it."

"And he's starting to get the idea of how to use the wind to search, and he's got a good start on his alert indication," Sam continued, "What's the next step?"

"You mean besides repeating all these exercises a few hundred times until he's got it down pat?"

"Well, yeah, that."

"I'm not worried about his ability to search," Sharon replied, "He's a, what, second cousin of Gunny's? He'll know how to hunt, no problem. No, I think the next step is to get him exposed to full body odor, which, as the learned Doctor Phillips has pointed out to me—repeatedly—is significantly different than any single sample of tissue or fluid."

"If you would listen to what I say the first time," Alicia chimed in, "I wouldn't have to repeat myself so often."

Watching the women talk, Rebecca was amazed that these two, who could be such hard-asses, were talking as easily and casually as old friends. *It has to be the dogs*, she thought, *there's something about working with dogs that brings people together.*

"Can't they just go to the Body Farm at Tennessee, I mean, you teach there Alicia," Sam said.

"Unfortunately, that's not an option," Alicia replied, "the University has a long-standing policy of not allowing dogs into the ARF, and they won't waive it, even for one of their Professors."

"I'm sorry, what's the ARF?"

"It's the Anthropological Research Facility at the University of Tennessee, which is the proper name for what your husband so crudely refers to as a Body Farm. It's the first of its kind in the world, and it's the source of a lot of the data used by crime scene investigators everywhere. It's an amazing facility, but some of its policies are a bit out-dated."

"But, uh, Alicia, weren't you instrumental in writing some of those policies?"

"Yes, Sam, that was before I went to Iwo Jima with you and Gunny and saw what these dogs can do. Now I'm up against some faculty members who are just as misinformed and pig-headed as I was. As you well know."

"Yeah, I know," Sam said, "I just enjoy hearing you admit it."

Alicia paused to give Sam the finger before continuing, "Now my only real option is to go to the cadaver dog training program at Western Carolina like you and Gunny did, but Iwo won't be old enough to get into their Spring course."

"I don't think that'll be a problem," Sam replied, "especially if you're willing to give your lecture on our search at Iwo Jima."

♦ ♦ ♦

Western Carolina University

Cullowhee, North Carolina

Friday, 16 March

The course started in the classroom. As Sam had predicted, Iwo had been welcomed into the program even though he was a month under the minimum age. Also, Alicia's seminar fee had been waived. The price was that Alicia once again stood before a room full of knowledgeable people and had to describe what had happened on Iwo Jima without talking about the ghost who had helped them or the demon who had tried to kill Gunny. It made for some tense moments, but Alicia thought that she had managed to bluff her way through it.

Classes on human decomposition and search theory took them to the lunch break. After lunch, Alicia was on stage again to give an overview of crime scene investigation. At two o'clock it was finally time to do something outside with the dogs, and everyone was eager to get started.

The rest of the day would be spent working on each dog's alert indication. Thanks to Sam and Sharon, Alicia thought that Iwo's was pretty reliable, but the difference here was that he would be working with much larger sources than he had seen so far. Not full bodies, not yet, but large enough.

The first time Iwo encountered a human leg inside a mesh bag hanging from a tree, there was so much more odor than he was used to he wasn't sure what to do. He hesitated to approach it and, when he did, just circled it sniffing rapidly.

The instructor assured Alicia that this was perfectly normal behavior and that Iwo was doing precisely what they hoped he would. She told Alicia to give Iwo a minute or two to check things out and get more comfortable with this new experience. After circling the tree several times, getting a little closer each time, Iwo finally stopped and looked back at Alicia.

"Alicia, tell him what to do and get ready to reward him."

"Iwo, sit!"

Iwo looked at Alicia as if he had no idea what she was saying. Alicia was about to repeat her command, but the instructor said, "Give him a second, he's processing."

A moment later, Alicia could literally see the light come on in Iwo's eyes as he put it all together. Iwo's face broke into a broad grin, he plopped his butt on the ground in a perfect "Sit," lifted his muzzle to the sky and gave three loud barks.

"Yes! Good boy! Good boy, Iwo!" Alicia cried as she walked quickly forward to give Iwo his treat.

"OK," the instructor said, "Now give him a treat right under the source. Good. Now right next to the source. Perfect. Good job both of you."

Before they left to go to the next station, Alicia had a question, "So, it's pretty stinky over there. I'm used to it, but don't you get some handlers here who haven't been exposed to large source cadaver odor?"

"Oh sure. That's why I keep a small jar of Vicks Vapo Rub handy. They can smear some under their nose, and it helps— psychologically, at least."

"Good idea. I've probably spent a month's salary on Vapo Rub for my students over the years. Hey, this was great. Thanks for your help."

"You bet."

They did three more training stations that afternoon. At each one Iwo was presented with a new odor source and went through a similar learning process. The *piece de resistance* was a large Tupperware container filled with human viscera. This source produced not only a lot of scent but an odor that was unique. Iwo was very unsure about this whole thing, but he was figuring things out. With just a little coaxing from Alicia, he sat and barked right next to the container.

That evening the trainees and instructors went out to dinner in Cullowhee. They got more than a few quizzical or disgusted looks from other patrons who were able to overhear their conversation.

The next day the class split into two groups. Alicia's would spend the day working with large odor sources in a variety of situations; in vehicles, in barns filled with manure, in buildings, and in trash dumps. The

48

plan was to expose the dogs and handlers to as many different odors and situations as possible. The idea was that if a dog could learn to ignore the smell of thirty years or so worth of manure and detect the source hidden behind the manure pile, they should be able to find their target odor just about anywhere.

The other half of the class went to the FOREST, the Forensic Osteology Research Station, Western Carolina's very own body farm. The next day it would be Alicia and Iwo's turn.

◆ ◆ ◆

FOREST

Western Carolina University

Cullowhee, North Carolina

Sunday, 18 March

The final day of the course again started in the classroom. Before anyone was allowed into the FOREST, they had to understand the protocols for appropriate behavior, especially if they were bringing a dog in with them.

Alicia learned that all of the bodies in the FOREST, and all of the remains that they had been working with for the past two days, had been donated by individuals for the advancement of science. Permission had been obtained from the donors or their families to include using their remains for the training of cadaver dogs. Part of the University's promise to the donors was that their remains would be treated with respect and dignity. Everyone entering the FOREST, including the dogs, would be expected to act professionally. Photography was strictly forbidden, and cell phones would be left outside.

The FOREST itself was small, a sixty-foot square surrounded by two fences, an inner privacy fence and an outer protective fence topped by barbed wire coils. There was no roof or overhead shelter, the intent was for the remains to be exposed to the elements. On this particular day, there were sixteen sets of remains inside the FOREST, thirteen on the surface and three buried. The newest remains had been there for two weeks and were well into advanced decomposition. The oldest was about two years old and completely skeletonized.

The placement of the remains depended upon the objectives of the research they would be supporting. Some were naked, some were fully clothed. Some were shaded under brush, some were in the open. While the dogs were working there would be students in the FOREST collecting data from various subjects.

Alicia wondered how Iwo would react to all this. There were a lot of ways that Iwo could do something inappropriate, and she'd have to watch him like a hawk. Most of the handlers, including Alicia, planned to work their dogs on leash to give them more control. This meant that the handlers would have to get up close and personal with the bodies. That didn't bother Alicia, but she could see that some of the others were apprehensive.

When it was all over, there had nothing to worry about. Iwo's natural curiosity had overcome his unease at being surrounded by so much odor of so many different types. He had been very wary approaching the two-week-old corpse, but when he did he sat and gave a loud bark, and the instructor said he had performed like a veteran.

The last thing Alicia did before leaving for home was to take Iwo for a long swim in the creek and then go to the gym, take off all her clothes and put them in a large garbage bag and take a long, hot shower. Back at the car, Iwo went into his crate, and the bag of clothes went into the rooftop carrier.

No sense smelling cadaver odor all the way home if I don't have to.

CHAPTER FIVE

Joseph Golden Eagle

"... nits make lice."

Colonel John Chivington of the Colorado Militia to justify the killing of Arapahoe and Cheyenne children at the Sand Creek Massacre November 29, 1864

Brigham Young University

Provo, Utah

Monday, 19 March

"GOOD MORNING. DOCTOR STEWART?" The man standing at the open office door was tall with reddish-dark skin. His black eyes had an Asian cast, and his large, hooked nose dominated his face. His long hair was coal black, streaked with gray and tied into a ponytail. He wore jeans, a plaid shirt, and cowboy boots. He was, very obviously, an American Indian.

51

"Yes! Doctor Golden Eagle, how nice to finally meet you."

"Joseph, please, Doctor," the man replied as they shook hands.

"Joseph, then. Jim Stewart. Please, have a seat."

As he took his seat, Joseph Golden Eagle took a moment to study the man he had come to see. Jim Stewart did not look like the photographs of him in the University directory. That man looked like a typical professor of history with bright, intelligent eyes, unruly blond hair, and a face that was a little soft and pudgy. The man who sat across from him now had the same eyes and hair, but his face was lean and tan. He looked fit, and his handshake had been firm. *This is a man who's had some significant change in his life. I expect I know what it was.*

"May I get you some coffee?"

"That would be great, thanks, but I thought that Mormons didn't drink coffee."

"Yes, you're right, but not everyone who comes to my office is a Mormon, and I try to be a good host. Do you take anything in it."

"No, thank you, black is fine." *He seems like a man who is confident and open to new ideas. I hope so, or he's going to think that I'm a fool, or crazy, or both.*

When they had settled into their chairs, Jim continued, "When we talked on the phone you said you had a problem that you hoped I could help you with, and you implied that it was an academic problem. I must admit that I'm not sure how a professor of Twentieth-Century History can help an esteemed professor of Social Anthropology, but I'm eager to hear what you have to say."

"Well, Jim, I've read a lot about you, and I'm here less because of what you do for a living than because of your other interests."

"Other interests? Such as?"

"First, I know that you're an avid student of the early history of the American West."

"Yes! That's been my hobby for many years. I know it sounds funny that someone would have a hobby so similar to what he does for a living, but I guess that's just the way my mind works. I've always been especially fascinated by cowboys and Indians, I mean Native Americans, sorry."

"Don't worry about the whole Indian, Native American thing. Most of the Indians I know don't care what your people call us. Those that do care would prefer to just be called by the name of their tribe."

"Thanks. And you're an Arapahoe, right? From up on the Wind River Reservation.?"

"Right. Northern Arapahoe to be precise but we've been called many names by many different people over the years, so we're not too picky."

"Back to why I think you can help me. Your interest in cowboys and Indians extends to the western outlaws, right?"

"Oh, don't get me started on outlaw stories, I could talk your ear off. Yes, they are a special interest of mine. Is that why you're here?"

"In part. I'm also here because of what you and your friends did on Iwo Jima."

"Really? Wow! That was one of the great experiences of my life. In fact, I think I would call it a watershed. Before Iwo Jima, I had thought that I could find out everything I needed to know by reading enough books. On Iwo, I learned that I got an entirely different perspective on things when I got down on the ground and got my hands dirty and was able to see things from the standpoint of the original participants. Now I try to get out to the scene of whatever I'm studying, and I've found that I enjoy it. What do you know about what we did there?"

"I know what I've read. That you and Professor Okada from the University of Tokyo were instrumental in identifying the most likely search areas and that you helped piece together the clues that led your team to find those five Marines and the Japanese officer."

"Well, we identified the general areas, but it was our dogs, Gunny and Luke, who get the credit for finding all the remains."

"Yes, and that's another reason I'm here."

"I'm not sure I understand."

"Let me continue, and I hope it will become clear. The last reason I'm here is a bit ... delicate. May I close the door?"

Jim looked warily at his guest but nodded.

"So, I need to give you some background. I'm sure that you're aware that all of the native tribes have some strong spiritual beliefs and that we believe in actual spirits. In particular, we believe that the spirits of the dead can be an ... unsettling, even evil influence."

Leaning forward in his chair, Jim looked straight into Joseph Golden Eagle's eyes, "Yes, I'm aware of that," *And I hope you're not going where I think you're going.*

Seeing the tension on Jim's face, Golden eagle continued, "Jim, I'm sorry. I don't mean to cause you any problems, and I give you my word that everything we say here, stays here. May I continue?"

After a moment Jim nodded slowly.

"There are some rumors going around in certain academic circles that some unusual things happened on Iwo Jima. Things that can't be explained by science. Spiritual things. And somehow, I have no idea how, these rumors got to our *hiitheinoonotii*, our medicine man, who also happens to be my uncle."

"What did your uncle say?"

"He told me, and this is a quote, 'Those people on Iwo Jima fought an evil demon to bring their warriors home. I think we need their help.'"

♦ ♦ ♦

Ogden Valley, Utah

Monday, 19 March

Three Hours Later

"Sam, Rebecca, thanks for seeing us on such short notice."

"Nonsense, Jim," Rebecca replied. "You're always welcome here."

Rebecca walked forward toward Joseph with her hand outstretched, "Hi, I'm Rebecca Webber. Welcome."

"Mrs. Webber, I'm Joseph Golden Eagle."

"Doctor Golden Eagle, what a pleasant surprise! I've read a couple of your books. This is my husband, Sam."

After everyone had settled in the living room, Sam spoke first.

"OK, Jim. What's so important that you and Doctor Golden Eagle had to rush up here from Provo for?"

"I think I should let Doctor Golden Eagle explain."

"I'll be happy to, but first, please call me Joseph. You may not think much of my academic credentials after you hear what I have to say."

Golden Eagle quickly recounted the conversation he'd had with Jim Stewart.

"Let me see if I understand this correctly," Sam said. "You've heard some stories about some unexplained things that certain people believe happened while we were on Iwo Jima, and because of those things, you think we have some special insight or ability to help you with a problem that concerns the Northern Arapaho nation. Is that about right?"

"Sam, that's a perfectly logical and rational summary of the situation."

"But your problem doesn't fit neatly into any logical or rational box. Right?"

"Exactly, and I particularly liked your use of the word 'insight' earlier. I think that's a critical point."

"You mean that if we have, or think we have, encountered ghosts, or spirits, or demons, or whatever before that we will be more likely to … what? Believe in them, know how to deal with them?"

"Perhaps some of both."

Looking to Sam, Jim said, "Now you see why I wanted to get you involved in this right away."

"Yeah. Look, I'm gonna get a beer, or maybe a glass of Jamison's Irish. Anybody else want anything?"

After they had settled back down Sam stared down into his glass of Irish whiskey for a long time before speaking.

"We're going to have to get the whole team involved in this, but here's what I'd like to do. Joseph, tell us about your problem. Go ahead and assume whatever you want about any special talent or ability you think we may have and tell us how you think we can help. Fair enough?"

"Yes, that'll be fine. I'll have to give you some background first. There's a lot of Arapahoe history that plays a role in my story. I'll try to just give you the highlights, but even those get complicated, so I've got some things here on my laptop that might help me explain." After a pause to collect his thoughts, Joseph continued.

"The best place to start is with the California Gold Rush of 1849. Before that time there had been conflict between the tribes and the white men moving west, but it had been more or less on a small scale. The men rushing west to the gold fields were followed by settlers, and they were followed by the U.S. Army who established forts to protect the emigrants. All of this, of course, violated the treaties and agreements that had been made between the U.S. Government and the tribes. The various tribes retaliated against both individual travelers and wagon trains, which brought more soldiers out leading to an ongoing state of warfare."

"It's important to note that the conflicts were not only between the white man and the red man. The various tribes had been fighting each other for as long as anyone could remember and alliances between tribes were constantly shifting, and some tribes were happy to ally with the whites against their Indian enemies. By 1851, it was a very violent and confusing situation."

"In 1851 at Fort Laramie in what is now Wyoming the government signed a treaty with eight of the Indian nations, including the Arapahoe, that was intended to solve all these problems by assigning separate territories on the Great Plains to each tribe. There was to be no white settlement in the tribal areas. In return, the tribes agreed to allow safe passage through their territories along established trails."

"Gather around where you can see my laptop, and I'll show you a map."

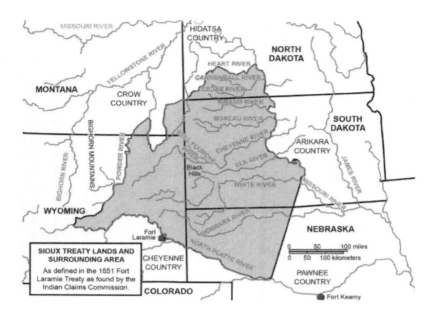

"The shaded area here is the land assigned to the Sioux. The other tribal areas are around this. The Arapahoe and Cheyenne shared the land to the west and south of the Sioux territory in what is now Wyoming, Colorado, and Nebraska."

"It's likely that the government agents who worked on this treaty acted in good faith as did the various tribal Chiefs, but there were too many differences between the two cultures for the treaty to have a hope of success. For example, the Indians never understood the white concept of private land ownership. To them, the land was the land to be used by everyone. On the other hand, the whites never understood that a Chief did not necessarily speak for everyone in his tribe. If someone disagreed with a Chief's decision, he was free to go his own way, and many Indians did not consider themselves bound by the treaty."

"Another problem was that the treaty gave the Black Hills entirely to the Sioux. All of the tribes considered the Black Hills to be sacred ground and this became the basis for a lot of fighting between the tribes."

"Of course the treaty was broken almost immediately by both sides. Most of the Indians never understood the boundaries assigned to them, and they continued to roam wherever their nomadic lives took them. At the same time, many of the whites traveling west settled wherever they found a pleasing piece of land even if it was in territory promised to the tribes, and that led to ongoing battles between the Indians, the settlers, and the Army."

"Between 1851 and 1864, the Arapahoe Nation as a whole never fought anything more than a few skirmishes with the whites as they advanced westward. The Arapahoe Chiefs knew that they were outnumbered and outgunned and that any conflict would end badly for them. Many of the young men disagreed, as young men always do, and went to fight with the Commanche, the Cheyenne, the Sioux, and others."

"The Arapahoe attempts to live peacefully with the white man were futile. On November 29th, 1864, a band of Arapahoe and Cheyenne who had settled peacefully in southern Colorado were attacked by a large Colorado militia force led by Colonel John Chivington. Chivington and his men killed over one hundred and fifty Indians, mostly women and children. This horrible disaster is known as the 'Sand Creek Massacre.'"

Golden Eagle paused for a moment.

"After Sand Creek, the Chiefs knew there was no chance of holding back the young warriors and they allied with the Cheyenne, the Lakota, the Kiowa, and others to resist the white invaders. Over the next two years, the combined tribes fought a number of small battles against the U.S. Army. Finally, in December 1866 a band of Arapaho, Lakota, and Cheyenne lured Captain William J. Fetterman and his men into an ambush on the eastern slopes of the Bighorn Mountains and killed eighty-one soldiers. The 'Fetterman Massacre,' as it was called by the whites, was second only to the

Battle of the Little Bighorn, which was fought ten years later, in the number of Army casualties."

"So," interjected Rebecca, "Chivington killed women and children at Sand Creek, and it was called a massacre, and the Indians killed eighty-one armed soldiers, and it was also called a massacre. Why is that?"

"I'll let Jim answer that one," Golden Eagle replied.

"Simple answer?" Jim replied, "The winners get to write the histories. However, most of the historians I know now refer to what happened to Fetterman and his men as, 'The Fetterman Fight.'"

"Thanks, Jim. So, after the 'Fetterman Fight,' the United States and the tribes signed the Fort Laramie Treaty of 1868, which gave the country in central Wyoming between the Powder River and the Bighorn Mountains to the tribes and prohibited any white settlement there. This could have worked out well. This was the Great Plains, buffalo country, although there were damn few buffalo left. There was water there, not much, but enough. The tribes could have made do, could even have done well there, but, of course, it was not to be.

"Gold was discovered in Montana and the Dakotas, and the Bozeman trail was established to get the miners to the fields. It ran right through the Powder River country. At about the same time, cattlemen in Texas and Wyoming started looking at the Powder River as a good place to run their herds. The Indians were in the way and would have to be moved.

"Over the next ten years the Arapaho were pushed steadily to the west, and their numbers were depleted continuously by battles, illness, and starvation. In 1878, the remnants of the great Arapahoe Nation, a few thousand starving Indians with a small horse herd were forced onto the Wind River reservation, which was already occupied by what was left of the Shoshone. The Shoshone and Arapaho had been enemies for as long as anyone could remember, but Chief Washakie of the Shoshone, who had been treated the same way by the whites, generously made room for the Arapaho.

"The next hundred years or so were the same story for the Arapaho as for most of the tribes. Forced into dependence on the government because the lands allotted to them could barely sustain life they became prey to the depredations of dishonest agents from the Bureau of Indian Affairs, many of whom grew rich by stealing the food and supplies intended for the tribes.

"Perhaps the worst thing the government did was to outlaw their language and religion."

"Wait a minute," Sam said, "The U.S. Government outlawed Indian language and religion?"

"Yes, Sam, it did. It's a long, sad story so I'll just give you some examples. Come on back around where you can see my laptop."

"Here's a quote from Hiram Price, the Commissioner of Indian Affairs, that pretty well sums up the government's position in the late nineteenth century.

"*...there is no good reason why an Indian should be permitted to indulge in practices which are alike repugnant to common decency and morality; and the preservation of good order on the reservations demands that some active measures should be taken to discourage and, if possible, put a stop to the demoralizing influence of heathenish rites.*"

"The tribes tried to resist. In 1890, the Sioux traveled to the sacred Black Hills to perform a Ghost Dance. They were met there by a large force of the Seventh Cavalry, the same Seventh Cavalry that the Sioux had annihilated at the Little Bighorn. Although it's not clear how the fighting started, the outcome is well known. Over one hundred fifty Indians, many of them women and children, were killed at what has become known as the Massacre at Wounded Knee.

"Finally in 1892 the practice of Indian religion was made a criminal offense, and a violator was subject to imprisonment. For example, anyone convicted of a second offense of practicing as a medicine man would be jailed for six months.

"After that, instead of direct resistance, the religious practices went underground. Many rites and beliefs were preserved, but others were lost. Various Christian churches sent ministries to the reservations. In most cases, the missionaries took up the cause of eradicating Indian religions and substituting the teaching of English for the native language.

"The Arapahoe and Shoshone on the Wind River Reservation were a little lucky in this respect. The Jesuit order of the Catholic Church established St. Stephan's Indian Mission. The Jesuit Fathers converted many of the Arapahoe, but they were tolerant of the old beliefs and did nothing to try to stop the Arapahoe from practicing their old religion alongside their new faith.

"As a result of this tolerant attitude our medicine men, like my uncle and my great-grandfather, were able to preserve both our language and traditional beliefs. And this brings us up to the current time and the problem I need help with.

"What do you know about what the whites call the Bighorn Medicine Wheel?"

When Sam and Rebecca were quiet, Jim Stewart spoke, "It's an ancient stone circle high up in the Bighorn Mountains that is similar to Stonehenge and other circles around the world. I don't think anyone knows for sure how old it is, but it's ancient, a couple of thousand years at least."

"Yes, Jim, exactly. Like Stonehenge, it is an astronomical calendar that the First People used to predict the seasons. We Arapahoe call it *Notoniheihii,* the Buffalo Wheel, and it has been sacred to our people for as long as anyone knows. It has always been a place of peace and safety, but since the time of my great-grandfather there has been a problem there."

"What kind of problem?" Sam asked.

"Since my great-grandfather's last days as medicine man, sometime in the mid-nineteen-thirties, there has been a disturbance there, a disquiet. My uncle believes that there is a spirit there that has not been able to travel on to the next world and is in anguish. He thinks that the pain this spirit feels is causing the disturbance that the medicine men can sense."

"Why would this spirit be trapped at the Buffalo Wheel, and why did this happen in the mid-thirties after all those centuries?" Sam asked.

"My uncle believes that someone was buried there improperly."

"What do you mean?" Sam asked.

"First, there should be no one buried in that sacred ground, and second my uncle thinks that the spirit belongs to a white man who was buried without the proper ceremony."

"Why would your uncle think that?" Sam asked.

"There have been rumors and stories on the reservation for a long time about two white men, and two white women who lived just off the reservation and the stories say that one of the white men was buried somewhere on Indian land."

"Does your uncle know who this man might be?"

"Yes, Sam. He thinks that it might be Robert Leroy Parker."

"Robert Leroy Parker ... why is that name familiar?"

"You would know him better by his outlaw name," Jim said.

"Outlaw name?"

"Yes, Robert Leroy Parker was Butch Cassidy."

As the people talked Gunny lay half-dozing under the dining table. He was curious about this new man. He smelled different from the others.

The difference was tiny, but Gunny could sense it as soon as he sniffed his hand. When he smelled it, he saw an image of wide, open spaces where the wind always blew. He didn't usually see pictures like that, and he didn't understand what he was seeing. He wasn't afraid of the man, but he was curious.

◆ ◆ ◆

Ogden Valley, Utah

Tuesday 20 March

"That's it. You guys know as much as Jim, and I do," Sam said, "Any questions? Tom? Steve? Alicia?"

"Questions? Only about a hundred, " Alicia Phillips replied, "The first one being, 'Do you think we can trust this guy?'"

"Trust him to do what?"

"Trust him not to tell the world if we talk to him about Robby Durance and Lieutenant Watanabe and the other ghosts on Iwo Jima."

"Yeah, I think so. How about you, Jim?"

"Yes, I agree with Sam. Doctor Golden Eagle's on the research faculty at the University of Wyoming Department of Anthropology, and he teaches pro bono at the Wind River Tribal College. Everyone I've talked to about him had nothing but good things to say."

"Where is he now?"

"He went for a long walk with Rebecca and Gunny to give us some privacy for this phone call."

"Rebecca likes him?"

"Yeah. I guess she's read a couple of his books and they've been talking non-stop since he got here."

"If Rebecca likes him, he's probably all right," Alicia said,"So, what do we tell him and what do we do next?"

"I guess the first thing, if you guys agree, would be for Jim and I to tell him what happened on Iwo, and then find out what he wants us to do. I assume he's going to want us to go to the Buffalo Wheel and look for Butch Cassidy's grave. Do any of you have a problem with us doing that?"

After a short silence, Steve Haney said, "I just have one question. When do you think he wants to do that? I'll be busy here at school until the end of May."

"Yeah, me too," Alicia said.

"I think it's going to be another deal like Iwo Jima. We're going to have a pretty tight window of time. I'm sure that they would like to have us finished before the Summer Solstice, which I think is the twenty-first of June, and the snow's not going to be melted off at that altitude until at least early to mid-June."

"That leaves me out, guys," Tom Sanders said, "I'm off to Europe on another Team Liberty search in June, and, on your recommendation Sam, I'm taking your friend Sharon and her dog with me."

"Crap, Tom, that's right I'd forgotten. We'll miss you, and I was thinking of asking Sharon to join us, but I'm not sure how she would have responded to our ghost story."

"Yeah, Sam, I'll miss you guys too, but I think they need me more over in Normandy."

"You're right, and Sharon and Rascal will do a good job for you."

"Here's the plan. Jim and I will fill Joseph in on what happened on Iwo Jima and find out what he wants us to do. Once we know that, I'll pass the word to all of you. In the meantime, Jim is going to do some research on Butch Cassidy so he can figure out if there's any chance he could be buried up at the Buffalo Wheel."

"Yeah, what about that?" Tom asked, "I thought Butch Cassidy and the Sundance Kid got killed down in Peru or someplace."

"You can't believe everything you see in the movies, and it was Bolivia, not Peru," Jim replied. "Paul Newman and Robert Redford may have gotten shot in San Vicente, Bolivia in 1908, but there's a lot of evidence that the real Butch and Sundance came back from South America alive. There are some theories about what happened to them, but this is the first time I've heard anything about a burial in the Bighorns so I'll have to do some digging. I'll know more the next time I see you."

"I guess that wraps things up. I hear Gunny barking, so it's time for Jim and me to tell our ghost story. I'll let you know how things work out.

◆ ◆ ◆

Ogden Valley, Utah

Tuesday 20 March

An Hour Later

"… and then those five ghosts just sorta faded away and left us all standing in the middle of Arlington National Cemetary with our mouths hung open and a glazed look on our faces."

When he'd finished his story, Sam looked at Golden Eagle for his reaction.

"Let me see if I understand. The three former military men on the team all had dreams where you re-lived the battle of Iwo Jima through the eyes of Robby Durance, one of the Marines you were looking for, and, Jim, you and Alicia Phillips, your forensic anthropologist, both saw his ghost."

"That's right," Jim replied.

"And you believe that the ghost of Robby Durance somehow influenced your dogs to help them find his remains and the remains of the other four Marines."

"Yep."

"And then this demon, the spirit of the Japanese officer who killed Robby, tried to kill Gunny before he could finish his search?"

"That's our story, and we're stickin' to it," Sam said.

"That's interesting."

"Interesting?" Rebecca asked, "Only interesting?"

"Rebecca, the Arapaho have believed in spirits for thousands of years. Our religion is at least as old as Judaism. We believe that animals, plants, and even some rocks have spirits and that these spirits can be invoked to help us. When we need help from a spirit, we go on a vision quest. We fast and pray and, if we are worthy, we will be given a vision that will help us to solve our problem or to grow and become a better person. The only difference I see between a vision quest and what happened to Sam, Jim, and the others on Iwo Jima is that a vision quest is voluntary. Their visions seem to have been imposed on them. That's why I find their story 'interesting.' It is also interesting that one of the places that many Arapaho and other Indians go on a vision quest is to the Buffalo Wheel."

"Do you think that because we had a 'vision' on Iwo Jima, we would be more receptive to whatever spirit might be at the Buffalo Wheel?" Sam asked.

"I don't know, but I think that may be part of the reason that my uncle is asking for your help. That and the dogs, of course."

"So, what's the story behind Butch Cassidy? Why does your uncle think he may have been buried at the Buffalo Wheel?"

"Rebecca, I think that's a story that I'll leave to my uncle to tell. He knows it much better than I."

"So, what's next. What do we need to do now?" Sam asked.

"I propose that you arrange with your team to meet out here in mid-June. We'll travel to the reservation and get the full story from my uncle and make a search plan. Then, as soon as the snow is gone, we go to the Buffalo Wheel to look for the burial place of Butch Cassidy, or whatever unfortunate individual was buried there improperly."

"Oh, by the way," Joseph continued,"my uncle has said that the Tribal Council has voted to use some of our oil lease money to pay your team's expenses and fees."

"Joseph, that's great," Sam said, "if you can help with expenses we appreciate it, but we won't charge any fees."

"That's very generous. We'll be sure to take good care of you. Do you think this will work?"

"I'll have to talk with the rest of the team, but I think that's in line with what we were planning to do."

"Great. We'll see you up on the rez sometime in June."

CHAPTER SIX

Rebecca

"The Marine Wife

Toughest Job in the Corps"

Popular T-Shirt on Marine Bases

Ogden Valley, Utah

Sunday, 10 June

STEVE AND ALICIA HAD FLOWN INTO SALT LAKE earlier that afternoon. They had both rented cars since they would need room for the dogs and their gear. It was a little over an hour from there to Sam and Rebecca's house in the Ogden Valley. They arrived just before dinner.

After a leisurely meal, Sam suggested that they take the dogs out for a walk.

"I'm kinda tired," Alicia said, "If you guys don't mind taking Iwo, I think I'll stay here and help Rebecca clean up and then have another glass of this good wine."

"Sure, no problem for me. Steve?"

"Yeah, let's go."

After the men and dogs had left, Rebecca turned to Alicia, "You don't look all that tired. Why do I think you have an ulterior motive for getting rid of the guys?"

"Because I do. You and I have never had a chance to just sit and talk. I'd like to get to know you a little better."

Rebecca suggested that they take their wine outside and enjoy the early summer evening.

"What about the dishes?"

"I cook, Sam cleans. He'll take care of it when he gets back."

When they had gotten settled, Alicia said, "OK, Rebecca, you and Sam have been married since about the end of the last Ice Age, and I know you've gotta have a bunch of great stories, so why don't you start."

"What do you want to hear?"

"Let's start with how you guys met."

"I met him at a rugby party at UVA."

"I thought Sam went to Notre Dame?"

"Yes, Sam went to Notre Dame. He was playing scrum half on their rugby team against Virginia."

"And you were at UVA? That's where Steve is."

"No, I was at Sweetbriar College, which, according to Sam, is a four beer trip south of Charlottesville. I had a date with this guy who played rugby at Virginia, Courtney something or other. He got drunk pretty quickly, and I went looking for someone to talk to. I ran into Sam, and the rest is history."

"Was he in the Marines then?"

"No. He had done four years as an enlisted Marine and gotten out. He'd already done his tours in Vietnam."

"Was it love at first sight?"

"No, but there was a definite attraction. We talked for a long time about a lot of different stuff. He got my phone number, and we agreed to see each other when he came home for Christmas."

"Home was where?"

"Well, I just found out talking to Sam that you and I both grew up in Chevy Chase and went to National Cathedral School about twenty-five years apart."

"Really? Wow, you went to NCS. Purple or Gold?"

"I'll have you know that I was the Gold Team captain my senior year."

"That's a big deal."

"Yeah, well you were your class valedictorian so I'd say we were even."

"I'll be damned. I had no idea."

"Yeah, I guess we're overdue for having this little talk."

"And Sam's from DC too. Right?"

"Yep. He lived over in Northeast."

"OK, so you got together at Christmas. Then what?"

"We started dating. We had a kind of long-distance romance with him in South Bend and me back east, but it worked out pretty well. Two years later, right after he graduated and got his commision as a Lieutenant, we got married."

"What was that like? I don't think I've known anyone who was married to a career military man."

"Well, it was very seldom dull, that's for sure."

"Did you move a lot?"

"Not as much as some. Let's see, we were at Camp Lejeune a couple of times, Monterey California – that was nice, Fort Knox, and Quantico. Plus, I stayed at home one year when he was in Okinawa. So, six moves in sixteen years. That's not too bad."

"I think most people would disagree with you on that. Did he have to go away very often?"

"Yeah. We call those deployments. Let me count 'em here; a year in Okinawa—that was his first tour and I went home and stayed with my folks, our son Mike was born nine months after he got home, a six month Med cruise—our daughter Maddie was born nine months after he got home from that, I mean almost to the day—a three month Carib cruise, two three month deployments to Norway, and six months in Okinawa and Korea."

"Wow!"

"Yeah, and that doesn't count the short ones. Four weeks to jump school, ten weeks to Ranger school, and more one and two-week deployments than I can remember."

"I'm guessing a Med cruise is the Mediterranean?"

"Yeah, the Second Marine Division keeps a battalion landing team aboard amphibious ships in the Med all the time."

"I didn't know that. And Carib is … The Caribbean? Do they keep Marines there all the time too?"

"No, they just do that for training."

"So you were like a single mom all that time. Wasn't that tough?"

"Yeah, but most of the time we were livin' on base or in a military community, so there were a lot of folks around who were in the same boat. And there were some nice compensations."

"Like what?"

"Both of our kids were born at the Naval Hospital at Camp Lejeune. Sam was in Force Recon then, and he was gone a lot, but there's no place better than Lejeune to raise kids."

"OK, two questions. What's Force Recon and why is Lejeune so great?"

"Force Recon is what they call a Special Operations unit today. Kinda the Marines' version of the SEALs. Lejeune is great because it sits right on the ocean with fantastic beaches. It has excellent schools and facilities for kids, and you've got twenty or thirty thousand Marines there, so it's gotta be the safest place in the world."

"Plus, like I said, we were all in the same boat. If I had a bad day, and there were more than a few, there was always someone there who could help with the kids, cook a meal, pour me some wine, whatever. And they all knew I'd do the same for them."

"The kids were babies our first time at Lejeune, and we went back when they were starting school. When they were in first and second grade, we could just send them out the door to walk a half mile to school. They had to cross two major roads, but there were MP's at each intersection, and they would stop all traffic whenever a kid had to cross. When they got home, they could just go out and play in the neighborhood. If they had a problem, they knew they could go to any house and get help."

"And, if they were being naughty, there was always someone watching, and Marine parents have no problem administering a little discipline to someone else's kid."

"So, you have a lot of fond memories of Lejeune?"

"Yeah, but there were some tough times."

"Like what?"

"Well, you know being a Marine's wife is kinda like being a cop's wife. When you send 'em out the door, you never know for sure when, or if, they're gonna come back."

"Can you give me an example?"

"It's been a long time since I talked about this stuff because most people just don't get it, but you work with cops all the time, so I guess you'd understand."

"I'll try."

"If you want to know about a tough time, October, 1983, sticks out. You were probably in grade school then."

"Yeah, I was. What happened?"

"It started on the morning of the twenty-third. Sam was gone, of course. He was the XO of First Battalion, Second Marines. They had deployed to Okinawa and then deployed from there to Pohang, Korea and they were in the field living in tents. So, he was just about as far away from me as he could be. I got a call at five-thirty in the morning. It scared the hell out of me because I assumed it was something bad about Sam. It was a friend who was frantic and saying, 'Turn on the TV! Turn on the TV!'"

"That was the day a terrorist truck bomb blew up the Marine barracks in Beirut, Lebanon. Two hundred and twenty Marines, eighteen Sailors, and three Soldiers were killed, which meant a whole bunch of brand-new widows and fatherless children. Another hundred and thirty or so were seriously wounded. The unit in Beirut was the First Battalion Eighth Marines from Camp Lejeune, so a lot of those widows and orphans were my neighbors."

"Our next door neighbors had two kids, a boy, and a girl. The boy was Maddie's age, and the girl was Mike's age. The kids played together all the time, and they were constantly in and out of our two houses. She and I would cook for each other, drink wine together, you know, the usual."

"Her husband was the same rank as Sam, a Major. He was the Operations Officer of One-Eight."

"Have you ever seen pictures of what happened?"

"Yes, it's something that's studied in forensic anthropology courses. I didn't recognize the date, but as soon as you said Beirut, I knew what it was. It was catastrophic."

"Yeah. I think they figured that there was something like ten tons of explosive in that truck. It was an eight-story building, and it was flattened."

"So, the problem was it took a long time to figure out who had been killed and who survived. Meanwhile, you've got all these women and kids who don't know if their husbands or daddies are ever coming home."

Rebecca paused and took a deep breath and a long drink from her wine glass.

"So that was pretty bad. We all chipped in, of course, and did what we could, but what can you do? I mean, really?"

"And then it got worse."

"What happened?"

"There was another battalion from Lejeune, Second Battalion, Eighth Marines, Two-Eight, that had left on the twentieth to replace One-Eight in Beirut. They had been at sea for a few days when they got orders to divert to the Island of Grenada to put down a Cuban-backed coup and rescue six hundred American students who were being held hostage at a medical school there."

"Grenada? I sorta vaguely remember that."

"Yeah, it was a big deal back then, but most folks have forgotten about it now. Except for anyone who was at Lejeune, of course. It was over in a few days. The Marines plus Army Rangers and some Special Operations guys took care of things pretty quickly, but another forty or so Marines were killed or wounded."

"Meanwhile, One-Eight in Beirut has taken about forty percent casualties, and they're calling for help, so they launched the air alert battalion to go to Beirut. I don't remember which battalion that was."

"What's an air alert battalion?"

"There's always a battalion at Lejeune ready to deploy anywhere in the world on short notice. I think the first company has to be ready to board aircraft in an hour and the whole battalion has to be gone in five or six hours. You can imagine how happy all those families were to see their Marines go rushing off to Beirut."

"How many battalions are normally at Camp Lejeune?"

"Nine. So, by the end of October, there were two battalions in Beirut, one in Grenada, and Sam's battalion in Korea. Pretty much everyone else was on alert, so there were hardly any men around, and the wives had to take over and get everything done. Yeah, October, 1983 was a pretty shitty month."

"What happened to your neighbor?"

"I think it was four or five days after the bombing that she was told that he was presumed dead. It was another month before they knew for sure. How do you explain something like that to a second grader? You can't. All you can do is hold them when they're crying."

"What was being done for all those families?"

"Each family of a killed or wounded Marine or Sailor was assigned a casualty assistance officer. This was a Marine whose job it was to do all the things the husband normally would. Everything from dealing with the bureaucracy to making sure all the bills got paid, and the grass was mowed."

"We all pitched in to help where we could. A lot of babysitting, a lot of hand-holding and anything else we could do."

"The interesting thing is that within a year-and-a-half a lot of those women had re-married Marines."

"Really? I wouldn't expect that after what they'd gone through. Why?"

"Who knows? I guess you get used to a certain type of life and a certain type of people, and Marines and the Marine Corps are definitely their own types."

When Sam and Steve got back with three happy dogs a few minutes later, they found Rebecca and Alicia chatting companionably.

"So, what have you two been talking about?" Sam asked.

"Beirut," Rebecca replied.

"Oh, shit! You OK Bec?"

"Yeah, I guess I need to purge my system every thirty years or so. Alicia was very nice to listen to me."

"What an amazing, terrible story," Alicia said, "I've always known that the military was tough, but I never realized how tough it could be on the families. Your wife is an extraordinary woman."

"Yeah, tell me something I don't know. Can we join you, or is this ladies only?"

"Have a seat. It's nice out here this time of the evening," Alicia said.

"Steve, I'm gonna grab a beer. You want one?"

"Sure, thanks."

A few minutes later everyone had settled in around a gas firepit on the patio. The sun was behind the mountains, and the first stars were coming out. It was getting a little chilly, and everyone had put on a jacket.

"Sam you retired from the Marines in 1988, right?" Alicia asked.

"Yep."

"So, Rebecca you could finally stop worrying every time he walked out the door?"

"Yeah, that lasted for eleven years until our son, Mike became a Marine Officer."

"Oh, lord! What's that like?"

"Most of the time it's not too bad, but the six months he spent in Fallujah were pretty tough."

"I can't even imagine."

"Your son's a Marine Lieutenant Colonel now, right Sam? He outranks you."

"Yes, Steve. Thanks for reminding me."

"Mike's a Marine lawyer," Rebecca said, "He was an infantry officer for nine years, and that's when he did his tour in Fallujah. Then went to law school. Now he and his family are finishing up a two-year tour in Abu Dhabi and getting ready to come back to the States."

"What's a Marine lawyer doing in Abu Dhabi?" Steve asked.

"When he made Lieutenant Colonel he was selected for command," Sam replied, "There ain't a lot of command billets for lawyers, so they put him in charge of all of the Marine Embassy Security Guards in the Middle East and South Asia. He's spent most of the last couple of years going to all the fun places where we have Embassies or Consulates over there. You know, Baghdad, Kabul, Peshawar, places like that."

"Sounds like a big job. Where's he going next?"

"National War College."

"Wow! That's a big deal. So he's on track to make General."

"Yeah, I guess so. If he doesn't screw up."

"Sam has forgotten to mention that Mike and Hannah have given us two wonderful grandkids, a twelve-year-old boy, and an eight-year-old girl," Rebecca added.

"What about your daughter?" Alicia asked.

"She's kind of a disappointment," Sam replied, "I don't like to talk about her."

Alicia was afraid she'd touched on a sore point, but when she turned toward Rebecca, she got a wink and an eye roll. *OK, not sure what this is about, but I'll play along.*

"What do you mean, Sam. What kind of disappointment?"

79

"First of all, when she finished high school all she could get into was some damn junior college out in California."

"There's nothing wrong with junior college …"

"Let me interrupt, Alicia. What Sam is referring to is the college in Palo Alto the full name of which is Leland Stanford Junior College."

"Leland Stan … Oh, Stanford. Got it. Well, Sam, that's not a bad school."

"It shouldn't be. It costs enough."

"Exactly how much did we pay per year Sam?"

"I forget. It was a lot."

Turning to Alicia, Rebecca said, "Maddie got a full scholarship. She was an outstanding gymnast. It cost us thirty-six dollars a year to pay for her post office box. Everything else was covered."

"So what did your bum of a daughter do after Stanford?" Steve asked.

"Well she couldn't get into a decent graduate school in the states, so she had to go to some little college overseas."

"And what little college would that be, Rebecca?"

"That would be Saint Antony's College, Oxford, Alicia."

"Wow, I see what you mean, Sam. If I had a daughter like that, I'd be disappointed too. Has she done anything else?"

"I'll take over the story now before Sam makes an even bigger fool of himself. She met a very nice man, a Norwegian named Knut, at Oxford. They married, have two beautiful daughters, and live in Oslo. Maddie got her Ph.D. from the University of Oslo a couple of years ago."

"OK, Mr. Comedian, we've bored these people enough, let's go to bed. You're the one who said we've got an early morning tomorrow, and I'm the one who'll be doin' all the cookin'."

After Sam and Rebecca had gone inside, Steve and Alicia sat quietly by the fire a little longer. After a few minutes, Steve spoke, "That was quite a show."

"Yeah, I get the feeling they've done this before."

"No wonder they've been married for forty-six years."

"Good people."

"Yeah."

CHAPTER SEVEN

The Outlaw Trail

"An outlaw can be defined as somebody who lives outside the law, beyond the law and not necessarily against it."

Hunter S. Thompson

Ogden Valley, Utah

Monday, 11 June

"OK," SAM SAID, "IF EVERYONE HAS COFFEE AND A PASTRY let's settle down so we can get started. Find a place where you can see the screen because I think Jim will have some maps and things to show us. It's great to have the team together again. It's too bad Tom can't make it. Rebecca will be joining us to help out in any way she can so she's part of the team now also.

"Today will be mostly Jim's show. He's going to give us some background on the western outlaws in general and Butch Cassidy, the

Sundance Kid, and Etta Place in particular, so we have a better understanding of who we're going to be looking for.

"Unfortunately, it looks like Jim isn't going to be able to go on the search with us. He has some obligations at BYU he can't get out of. We'll miss having him along."

"Crap, Jim, that's too bad," Steve said.

"Yeah," Alicia said, "Who'm I gonna get to help me sort out any bones we find?"

"Thank you," Jim replied, "Believe me, if I could go I would, but it looks like all I can do is help you get ready."

"And we're lucky to have your help today, Jim. Thanks," Sam said.

"When Jim is finished," Sam continued, "I'll wrap up with a little information about the Buffalo Wheel focusing on the terrain and the expected weather so we have an idea about how we might structure our search.

"I'm looking forward to this for a couple of reasons. First, it's a fascinating problem and a potentially high-profile search given the historical background. Second, it's going to be fun working with three great dogs.

"Tomorrow we'll travel up to the Wind River Reservation to link up with Joseph Golden Eagle, his uncle, and others. That's where we'll hear why Joseph's uncle thinks that Butch Cassidy might be buried at the Buffalo Wheel and why the Arapaho believe it's important that he be recovered and re-buried elsewhere.

"Wednesday we'll travel up to Medicine Mountain and start our search there at around noon or one o'clock. When we're done, we'll get settled in the lodge where we'll be staying, and re-start early Thursday morning.

"The Arapaho, with agreement from the Shoshone and other tribes, and the Forest Service, will keep everyone out of the area around the Buffalo Wheel until the afternoon of the twentieth when they will begin to set up for the solstice ceremonies.

"Steve and Alicia have to leave to get back to their schools on Sunday the seventeenth. That means we'll only have three full search days. A half-day on Wednesday, a full day on Thursday and Friday, and another half day on Saturday. The bad news is that's seven days less than we had on Iwo. The good news is that we'll have three search dogs instead of one, and we won't have to worry about clearing unexploded ordnance."

"And we won't have Commander Matsuyama screwin' around with us," Steve said.

"Yeah, that too," Sam replied, and then continued, "Rebecca, and I can stay until the twentieth, but I'm hoping that won't be necessary."

"Any questions?"

When he heard no response, Sam concluded,"Let's get started. Jim, you're up."

"Thanks, Sam."

"Robert Leroy Parker, Butch Cassidy, was born in Circleville, Utah on 13 April, 1866. He is reputed to have been killed in a shootout in San Vicente, Bolivia on 6 November, 1908 along with Harry Longabaugh, the Sundance Kid. There is now a significant amount of evidence that the outlaws killed in Bolivia were not who the movies say they were, and that Butch and Sundance returned to the States and died here years later. I'll get to that in a few minutes, but first, as you know, I'm a history professor, so I have to start with a little history lesson. I think it's important that we all understand what it meant to be an 'outlaw' in the western US in the mid-nineteenth century.

"Butch Cassidy's life coincided with a technological revolution that was radically changing both the land and the way of life on the western Great Plains. The first patent for barbed wire was issued in 1867, a year after Butch was born. For the millions of years before that, the Plains had been open range and the animals that lived there, from mastodons to buffalo to cattle, roamed freely.

"It took ten years after the wire was invented to perfect it to the point that it could be manufactured in large quantity, but by the time Butch left home in 1882 at the age of sixteen to begin his outlaw life, 'the wire' was starting to change everything.

"Cowboys talk about 'the time before the wire' when cattle spent most of the year grazing on the open range. In the semi-arid climate of the Plains, it took forty acres of land or more to support a single cow so the cattle would spread out over vast distances looking for forage. When it came time to round up the herd and brand the calves and castrate the young bulls, these cows were essentially wild animals. It was tough work being a cowboy back then, and if at the end of the roundup you had a few head with the wrong brand nobody paid too much attention to it, and a calf without a brand became the property of whoever branded it first.

"Taking an unbranded calf was called 'rustling,' and if you had cows in your herd with someone else's brand on them then you were, technically speaking, a cow thief. Cow thieves were considered outlaws, but since almost every rancher had a few cows that didn't belong to them, nobody got too upset about it. Not until 'the wire' and the winter of 1886-1887.

"With barbed wire, the big ranching outfits, those who could afford it, started claiming large tracts of land that had been open range before. Because of this, the poorer ranchers were being pushed into smaller and smaller areas and onto less desirable grazing land. For them, a few head of cattle could mean the difference between making it through the winter or starving, and so they kept to their old habit of not looking too closely at the brands on all of their cows.

"The big ranchers, who mostly lived in Cheyenne and left the running of their herds to field managers, often railed publicly against the 'outlaws' who were stealing their cattle, but in private they knew that there was little that they could do about it and considered it just a cost of doing business. Occasionally, someone would be caught red-handed with cows that didn't belong to him and be shot or hung, but that was the exception.

"And then came 1886 and one of the worst winters ever recorded. Tens of thousands of cattle died. The harsh winter was followed by a dry, hot summer and more cows died. Now the big outfits were concerned about each and every one of their cows and began to employ hired guns to protect their herds and punish anyone they caught rustling or with a cow that had their brand.

"Under these conditions, the small ranchers evolved into a community of outlaws.

"Let me show you a quote that I think makes an important point.

> *The guerrilla must swim like a fish in the sea of the people.*
>
> *Mao Tse Tung*

"Why am I showing you a quote from Chairman Mao when I'm supposed to be talking about the American West? It's because the western outlaw, in many cases, was like one of Mao's guerrillas. He, and sometimes she, was dependent upon the goodwill and support of the populace, and, more times than not, that support was freely given."

"So, what kind of support are we talking about?"

"Good question, Alicia. Let me give you an example. In 1889 after Butch, along with Tom McCarty and Matt Warner, had robbed the bank in Telluride, Colorado, Butch was on the run. He and the other two had gotten away from the Colorado posse, split up the loot, and gone in separate directions. Butch headed to Brown's Hole.

"Brown's Hole, which is now called Brown's Park, sits on the border of Utah, Wyoming, and Colorado, and one advantage it had was there was always confusion over which state had jurisdiction there. Remember, we're talking about a time before there were any national law enforcement agencies like the FBI. A Colorado Sheriff could get in a lot of trouble for arresting someone in Utah or Wyoming.

"Brown's Hole is actually a high valley surrounded by rugged mountains with the Green River flowing through it. There are only a couple of entrances through steep, narrow canyons that can be easily blocked or defended. It's good cattle country, but because it's so remote the big ranch outfits weren't interested in it. That made it ideal for small ranchers, especially if they had a few cows that technically didn't belong to them.

"Butch worked as a cowboy in Brown's Hole when he first left home. He was well-known and popular there, and he met two people who would be important to him for the rest of his life, Elzy Lay, and Annie Bassett. Elzy Lay and Butch became partners-in-crime long before Butch met Sundance, and there are stories that Butch and Annie, who became known as the 'Queen of the Outlaws' were lovers.

"Butch could always depend on getting help in Brown's Hole. If he was on the run and needed a fresh horse, he could stop at almost any one of the ranches, take a horse, and leave his worn horse behind. Later, when things had quieted down, he would come back and exchange horses again and leave something for the rancher, a small purse or a side of beef.

"Anyway, back to the story. Somehow, the Sheriff of Daggett County, Utah found out where Butch was heading and set out after him. Butch was in trouble when he got to Brown's Hole. He had a tired horse, and the Sheriff was close behind him. He knew what he had to do."

♦ ♦ ♦

John Jarvie Ranch

Brown's Hole Utah

Monday, 1 July, 1889

"All right, mister, whoever you are, keep yer hands where I can see'em and climb down slow off that horse."

"John, be careful where you point that shotgun. It's just me, George."

"George? George Cassidy is that you?"

"Yessir"

"Well, you know better'n to give folks a fright at night charging up here like that. What's goin' on?"

"Well, John, I'm in a bit of trouble and could use some help."

"You mean trouble with the law?"

"Yessir. I'm afraid Sheriff Jenkins is looking for me, and he's getting' close."

"Nellie, git out here. It's George."

"George, how good to see you."

"No time for talkin' woman. Take George's horse down across the ford and get him in the corral. Make sure his saddle is hid in the sagebrush and then git back here as quick as you can."

"What are you gonna do, John?"

"I'm gonna hide him in the dugout. Now quit talkin' and git moving."

Before Nellie took his horse, Butch Cassidy, whom folks in the Hole knew as George when he'd cowboyed there, took his saddlebags off and slung them over his shoulder.

"I sure appreciate this, John."

"Let's just get you hid before that sheriff gets here. You hungry?"

"Yeah, I am."

"Grab a mug of coffee off the stove. I'll wrap some meat and biscuits for ya."

John Jarvie had been in Brown's Hole for almost ten years. He now lived in a comfortable stone house and ran the only store for many miles around, but things had been different when he and Nellie first arrived. Their first home was a cave dug into the side of a small hill. They called it a dugout, and it was roomy and kept them warm in the winter, but there were no windows, and it could get a bit gloomy after a while. After they had built their house and store, they kept the dugout for guests and emergencies.

After John had put some food together, he lit an oil lamp and led Butch over to the dugout.

John and Nellie had just gotten back into the house when Sheriff Jenkins rode up on a lathered horse. John greeted the sheriff the same way he had Butch, with a loaded shotgun pointed at his chest.

"Easy there, Mr. Jarvie. It's Sheriff Jenkins from over to Manila. I'm just here chasin' an outlaw."

"What outlaw would that be?"

"Butch Cassidy"

"Don't know any Butch Cassidy."

"Mr. Jarvie I'd feel a lot more comfortable if you'd lay that shotgun aside. I'd hate to die from a finger twitch."

Jarvie slowly lowered the gun to his side. "I don't mean you no harm, Sheriff, I just don't like folks who come riding hard up to the house in the middle of the night."

"I'm not here to bother you, Jarvie. I'm just lookin' for Cassidy."

"Well, he ain't here."

"Well, Sir, I'll just have to make sure of that."

"You do what you please, just don't bother nothin'," Jarvie said as he walked back into his house.

Fifteen minutes later the sheriff knocked on Jarvie's door.

"What you want now?"

"How come you got a lock on the door of that ol' dugout of yours?"

"We store some things in there from time to time."

"Well, I need to look in there."

"There ain't no outlaw in my dugout."

"I'll just need to see that for myself."

"All right let's go then."

After he got his key and a lamp, Jarvie led the sheriff to the dugout and opened the door. "There ya go, Sheriff."

"No sir, you go in first and remember, I got my hand on my forty-five."

Jarvie walked through the low, narrow entrance and into the dugout.

"Shine yer light around here so's I can see."

Jarvie carried his light to the corners of the small room as the Sheriff watched from the doorway.

"This is a small place. How long did ya live here."

"Me an' the wife was in here 'most a year."

"I don't see no bed."

"No room. We just put a pallet down on the floor at night."

"Livin' in a place like this would drive me crazy."

"We made do. Are we done here? Can I get back to a real bed now?"

"Yeah, Jarvie, we're done for now, but I think you know a lot more'n you're tellin'. I wonder what would happen if I came back and rode out to your herd and checked some brands. I wonder what I might find?"

"I don't know, Sheriff, but I'd be mighty careful about that if I were you. You might get mistook for an outlaw, and folks aroun' here don't take kindly to outlaws."

When Jarvie was sure that the Sheriff had ridden off, he went back into the dugout. With difficulty, he slowly pushed the large cabinet aside revealing the door to the second room, the bedroom.

"OK, George, it's clear c'mon out."

"John, I can't thank you enough. You and Nellie are good people."

"It's OK, George. Never did like that Sheriff much."

"Well, anyhow here's a little somethin' I found in my saddlebag. It ain't much, but it oughtta help make a few mortgage payments."

"Thank you, George. You'd better get goin'. You know my horses. Take one that suits you, and we'll swap back next time you're through and got a little time to visit."

"Thanks, John. Tell Nellie next time I see her I'll bring somethin' nice from Laramie."

"OK, George, good luck."

♦ ♦ ♦

Ogden Valley, Utah

Monday, 11 June

"So," Alicia asked, "didn't Butch Cassidy have a couple of hideouts? Wasn't there a place called 'Hole-in-the-Wall'?"

"Yes, there were many places where Butch and other outlaws could go to be safe from the law. Here, take a look at this map."

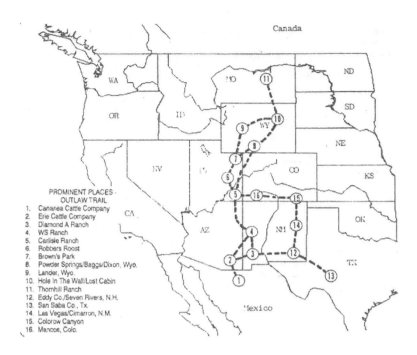

Canada

PROMINENT PLACES
OUTLAW TRAIL
1. Cananea Cattle Company
2. Erie Cattle Company
3. Diamond A Ranch
4. WS Ranch
5. Carlisle Ranch
6. Robbers Roost
7. Brown's Park
8. Powder Springs/Baggs/Dixon, Wyo.
9. Lander, Wyo.
10. Hole In The Wall/Lost Cabin
11. Thornhill Ranch
12. Eddy Co./Seven Rivers, N.M.
13. San Saba Co., Tx.
14. Las Vegas/Cimarron, N.M.
15. Colorow Canyon
16. Mancos, Colo.

"This is the famous, or infamous, Outlaw Trail. The Outlaw Trail was a series of hideouts where outlaws could go when the law was after them and where they would be relatively safe. The few people who lived in these areas were, if not friendly to the outlaws, at least they were unfriendly to the people trying to catch them. They provided the friendly sea in which the outlaws could safely swim."

"So, we just talked about Brown's Hole, which is number seven on the map, and it was a perfect example of an outlaw hideout, and it was Butch Cassidy's favorite."

"The next place on the trail I want to talk about is number nine, Lander, Wyoming, where we'll be going tomorrow. Lander itself is not too important to us, but it sits right on the eastern border of the Wind River

93

Reservation. The Arapaho and Shoshone had been considered outlaws by the white man for generations, and so men like Butch could easily find people on the reservation who were happy to help, especially since Butch became known for his generosity to those who befriended him."

"Northwest of Lander, tucked between the reservation and Yellowstone National Park, is the town of Dubois. Dubois is of interest because Butch bought a ranch and lived there for a few years around 1890 in one of his several attempts to go straight."

"Excuse me, Jim. How do you spell the name of that town?"

"I know what you're getting at, Alicia," Jim replied. "Dubois is spelled, D-u-b-o-i-s and you would expect it to be pronounced as the French would, *du bwa'*. Instead, it's pronounced *du' boyz*, and there's an interesting reason why, if I can digress for a moment."

"I know the story, Jim," Sam said, "It's pretty good. Go ahead."

"Wyoming became a state in 1890. Before that, the town of Dubois was known as 'Never Sweat,' probably because it sits up in the mountains at about seven thousand feet and it's always cold. Evidently, the folks in the Territorial Government back in Cheyenne didn't think that 'Never Sweat' would be a good name for a town in their new state, so they renamed it after a legislator named Dubois, whose name was pronounced in the French manner. This made the folks in Never Sweat angry, and they insisted on pronouncing their town's new name as *du' boyz*, and that's the name that's stuck."

"And the moral of that story," Steve said, "is, 'Don't piss off the folks in Wyoming!'"

"Yeah, especially if they think you might be French," Sam added.

After everyone had a chuckle, Jim continued.

"Now we get to the most famous place on the Outlaw Trail, the one you mentioned, Alicia, the Hole in the Wall. As you probably know, Butch was considered to be the leader of the Hole in the Wall Gang, and that's how he was portrayed in the movie. As is often the case in popular mythology, that depiction is somewhat misleading. Butch never had a 'gang' *per se*; it was more a loose confederation of like-minded men. Butch, Elzy Lay, Kid Curry, and, later, Sundance, were regulars, but there were others, and gang members would drift in and out. Butch was never identified as the leader, but he was definitely the brains of the outfit."

"The Hole in the Wall was not, as its name suggests, a cave or opening in a rock face. It was a smaller version of Brown's Hole, and the name Hole in the Wall refers to the entrance into this small valley which is a narrow slot canyon."

"The main advantages of the Hole in the Wall were that it was remote and difficult to get into and that it was located in Johnson County, Wyoming where everyone hated the big ranchers and the government because of the 'Invasion of 1892.'"

"That's a new one on me," Sam said, "What was the 'Invasion of 1892'?"

"The Invasion of 1892 was the most significant part of the Johnson County Cattle War that raged between 1888 and 1893. I could talk about this for the rest of the day, but I'll try to just hit the highlights."

"Remember that I said earlier that the big ranchers decided they had to do something about the outlaws and rustlers after the winter of 1886 – 1887? Well, the Wyoming Stock Growers Association was formed to deal with the outlaw problem. In 1892 the WSGA hired forty gunmen led by the infamous killer Tom Horn to solve the outlaw problem once and for all. The WSGA made up a list of sixty or more 'outlaws' who were to be killed without benefit of a trial. Horn led his mercenaries into the Powder River country in Johnson County and onto the KC Ranch to find his first victim, Nate Chapman."

"Nate Chapman turned out to be a hard man to kill. He fought the gunmen for three hours before they were able to put him down. This allowed time for riders to get the word out to the small ranchers in the area who quickly put together a sheriff's posse of over three hundred men. A few days later Tom Horn and his gang were surrounded on the TA Ranch and about to be wiped out. At this point, Wyoming Governor Barber, with the approval of the President of the United States Benjamin Harrison, dispatched the U.S. Cavalry—to save the gunmen!"

"Tom Horn and his men were taken under guard to Cheyenne. After a few months, enough judges had been bought off that the invaders were set free to return to Texas or wherever they came from. No one was ever charged for this attempt at wholesale murder."

"To this day, the people in Johnson County refer to what happened in 1892 as, 'The Invasion.' If you'd like to learn more about this, I'd suggest a trip to Kaycee, Wyoming, a town about an hour north of Casper on the site of the old KC Ranch where Nate Chapman was murdered. Just up the street from the cabin where Chapman died is the 'Hoofprints of the Past' museum, one of the best, small-town museums in the country. You can learn the whole history of the Johnson County Cattle War and quite a bit about the Hole in the Wall Gang. When you're ready for lunch, take a walk across the street to the best restaurant in town."

"It's called, 'The Invasion Bar.'"

"Wow! Those folks have long memories," Steve said.

"Yes," Jim replied, "You can imagine how they felt about the government and the law back in the 1890's. Butch knew that when he made it to Johnson County, he'd be safe."

"There's one more point I'd like to make about why Butch and the other outlaws enjoyed so much support among the populace. Butch never killed anyone, and only a couple of people were killed by any of the other outlaws he associated with. Because of this, the ordinary ranchers knew that they had nothing to fear from Butch, and, in most cases, they had more to fear from the government, banks, and the big ranchers."

"So, that's Butch's background. Maybe we could take a break and then I'll talk about how it's possible that he survived in Bolivia and made it back to the States."

"Jim, that was great," Sam said, "Rebecca has coffee, tea, water, soft drinks and so on for us. Let's take fifteen minutes and then we'll hear the rest of Jim's story."

As everyone got up, Gunny barked three times.

"Oh yeah, let's make that thirty minutes so we can get the critters out for a little while."

Ogden Valley, Utah

Monday, 11 June

Thirty Minutes Later

After everyone had gotten resettled after the break, Jim began, "Now I'll talk about why many people believe that Butch and Sundance came back alive from Bolivia, but first I'll have to explain why they were down there in the first place.

"In the days before fingerprints and identification cards and the widespread use of photography, it was easy to change your name, move to a new area, and assume a new identity. Butch was very good at this. So good that in the years 1889 to 1908, his most active time, Butch only went to jail once and that was for stealing a horse that he had actually paid for.

"As I mentioned before, there was no national police agency back then and very little coordination between states and even counties within states. That began to change with the rise of the Pinkerton Detective Agency. The Pinkertons started as Abraham Lincoln's primary intelligence service during the Civil War. After that, they expanded into private practice and became very successful. Their logo was an all-seeing eye, which became the basis for the term 'private eye.'

"The Pinkertons first became interested in Butch after a Union Pacific train was held up near Wilcox, Wyoming in June 1899. This is the train robbery that was depicted in the 1969 movie, the one where they used too much dynamite and blew the baggage car apart. Interestingly, we don't know if Butch was there at the train. He certainly planned the robbery and took a share of the loot, but he may not have been one of the robbers at the scene.

"The take from this robbery may have been as much as fifty thousand dollars, a good-sized fortune at that time. After this robbery, the Union Pacific and several other railroads and banks pooled funds and hired the Pinkertons to rid themselves of the troublesome outlaws.

"The Pinkertons had several advantages over the law enforcement agencies of the day. First, there were no jurisdictional issues, they could follow an outlaw wherever he went. Second, they took advantage of the available technology. They used the telegraph to pass information from one Pinkerton agency to another, and they made extensive use of photography to identify their subjects regardless of how many aliases they might invent.

"In fact, photography played a significant role in Butch's downfall. In 1900, after another train robbery near Tipton, Wyoming and a bank robbery in Winnemucca, Nevada, Butch, Sundance and several others escaped to Brown's Hole and laid up there for a while until they felt it was safe to travel. They then headed down to San Antonio, Texas for what amounted to a vacation. They set up camp at Fanny Porter's whorehouse and had an enjoyable time spending their ill-gotten gains. At some point, they went to Fort Worth, and they all bought new sets of clothes. Feeling like fine gentlemen, they decided to have their picture taken.

"This is the famous photograph of the Wild Bunch. Butch is on your right and Sundance is on the left. Between them is Ben Kilpatrick. Behind Butch is Kid Curry, and behind Sundance is Will Carver.

"After the gang left Fort Worth, the photographer, seeing an opportunity to get some publicity, sent the picture to the local paper. It quickly came to the attention of a Pinkerton agent, and it was soon distributed to all Pinkerton offices and published in newspapers across the West. It was now going to be much harder for Butch and the others to hide in plain sight as they had done for so long.

"It became evident to Butch that he had to leave the country. At that time Argentina was offering land at good prices to anyone who wanted to homestead. Butch probably saw this as an opportunity to get away from the law and get back to his first love, running a ranch and being a cowboy. On March 23, 1901, Butch, Sundance and Etta Place arrived in Buenos Aires.

"Butch's judgment was sound. Within a few months of the time Butch and Sundance left the US, the other three outlaws in the Fort Worth photograph were dead or in jail courtesy of the Pinkertons.

"Etta Place is the most enigmatic character in this story. No one knows for sure who she was or where she came from. The Pinkertons thought she was from Texas but had no idea what her real name was. Place was Harry Longabaugh's mother's maiden name, so it's probably an alias. Some people believe that Etta and Annie Bassett, the 'Queen of the Outlaws,' were one and the same, but that theory has been pretty well disproved. Etta was Sundance's girl, but she may have also had a relationship with Butch.

"When they arrived in Argentina, Sundance deposited $12,000 in a local bank, an amount worth over $300,000 today and worth much more than that in the Argentine economy of the early twentieth century. Butch, under the name James Ryan, used some of that money to purchase an *estancia* of around six thousand acres bordering a river in the Cholila Valley of Patagonia. They would eventually acquire large herds of sheep, cattle, and horses.

"Their ranch was remote, more than four hundred miles from the nearest railroad. There is little doubt that Butch and Sundance were trying to put their past as far behind them as they could.

"The Pinkertons tracked them to Argentina and learned about the ranch. When they reported that Butch and Sundance were safely tucked away in a remote corner of South America, the banking and railroad consortium that hired them were satisfied and terminated the Pinkerton contract. As long as the outlaws weren't bothering them, they didn't care where they were or what they were doing.

"But the Pinkerton's didn't quit."

"So, in the movie, when Paul Newman asked Robert Redford, "Who are those guys?", he was talking about the Pinkertons?" Rebecca asked.

"Good question. That's exactly right, and it brings up another point."

"We don't know why the Pinkerton Agency continued to chase after Butch and Sundance even when they were no longer being paid for it. Maybe they wanted to bolster their reputation that they always got their man, or perhaps it was stubborn pride, but the result was that they continued to monitor Butch and Sundance the entire time they were in South America.

"At that time Patagonia was in some ways a new American frontier. It attracted people from North America looking for cheap land and a chance to run their own farm or ranch. It also drew men like Butch and Sundance who were on the run from the law. Not all of the North American outlaws who came south were interested in going straight.

"At the beginning of the twentieth century, Argentina was at least twenty years behind the US in terms of law enforcement. Technologies like the telegraph and photography were still very new and not in extensive use. There were vast areas of open land and not many *policia*. In some ways, it should have been easy for a North American outlaw to get rich, but there was one significant disadvantage.

"The North American outlaws looked, acted and spoke differently than the people around them and were never able to gain their support. For this reason, the careers of many of the transplanted outlaws tended to be short and end violently.

"The Pinkertons took advantage of this. Every time a *Norte Americano* was believed to be involved in a crime, the Pinkertons saw to it that Butch and Sundance got the blame. While there were few photos of the other outlaws, the Pinkertons had plenty of pictures of Butch and Sundance. Since one *Norte Americano* looked pretty much like any other to a typical Argentine peasant, it wasn't too hard to get eyewitnesses to swear that Butch and Sundance were the robbers.

"In February 1905 two men, Brady and Linden, robbed the bank in Rio Gallegos. Although it is possible that Butch and Sundance may have known the robbers and could have given them some ideas about how to rob a bank, they were on their ranch hundreds of miles away at the time of the robbery. Nevertheless, they came under immediate suspicion, and Butch knew that their ranching days were over. Butch and Sundance began selling off their herds and property.

"At about this same time Etta Place disappears from the story and is lost to history. There are theories that she went to San Francisco, but no one knows what happened to her.

"Near the end of 1905, the bank in Villa Mercedes was robbed by four, 'English ranchers,' who were probably Butch and Sundance along with Brady and Linden. They were hotly pursued by a police posse from Villa Mercedes and just managed to make it across the border into Chile.

"Butch then traveled north into Bolivia and found work at the Concordia Tin Mine located at an altitude of sixteen thousand feet in the Bolivian Andes. Butch, using the alias J. P. Maxwell, started work by running the mule teams that brought supplies to the mine and quickly earned the mine manager's trust. Butch was soon transporting the mine's payroll. A little later he was joined at the mine by Sundance.

"And now we get to the part where we can start to talk about what may have happened to Butch and Sundance in Bolivia. There are many theories, but I'll focus on the one that makes the most sense to me.

"The mine manager was an American, Percy Seibert, and he soon figured out who his two new employees were. Despite this, he became close friends with both of the outlaws, and he believed them when they said that they would never steal from the mine or do anything to cause him trouble. He would often have Butch and Sundance join his family for dinner.

"That Percy and Butch were friends is a fact. Now, here comes the conjecture. Butch knew that the Pinkertons were going to hunt him until he was captured or killed. He didn't want to be caught, but what if he could convince them he was dead? I think that Butch and Percy made a plan and then waited for a couple of outlaws to be killed in a robbery. They didn't have to wait long.

"On November 4th, 1908, two men robbed the Aramayo and Franke pack train that was carrying the company's payroll. Two days later, two outlaws were killed in San Vicente, Bolivia. Both of these events were recounted in the 1969 movie. What is different from the movie is the fact that there is no credible evidence that Butch and Sundance were at either of these places!"

◆ ◆ ◆

Concordia Tin Mine

Andes Mountains

Near La Paz, Bolivia

20 November, 1908

"Mr. Seibert, I'm … I'm … Josh Phillips the Pink … Pinkerton agent from Buenos Aires. My god … how do people breath up here?"

Hiding his smile, Percy Seibert said, "Yes, Mr. Phillips, we've been expecting you. You made good time getting here. Please come in out of the cold, have a seat."

"I'm sorry you had to come all the way up here, but we're getting ready to start up operations at the mine after a long winter, and I've been much too busy to get away. That little trip to San Vicente took up all the spare time I have. Can I get you some water? Maybe a glass of whiskey would help?"

Collapsing into a chair, Phillips replied, "No, … no whiskey. Just water … please."

After Phillips had rested long enough to get his breathing under control, he asked, "So, what did you find in San Vicente?"

"Well, it was a very unpleasant business. The authorities agreed to dig up the bodies that had been in the ground for almost ten days, and I can tell you it wasn't very pretty, but I could recognize them well enough. It was Maxwell and Ingersoll all right."

"Well, I appreciate you doin' that Mr. Seibert, and I'll see your expenses get paid like I promised. Now take a good look at this photograph here. Do you see your men, Maxwell and Ingersoll here?"

After looking carefully for a minute, Seibert replied, "Why, yes. The fellow sitting on the right is J.P. Maxwell and the one sitting on the left is Ingersoll. I never could remember his first name."

"Well sir, the picture you're lookin' at was taken in Ft. Worth, Texas and that's the Wild Bunch. Your Maxwell and Ingersoll are actually Butch Cassidy and the Sundance Kid."

"No! That's not possible! I thought that the Wild Bunch had been wiped out."

"The rest are all dead or in jail, but Cassidy and Longabaugh have been robbing and killin' all over Argentina and Bolivia for the last five or six years, and the Pinkerton Agency has been tryin' to bring 'em to justice."

Butch and Sundance never killed anyone, and you know it, you lyin' S.O.B.

"But they've been good workers and easy to get along with. I've had 'em to supper with my family! They've been carryin' the payroll up from La Paz, and I never lost a penny. It can't be true!"

"Don't be too upset Mr. Seibert. Those men were professional outlaws. Lyin' and cheatin' come as natural to them as breathin'. You should be happy they've finally been put six feet under where they belong."

"I still can't believe it. What happens now?"

"Now I telegraph my report to headquarters in Washington, and maybe I can finally go back to the States."

"Yes, I understand. This is just too much. I'm going to have a glass of whiskey. Will you have one?"

"I'd like to celebrate with you, but I'm just feelin' too poorly. I need to lie down."

"I understand. It's difficult when you first come up to this altitude. We'll get you over to the guest cabin. That where Maxwell … I mean Cassidy and Sundance lived. Try to get some sleep. We'll get you headed down first thing in the morning. You'll feel better when you get lower."

After Phillips had left, Seibert's wife, Susan, came in from the kitchen where she'd been listening.

"Percy Seibert, if I'd known what a liar you are I'd never have married you."

"Darling Susan, I have no idea what you're talking about. What lies do you mean?" Seibert replied grinning.

"Well, for one thing, we've known all along about Butch and Sundance, and for another, you know as well as I do that they're in Chile lookin' for a boat to take them home."

"Should I have told Mr. Phillips that?"

"Oh god, no. That man made my skin crawl. That smug, self-righteous… well, I won't say the word, but you know what I mean."

"Yes. It's interesting how we came so quickly to trust two men we knew were wanted outlaws and so immediately to dislike the man who was supposed to be upholding the law."

"I just hope your plan works."

"Yes, me too, and I think it will. Butch and Sundance have enough money to last them a good while. If they can stay on the straight and narrow and not call attention to themselves, I think they'll be all right."

"And Mr. Phillips?"

"I think Mr. Phillips will have a very long, very uncomfortable night. I warned him to take his time coming up here, but he wouldn't listen, and now he's payin' the price. I'm sure he'll be as anxious to leave as we will be to get rid of him."

◆ ◆ ◆

Ogden Valley, Utah

Monday, 11 June

"So, your theory is that Butch Cassidy and the Sundance Kid faked their deaths in Bolivia and made it back to the States. Is there any evidence to support that?"

"Well, Alicia, it's not my theory, it's just the one out of many theories that makes the most sense to me. And, yes, there is evidence to support it; quite a bit of evidence."

"Such as?"

"Well here's something that should appeal to you as a forensic anthropologist. In 1992 a team went down to San Vicente to do a documentary on Butch and Sundance for the PBS 'American Experience' series. It's an excellent documentary, by the way, and Sam can get it on Netflix if we want to watch it later. Anyway, this team uncovered the remains of the two men who had been identified as Butch and Sundance and took samples for DNA testing. They had to re-write the ending of their documentary when they discovered that they got no match for any of Butch or Sundance's relatives or their descendants."

"Well," Alicia replied "assuming that no one screwed up the samples or the testing, that's pretty conclusive, but all it proves is that those two specific bodies were not Butch or Sundance, it doesn't say anything about what may have happened to them."

"No, you're right, of course, but there's more. Bill Bentenson wrote a book called "Butch Cassidy My Uncle." Mr. Bentenson is Butch's great-grandnephew, his great-grandmother was Lula Parker, Butch's youngest sister. Mr. Bentenson has exhaustively documented the life of Butch Cassidy. He traveled to every place in the U.S. and South America where any event of major consequence in the outlaw's life occurred. In the process, he debunked many myths and half-truths. Of particular interest to us is the fact that Mr. Bentenson's great-grandmother told him that she saw her brother, Robert Leroy Parker, when came to visit his family in Circleville, Utah in 1925, seventeen years after he was supposedly killed in Bolivia!"

"Wow! Do you think that's reliable?"

"Yes, I do. In addition to a detailed account of Butch's visit to his family, Mr. Bentenson recounts meetings between Butch and many others who knew him well in the late Twenties and early Thirties. Throughout his book, Mr. Bentenson's research is meticulous, and I think that it's highly unlikely that he would have been misled on something like this. Furthermore, Lula Bentenson is a reliable witness. She went from being the youngest child on a remote farm to becoming the first female state representative in Utah. She wrote her own book, "Butch Cassidy, My Brother," when she was ninety-one. When she was eighty-four, she was invited to the film scene of "Butch Cassidy and the Sundance Kid," where, by all accounts, she completely charmed Robert Redford who became her friend for the rest of her life."

"So," Sam asked, "why did he wait until 1925 to see his family? He'd been gone, what, forty-some years?"

"There were probably two reasons. Lula said that he was ashamed of all the trouble he had brought on his family and he wasn't sure if they would want to see him. Remember, the Parkers were a religious Mormon family, and they had probably suffered because of Butch's reputation. Also, it's likely that Butch wanted to be sure that no one was still looking for him before he went back to his home grounds."

"What about Sundance?" Steve asked.

"Sundance didn't have someone like Bill Bentenson to chronical his life, so much less is know about him. However, I believe that it is likely that he and Butch both escaped from Bolivia and made it back to the States. What happened after that, I don't know. Maybe we'll learn some more tomorrow at Wind River."

"Any information on whether he could have ended up in the Bighorn Mountains?"

"No, Sam, I haven't been able to find any sources on that. Butch Cassidy's whereabouts after he came back from Bolivia are a mystery other than the fact that he spent some time traveling around Wyoming catching up with old friends."

"So, that's it. I apologize for taking so long to get to my point – that Butch Cassidy and, probably, the Sundance Kid did not die in Bolivia in 1908 and that Butch was alive as late as the early Thirties – but know I hope you have a better understanding of who these people were and that may help us in planning our search for Butch's remains."

"Jim, thank you very much, that was great. I don't know about the rest of you, but I learned a lot."

After the team had given Jim a round of applause, Sam continued, "As you have probably figured out from the great smells coming from the kitchen, Rebecca has a big pot of spaghetti ready for us, and we'll get to that shortly. Alicia, you've got the downstairs bedroom here, Steve, you'll be upstairs."

"We'll want to get on the road no later than zero-seven-hundred tomorrow to get to Lander before noon. We'll meet Joseph Golden Eagle there, and he will guide us onto the reservation where we'll meet his uncle and learn the rest of the story."

"I hope everyone remembered to bring cold weather gear with them like I suggested. We'll be working up at ninety-six hundred feet, and it can get cold. I've checked the weather forecast, and there's a chance of a storm and, at that altitude up in the Bighorns, it could be snow, maybe a lot of snow. If anyone needs some gear, let me know, and we'll fix you up."

"Does anyone have any questions or is there anything I've missed?"

"What have you done about getting permission to disinter any remains we might find?" Alicia asked.

"Uh … nothing?"

"Yeah, I thought so. We have two potential problems that we need to take care of. If we find any Native American remains we will need permission from the tribes to remove them. If they appear to be very old remains, then we have to worry about the Antiquities Act."

"What does that mean?"

"It's a long story, let me finish."

"If the remains are Caucasian, then we need to make sure that we have permission from whatever law enforcement agency has jurisdiction because it's a crime scene."

"Why would it be a crime scene?" Jim asked, "There's no evidence that a crime was committed."

"It doesn't matter. Any unobserved or suspicious death is treated as a possible homicide. The local law will want to be involved."

"I hadn't thought about any of this," Sam said.

"I know. Good thing you've got me. I know some folks at the Wyoming Department of Criminal Investigation. I can make some calls and get that side of things sorted out. Sam, you or Jim are gonna have to talk to your Arapaho friends and make sure they smooth things out with the tribes."

"I'll take care of that, Sam."

"Thanks, Jim."

"I've gotta tell you though, if we find very old native remains, we're going to have to leave 'em in place, and there's a good chance we'll get in the middle of a legal mess."

"Is there anything we can do about that beforehand?"

"I don't think so."

"We'll worry about that when, and if, it happens."

"Are there any other minor details I may have overlooked?"

When he got no reply, Sam continued, "I was going to brief you on the terrain and everything up at the Buffalo Wheel, but it's been a long day, and it will be better to get briefed up there by someone who knows the area. Let's take a few minutes to get settled and then it'll be time for dinner."

◆ ◆ ◆

Ogden Valley, Utah

Monday, 11 June

Later That Evening

It had been a long, dull day for Gunny and the other dogs. All they had to do was lie around while the people talked and talked. A couple of short walks and a little playtime was all the dogs got. At least The Man remembered dinner time.

As he did most nights, Gunny hoped that he would see the Good Man and his dog Rusty again, but they never came. Gunny thought about the Good Man often, and he sometimes dreamed about him, but he wasn't really there like he had been before. Now his dreams were a combination of odors; The Man, and the Good Man and Rusty who both smelled like Old Bone, and his old puppy dream of the first hand that had held him. He was happy with these dreams and began to drift into a deeper sleep.

And then there was a new smell. It was a wild smell that Gunny had gotten some whiffs of before when he and The Man had gone far up in the mountains to Go Find or Adios. It was a smell like a dog, but not a dog— something older than a dog. It was a smell that Gunny instinctively knew was dangerous, but, for some reason, he did not feel frightened. After a minute an image began to form. It was pale and hazy, its outline was blurred. It was shaped like a dog, but it was bigger than any dog Gunny had ever seen. As the image became clearer, Gunny could see that its fur was gray and white, and its legs were long, and it was lean and strong-looking. Gunny began to be worried, but then the Dog-not-Dog looked at him with calm, dark eyes and Gunny knew that he did not have to be afraid. Then the Dog-not-Dog lifted his muzzle to the sky and made the most exciting sound Gunny had ever heard, a long, mournful howl that made the fur all over Gunny's body come erect. As the howl faded and the Dog-not-Dog trotted away, Gunny wanted to follow him, but he didn't know how.

Luke and Iwo also dreamed of the Dog-not-Dog that night. Like Gunny, they knew that they, too, wanted to follow him, but why? What did he want them to do?

◆ ◆ ◆

St. Stephen's Mission

Wind River Indian Reservation

That Same Evening

"Bless me, Father, for I have sinned. It has been, uh… a long time since my last confession. I am heartily sorry for the following sins."

Yes, I haven't heard this voice for quite a while, thought Father Jim Smithers, *but I know it. Eldon White Dear has been gone from the Church for a long time. Please, Dear God, let him be back for good.*

"Father, I've been doing drugs and selling drugs and a lot of other things, and I wanna stop, but I don't know how."

"My son, coming here and admitting what you've done is a good first step. If you're truly sorry for your sins, I can give you absolution, and God will forgive you. But if you want to straighten out your life, it will take a lot of work. I can help you, but you'll have to do most of it on your own."

"What do I have to do, Father?"

"We have a program here at St. Stephens for young men struggling with drugs and alcohol. It has helped many others."

"I can't do anything in public Father. There's this white guy, a meth dealer, and he's a real bad guy. If he thinks I'm tryin' to go straight he'll … I don't know what he'll do, but it won't be good."

"Have you talked to the police?"

"Oh no, Father. He'd find out and kill me for sure."

"Well, you know where to find me. I will be happy to talk with you anytime you need help."

"Thanks, Father. I gotta run."

"Wait! Are you sorry for what you have done?"

"Yes, Father. I've screwed up my life, and it's killin' my mother. I'm really sorry."

"Then I absolve you of your sins in the Name of the Father, and of the Son, and of the Holy Spirit. Amen. For your penance I want you to set aside some time every day to say a good Act of Contrition and pray the Rosary. Maybe, with the Lord's help, some daily prayer will help you focus on what you have to do to change your life for the better."

"Thank you, Father. I'll do it. I'm gonna try real hard."

Before Father Smithers could reply, Eldon White Dear rushed out of the confessional and ran out of the church.

CHAPTER EIGHT

Dubois

"Now the old Double Diamond lay out east of Dubois, in the land of the Buffalo."

"The Old Double Diamond" lyrics by Gary McMahan

Activities Building

St, Stephen's Indian Mission

Wind River Indian Reservation

Tuesday, 12 June

IT HAD BEEN A LITTLE OVER FOUR HOURS from Sam's house to Lander where they met Joseph Golden Eagle for lunch. After that, they followed him out Seventeen Mile Road to St. Stephen's Mission. When they arrived, Golden Eagle asked them to wait while he talked with his uncle and Father Smithers to find out what they wanted to do. Sam said that they'd let the dogs out for some exercise and be back at the cars in ten minutes or so.

When they got back to the cars and were about to put the dogs up in their crates, Golden Eagle trotted up with his hand raised as if to stop them.

"My uncle and Father Smithers would like you to bring the dogs in with you."

Sam shrugged. "Fine. They'll be more comfortable inside. It's getting pretty warm out here."

The meeting room was pleasantly cool. Near the front stood two men who both looked to be in their sixties or early seventies but were otherwise total opposites. The nearer was small, about five-six, with a dark brown, wrinkled face and long black hair, liberally mixed with white, hanging in ponytails on either side of his head. He wore jeans and cowboy boots and a flannel shirt. The other man was tall and trim with close-cropped white hair and a remarkably smooth face. He was dressed in the black clerical garb of the Jesuit order.

Joseph Golden Eagle made the introductions. "Sam, Rebecca, Alicia, and Steve, this is my uncle, Old Man Sees Wolf and Father Jim Smithers."

As they shook hands, Joseph's uncle said with a wry smile, "They have been calling me 'Old Man Sees Wolf' for the last ten years or so, but I'm happy with just 'Sees Wolf.' I don't know why people think I'm old. I'm the same age as this young priest here. My white name, or, as you would say my Christian name, is Edward, and you can call me whatever you like."

As they had been shaking hands Sam, Steve, and Alicia had not been paying much attention to their dogs. They were now surprised to see the three of them sitting just in front of Sees Wolf looking at him attentively with their noses working rapidly.

"And hello to you my brothers. I see that you are interested in my scent. Here smell."

As Sees Wolf held his hand out for each dog to smell the dogs quivered with excitement and yet stayed in a perfect 'sit.'

Gunny thought, *It's very faint, but it's the same smell, the smell of Dog-not- Dog. Why is that?*

"Ah! Very good!" Sees Wolf said. "I see you have good noses. That is well, you will need them. Wait here."

Sees Wolf walked over to the corner of the room where a shallow copper dish sat on a table. Fragrant cedar smoke was coming from embers burning there. Sees Wolf brought the dish over and stood in front of the dogs whose eyes had never left him.

"Please, tell me their names."

"That one's Gunny, the one in the middle is Luke, and the young one is Iwo," Sam replied.

Going up to Gunny, Sees Wolf bent over him and softly sang a chant. The only word Sam could recognize was Gunny's name. When he had finished chanting, he held the dish with the cedar embers in front of Gunny's face and gently blew the smoke directly into his muzzle.

Wow! Gunny usually can't stand to have anyone blow into his face, but he's acting like he's lovin' this.

When he had finished with Gunny, Sees Wolf went to Luke and then Iwo and performed the same ritual. The other dogs acted just as Gunny had.

When Sees Wolf had finished, Father Smithers said, 'Well, I can't let the heathen Indian do all the work. Do you mind if I bless your dogs also?"

Sam and the others were taken aback, but then Sees Wolf said, "Watch out! If he starts talkin' Latin, we're all in trouble," and the two men grinned at their private joke.

Smithers went over to the same table where there was a small pail with a thick, silver rod sticking up out of it. Sam recognized it from his altar boy days as an aspergillum, used for sprinkling Holy Water. It was apparent that the medicine man and the priest had planned this ceremony together, probably right down to which insults they would exchange.

When he came back, the three dogs were still sitting quietly, almost respectfully. Standing in front of them, Father Smithers began by dipping the aspergillum in the pail of Holy Water and sprinkling it over each dog. Then, with a sly smile directed at Sees Wolf, he began.

"In Nomine Patri, et Filii, et Spiritus Sancti," and then continued, "Gunny, Luke, and Iwo, may the Lord bless you and bring his light to shine upon you, and may he keep you safe and make you successful in your search. Amen."

When Father Smithers had finished, Sees Wolf said, "All right, now it's time for me to tell my story. There's coffee and good fry bread. Get yerself somethin' and get comfortable. This may take a little while."

When they had settled in Alicia spoke first, "Sees Wolf, may I ask a question before we begin?"

"Of course, Doctor Phillips. As an anthropologist, I suppose you want to know what all that mumbo-jumbo was with the dogs."

"Well, I understand the blessing and thank you both for doing that, but what was it they were smelling on your hand? It was obvious that it was something fascinating. Oh, and, please, call me Alicia."

"Very perceptive of you to notice that, Alicia. Did the rest of you pick up on it also?"

When everyone had nodded, he continued, "I don't know this for certain because I don't have the nose of a dog, but I suspect that they were smelling my wolf."

"You have a wolf?" the four team members exclaimed almost in unison.

"Yes … in a manner of speaking. I do not have a physical wolf, but since I was a young man I have often been visited by a Spirit Wolf, which is why I'm called Sees Wolf. Sometimes when it is very quiet, and he is sitting next to me I can smell him, and I think that his scent has become part of my scent."

Seeing the expressions on everyone's face, Sees Wolf continued, "Is this strange to you? Is it any more strange than the ghost of that young Marine that you saw and dreamed of on Iwo Jima?"

"How do you know about that?" Sam asked.

"That is a story for another time, let's just say that I'm not as rustic as I may appear and that I have some friends at the University of Tokyo. Doctor Ed Akiyama and I had a very interesting talk a few months ago. By the way, he asked me to send you his regards. Anyway, I can see by your reaction that my information is correct."

"Yes, it is, and I'm beginning to understand why you asked for our help specifically. So, let me see if I've got it. You have a Spirit Wolf, and this spirit has a physical scent that dogs can detect. Is that as strange as it's going to get, or is there more?'

Sees Wolf smiled, "First, I do not have a wolf. The wolf is my brother, and I am his brother. Second, no. I'm afraid that the strangeness has just begun. Perhaps it would be best if I told you my story from the beginning."

"Yes, of course," Sam said, "please go on."

"Thank you."

"Like most tribes, we Northern Arapaho here in Wind River have an elected tribal council that works much like a city council that you whites would have. By the way, we tend to lump all people who are not Arapaho or from another tribe together as 'whites.' I hope that doesn't offend you, Mr. Haney."

"Well, I'm pretty sure no one has ever called me 'white' before, but I understand what you mean, so, no, that's fine with me."

"Thank you. So, as I was saying. The tribal council is in charge of the day-to-day running of the tribe and the reservation. We have our tribal police and fireman, we run a hospital, and all the other services you would expect."

"In addition to this council, we have another set of leaders that you might think of as our spiritual or cultural leaders. At the head of this group are the Four Elders who are elected from among the oldest and wisest members of the tribe. Their role is not as clearly defined as the tribal council, they're mainly concerned with the spiritual health of the people, and that includes preserving our customs and language among other things. One of the Elders is what you would call a medicine man, and I'll need to explain that a little."

"Medicine men are healers and spiritual guides. We are the original practitioners of what you call today 'holistic medicine.' We heal by a combination of traditional medicines, mostly herbs and plants, and by using a variety of blessings and other ceremonies to cleanse the spirit of evil influences that can cause physical suffering. We also work with the Four Elders to maintain our language and culture and to try to lead our people along a more spiritual path."

"Where does Father Smithers fit into this, if at all?" Sam asked.

"I'll answer that, if I may, Edward?" Father Smithers said.

When Sees Wolf nodded, Smithers continued, "The Arapaho believe in a single God, the Creator, whom they call *Hichaba Nihancan*. They also believe in many spirits, especially animal spirits. Edward's spirit wolf is a perfect example. The Arapaho pray to their spirits for help and guidance which is not that different from the way a Catholic prays to one of the Saints. If an Arapaho chooses to accept Jesus Christ as his Lord and Savior, he or she has done nothing against the Arapaho religion. If an Arapaho Catholic chooses to participate in an Arapaho ritual to ask the spirits for rain or some other blessing I have no problem with that, and I'm pretty sure that the Pope would back me up. The important thing as Sees Wolf and I see it is to get people to lead a more spiritual, less materialistic life. Do you agree, Edward?"

"Yes, I couldn't have said it better myself, except that I could have said it in Arapaho."

"Yes, well, I could have said it in Latin, so there!"

These two really like each other Sam thought.

"Excuse me, Sees Wolf, but I have a question also."

"Go ahead, Alicia."

"You practice holistic medicine, and that's great, and I know it has many benefits, but what do you do if, for example, you come across someone with a serious injury?"

"I do what you would do. I take out my cell phone and dial 911. That's a good question, and it brings up another point."

"Someone in my family has been a medicine man for as long as anyone remembers. My grandfather, who was born in 1890, was a medicine man from about 1915 to 1945. He remembered the old times when our religion was outlawed, and everything had to be done in secret. It was a great struggle for him and the Four Elders to preserve the old ways. It was necessary for them to avoid the white man, and, as a result, he knew little of the white man's world."

"My grandfather was called Sees Buffalo because his spirit animal was a buffalo."

"Are all of your medicine men named after their spirit animal?" Alicia asked.

"No. My grandfather and I are unusual. Not all of our medicine men have a spirit animal. My father didn't. He was called Wild Pony when he was young and then Horse Rider when he was older because, well, because he was such a good horse rider."

"My father was born in 1915, and his life was a little different. Things were beginning to change, and there was more interaction between the two cultures. His eyes were opened when he joined the Army and went off to fight in Europe. When he came home in 1945 and took over from my grandfather, he knew that the Arapaho would have to learn more about how to live in the white man's world. When I was born in 1946, he decided that I would be the first in our family to get a college education whether I was to be a medicine man or not."

"Where did you go?" Steve asked.

"University of Wyoming, Class of 1968. Go, Cowboys!"

After everyone had a chuckle, Steve asked, "How was that for you?"

"If you mean, 'Was there prejudice and discrimination?' sure, but probably not as much as there was for a black man at about the same time. Also, I did a little rodeo, and that helped me to be more accepted."

"I'm sorry, but I have to interrupt here," Joseph Golden Eagle said. "My uncle has a tendency toward excessive modesty. He did not do, 'a little rodeo.' He went to Wyoming on a full scholarship and was the NCAA champion bronc rider for three years in a row. At Wyoming and the other schools out here, that's a big deal."

"Yes, well," Sees Wolf continued, "if you want to be accepted at Wyoming as an Indian, you've gotta out-cowboy the Cowboys."

"So, Alicia, that's the long answer to your question. One of the most difficult things I have to do is to reconcile our culture with the modern world. To try to take the good parts of both and use them to help my people have a better life."

"Now, back to my story."

"I understand that Doctor Stewart has told you why he believes that Butch Cassidy and the Sundance Kid did not die in Bolivia but made it back to this country and disappeared. I can tell you that Doctor Stewart has the story almost exactly correct, and, furthermore, I can tell you what happened to them when they came home.

"Really?" Alicia said, "That's great! Can you tell us the source of your information?"

"Yes, my grandfather became a good friend to Butch, Sundance, and their two wives."

"Amazing! But that just opens up so many questions."

"I understand, and I think that the best person to answer those questions is my grandfather."

Sees Wolf handed each member of the team a folder that contained several typewritten pages.

"These are the transcripts of a recording that my father made of my grandfather telling his story about Butch and Sundance in the late 1940's. I think it's best if you learn the story in my grandfather's own words. Take as much time as you need to read this, and then I'll try to answer any questions."

Sam and the others took the papers out and began to read.

When I was a young man in 1906, word spread that a white woman had moved onto a small ranch between the reservation and Dubois. This was important to the Arapaho for two reasons. We had learned the hard way to keep a close eye on any whites living near us. And, it was unusual for a woman to be on a ranch alone.

Back then, my uncle was the hiitheinoonotii, the medicine man, and he was training me to take over his role. The Four Elders decided that he should approach this white woman to try to find out if she would be a friend or a problem for the people. He decided to take me with him as part of my training.

We rode to the ranch tryin' hard not to look dangerous. The woman met us at the house with a shotgun, but, when she decided that we were friendly, she invited us in for coffee. I could tell that this was a woman who had lived in our country and knew how to deal with Indians.

She told us that her name was Annie Porter and that her husband had bought this ranch back in the 1890's but they had never lived there because he had to travel a lot for his work. She never said what his job was. Her husband, George Porter and his brother Robert were finishing some work in South America and would be coming to the ranch soon along with Robert's wife, Ethel.

Mrs. Porter said that the two men had some money put aside and that they just wanted to go back to what they had grown up doin'—running a ranch and raising some cattle and horses.

Now, that ranch was up high, in-between the Wind River and Absaroka mountains. Because of that, it got enough rain and snow that even as small as it was, you could still run a decent herd of cattle. It was better land than most of the places on the reservation, which, of course, is why the whites had not seen fit to give it to the Indians.

So, me and my uncle found out what we needed to know, and we left Mrs. Porter. But before we went, my uncle told her that I was a good hand with cattle, and I'd be happy to work for them if they needed any hired help. My uncle thought that if I could work on the ranch, I could keep an eye on the new whites and earn a few dollars for the family at the same time.

And that's the way it worked out. I went to work on the ranch and ended up spending a lot of time there. I had two jobs; working cattle and horses on the ranch and learnin' to become a hiitheinoonotii when I was back home.

Then sometime early in 1909, I remember there was still snow on the ground, the other three whites came to the ranch. George Porter was friendly, and a good rider and a good hand with cattle and I enjoyed working with him. His brother Robert wasn't as friendly, and he could go a whole day without saying anything except to the cows or his horse. Robert's wife Ethel was real pretty, and the two women kept me well-fed when I was livin' at the ranch. You could almos' say that the four of them treated me like a white man.

That spring my uncle came to the ranch and was invited to dinner. His first words when he met George Porter were, 'You're George Cassidy!'

Now it turns out that George Cassidy was one of the names that Butch Cassidy, the outlaw, used when he came to Wind River to hide out during the 1890's.

After that, it didn't take long for us to figure out who the four really were. George Porter was Robert Leroy Parker, Butch Cassidy, and Robert Porter was Harry Longabaugh, the Sundance Kid. Sundance's 'wife' was Etta Place and the other woman was Annie Bassett, who the whites called the 'Queen of the Outlaws,' from Brown's Hole, Utah.

It didn't bother me none that they was outlaws. Far as I knew they'd never done anything wrong to an Arapaho. They was always real generous to us. If a baby was sick and needed medicine or a family was down on its luck and needed some money, they'd always help out. If some of that money happened to belong to some other white people that weren't none of our business.

I kept workin' at their ranch for few years until it was time to take on being a hiitheinoonotii. After that, other Arapahoe, and, sometimes a Shoshone would work there. I stayed close with them, and they were my only white friends.

Butch was always askin' questions about what we Arapaho believed and what our religion was. We spent hours and hours talkin', and I tried to teach him some of the things I was learnin'. Butch came to a lot of our tribal dances and other ceremonies, and he always left a generous gift.

Sundance and Etta left the ranch sometime in the early 1920's. I wasn't there when they left, and Butch never told me why they left or where they went. It could be that Sundance died and Etta went home to Pennsylvania, but as far as I know, no trace has been found of her or Sundance.

The last time I visited them I took my boy, Wild Pony, along. Butch was real sick and in bed. He told us that he expected to die soon and that he was worried about what would happen. He said that he didn't want Annie to have to deal with takin' care of his body.

The other thing that worried him was that he would go to hell if he couldn't be buried in sacred ground. He had been a Mormon a long time before, but they had kicked him out, and he couldn't get back in the Church without tellin' 'em who he was. The priest at St. Stephens then was pretty strict, and he and Butch had never gotten along so he couldn't be buried there. I told Butch that I didn't know anythin' about the white man's burial ceremonies and I couldn't help him, but that last time I saw him he told me he wasn't worried no more and he had it figured out.

Sometime in the Spring of 1936, Annie drove out to my ranch. She told me that the week before she had gone into Dubois to buy some supplies and that when she came back, Butch was gone. She said that she knew he was dead, but that he had arranged to have everything taken care of.

When I asked her where he was buried, she said she didn't know, but that it would be all right.

A month or so later Annie showed up at the tribal council office and signed over to the tribe the deed to the ranch. Turns out that the ranch had been in her name all along. She said that she was going back to Brown's Hole to be with her family. A few days later, she was gone, and that's the last I ever saw of her or any of the others."

When everyone had finished reading, Sam asked the first question, "Do you mean to say that four of the most notorious outlaw figures in the history of the West decided to hide out next to the Wind River reservation?"

"Yes, that's right, and I think you can understand why. The Arapaho and the Shoshone had no reason to want to help the white lawmen who had always mistreated them. Butch had been able to hide on the reservation before, and not much had changed in the next ten or fifteen years. What's more, the white people in Dubois had no great love for the law of the State of Wyoming. Do you know the story of how Dubois got its name and why it's pronounced the way it is?"

"Yes, Jim told us," Alicia said. "So, this part of the world was still pretty lawless?"

"If you're referring to white law or Wyoming law, yes. We on the rez had our own law and the few people who lived in Dubois had worked out a way to get along without needing a lot of adult supervision."

"What about the rewards for Butch and Sundance?" Steve asked.

"For the most part, those had expired. It didn't matter though, because, as my grandfather said, the Arapaho and Shoshone soon learned that the four new white people were generous neighbors, always willing to help out when there was a need. Anyone who turned them in would have been outcast."

"Your grandfather never found out where Butch was buried?" Sam asked.

"Not as far as I know," Sees Wolf answered, "If he did, he never told anyone."

"And no trace still of Sundance or Etta?" Rebecca asked.

"No. Etta seems to have just vanished. A body was exhumed in Duschene, Utah a few years ago that some think is Sundance, but the DNA results are inconclusive."

"So," Sam asked, "How did you get the idea that Butch was buried at the Buffalo Wheel?"

"That took a long time and a little luck."

"My grandfather first noticed the strange disturbance at the Buffalo Wheel during the summer solstice ceremonies that year after Annie had left. He didn't tell my father about it until a couple of years later when my father participated in the solstice ceremony as a medicine man for the first time. After the ceremony, my father asked my grandfather if he had noticed or felt anything unusual. My grandfather answered, 'Maybe. Why?'. When my father told my grandfather what he had experienced my grandfather just nodded and said, 'Yes. There is something wrong.'

"At that time, my father had no reason to think that there was a connection between the problem at the Buffalo Wheel and Butch Cassidy's disappearance, and if my grandfather suspected anything, he never told my father.

"And that's the way things stood for many years. My father took over from my grandfather in 1945, and I took over from him in 1979. I noticed the disturbance the first time I participated in the solstice ceremony in 1965, just as my father had. When I asked him about it, he just nodded and said, 'Yes.'

"When I asked my father what he thought the problem might be all he could do was to tell me that the disturbance had started in 1936 and that he and his father both believed that the source was an unquiet spirit that had somehow become trapped there. Who or what this spirit might be or how it came to be there they didn't understand.

"My father and I often talked about the problem, but we couldn't find a solution. We tried different blessing and purification ceremonies with no luck. When my father passed away in 1994, we were no nearer a solution than he and my grandfather had been."

"Has the problem gotten worse over the years?" Alicia asked.

"No, but the need for the spiritual peace of the Buffalo Wheel has gotten greater. The Arapaho and Shoshone, like most of the tribes, suffer from all the ills of the rest of the country, but somehow these problems, especially the effects of drugs and alcohol, are magnified for us. I don't think that the Buffalo Wheel will solve all our problems, but I believe that it can help. But to be truly helpful it must be whole, without the distraction of whatever this spirit might be.

"That was the situation up until about a year ago when we were cleaning a bunch of junk out from an old storage shed that we were gonna tear down before it fell down. In a back corner, I found a small box that had been wrapped in a part of an old, rubber poncho. Out of curiosity, I opened it up and inside I found a bunch of old papers and letters wrapped in oilskin. On several of the letters I saw my grandfather's name, and I knew that I had found something interesting.

"When I had time to sit down and go through it I found that everything in the box was addressed to or mentioned Sees Buffalo. Most of the letters were about mundane things, some of it appeared to be about tribal business, and there were a few bills or notices. Among all of this was a sealed envelope that was addressed to 'Sees Buffalo, Arapaho Reservation, Wind River Wyoming.' The return address was, 'Annie Bassett, Brown's Hole, Utah.' There were stamps on the envelope that had been postmarked in May 1936, and, as far as I could tell, the envelope had never been opened.

"The envelope contained two hand-written letters, each on a single piece of paper. The first was from Annie to my grandfather, and the second was from Butch to Annie. The handwriting on both was somewhat faded and hard to read so I've transcribed them and made copies for each of you. I think you should read Butch's letter first.

Dear Annie,

By the time you read this I'll be dead. You know my time is up so I hope this doesn't make you too sad. I have been in too much pain for too long and I know it has hurt you almost as much as me. I have hired a couple of boys to take me to my burying place. You don't know them so don't bother asking around. I'll put an end to things once I get there and they'll bury me.

I don't want you to know where I'm buried. I want you to go back to your family and forget about me and all the trouble I've caused you. Thanks to Sees Buffalo I've found a sacred place to be buried so I can go to heaven. He don't know where it is, but he gave me the idea.

Annie, these last years on the ranch with you have been the best of my life. Maybe if I'd a been smart enough to marry you when we first met so long ago everything would have been different. But I was a young kid full of wild ideas and I took to the outlaw life. I have always loved you and I always will and I hope to see you in heaven.

Butch

"And here's Annie's letter."

Sees Buffalo,

Butch has gone and killed himself and he's been buried and I don't know where. He says you gave him the idea for a sacred place. I want to find his grave and put up a stone but I don't know where to look. If you know please send me word as soon as you can.

Your friend,

Annie Bassett

"Sees Wolf, why wouldn't Sees Buffalo have opened a letter from Annie Bassett?" Alicia asked.

"I've thought about that a lot and couldn't come up with an answer until I remembered something that my father had told me. Because my grandfather had spent most of his life avoiding whites and working to preserve our language and religion, he had never gone to school. Sees Buffalo couldn't read. Although his reasons were honorable, he was always embarrassed by this, he thought it was a form of weakness. I think that he understood that these letters were things of importance that he couldn't bear to throw away, but he didn't want to admit that he couldn't read by asking someone to read them for him."

"That's sad," Rebecca said.

"Yes, it is," Sees Wolf replied. "But it explains a lot of things. As soon as I read those letters I was convinced that I knew where Butch Cassidy was buried."

"Because you started experiencing the ... unquiet spirit at the Buffalo Wheel shortly after his death."

"Yes, Sam, exactly."

"But why do you think his spirit has been trapped there for so long?" Jim asked.

"There are two reasons. First, the Buffalo Wheel is sacred ground, and there should be no burials there. My guess is that Butch misunderstood some of the things that my grandfather told him. He understood that the Buffalo Wheel was sacred ground, but he didn't understand exactly what was meant by that. We Arapaho don't have cemeteries that have been blessed and sanctified as you do, so 'sacred ground' means something different to us than to others. No Arapaho would think of burying a body at a place like the Buffalo Wheel."

"In addition to being buried on sacred ground, it was unlikely that Butch was buried with any ritual. His letter says that he, '…hired a couple of boys …,' to take him to be buried. It is highly unlikely that these 'boys' were Arapaho and it is certain that they were not anyone who would understand our burial rituals. Under these conditions, I would expect that Butch's spirit would be trapped until his body was moved and re-buried elsewhere with an appropriate ceremony."

"That's where we come in. Three cadaver dogs and three people who have had some experience with, …'unquiet spirits' …," Sam said.

"Yes, exactly."

Turning to the rest of the team Sam asked, "Anybody have a problem with this?"

"No, … nope, … not me."

"OK, Sees Wolf, I guess we're in."

"Thank you, Sam. Thank all of you."

"So, what's next?" Sam asked.

"So, now we go up to the Buffalo Wheel. Tomorrow is Wednesday, and I understand that you are all available until Sunday and then Alicia and Steve have to leave. Is that right?"

"Yes," Steve replied, "Alicia and I have flights out of Salt Lake on Sunday afternoon."

"We'll need to get you back to Lander by Saturday evening. Sam, will you and Rebecca be able to stay longer?"

"Yes, but I'd be surprised if there will be much need for us. Unless I'm mistaken, we're looking at a fairly small area for three dogs to cover, and I'm pretty confident we can cover it very well in three days."

"That's assuming that everything goes well," Sees Wolf replied, "Things can happen quickly up in the mountains. In fact, there's a chance of a storm on Friday or Saturday with the possibility it could bring some snow. I understand that you all came prepared for bad weather?"

"Yes, we did," Sam said, "But if we get any significant amount of snow, more than a couple of inches, it's going to make it hard for the dogs to search effectively."

"What about Gunny?" Joseph Golden Eagle asked, "Isn't he trained for avalanche search?"

"Sure," Sam replied, "But in an avalanche, he's searching for the fresh scent of a person who has been recently buried. Up there he'll be looking for the very faint scent of an eighty plus-year-old burial. Even an inch or two of snow could be too much. But, back to your question, we'll stay as long as necessary to make sure the area is searched properly."

"I guess we'll figure all that out as we go along," Sees Wolf said.

"Tomorrow," he continued, "We'll get an early start and drive up to the Buffalo Wheel. It's gonna take about four-and-a-half hours from Lander, so I'd like to be on the road no later than seven."

"Father Jim, do you have that projector working?"

"I do. Let me just get this … OK, here we go."

"All right, take a look at this. It's a Forest Service map image of the area immediately around the Buffalo Wheel, which is called by its white name, Medicine Wheel, here.

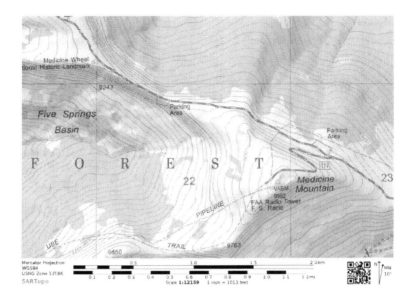

"Wow," Alicia said, "I'm impressed."

"Not all of these savages are as ignorant as they appear, Alicia," Father Smithers said.

After everyone had a brief laugh at his expense, Sees Wolf continued. "The three main features in the area are shown here; the Buffalo Wheel itself, the parking area, which is as far as we will be able to take any motorized vehicles except in emergencies, and a radar station run jointly by the FAA and NORAD."

"It's important to note the area just south of the Buffalo Wheel. There's a line of cliffs there, you can see how close together the contour lines are. These are very steep and fall two or three hundred feet. It's a dangerous area so be careful near there."

"From what I understand, there are a lot of patches of snow there now, and some of them are large, and the snow is deep in places. The area around the Buffalo Wheel itself is clear so it shouldn't cause a problem. Most of the snow is on the north-facing slopes and in the trees."

"So, we won't be able to drive past the parking area?" Alicia asked. "How far is it to the search area?"

"No, we can't drive there. That's a restriction that was agreed on between the tribes and the Forest Service to preserve the nature of the Wheel. You can see a second parking area near the center of the map, but that's no longer in use."

"It's about a mile-and-a-quarter to the Buffalo Wheel from the parking area, but don't worry. We want you and the dogs to be fresh so we'll have horses for each of you and a horse to pull a cart where the dogs can ride."

"Uh, I'm not much of a horse rider," Sam said.

"I'm OK," Rebecca said."

"What about you two?" Sees Wolf asked.

"I grew up riding," Alicia replied.

"Me too," Steve said, "My family has a dairy farm."

"OK, a gentle horse for Sam and unbroken mustangs for everyone else."

"At the Buffalo Wheel," Sees Wolf continued, "We'll have some tents set up where you can keep your gear, and for when you need to rest and for eating so we won't have to travel back and forth to the cars."

"What's up at the radar dome?" Sam asked.

"It's a pretty big facility, three buildings, and the large radar dome. It's manned all the time, year-round, and I think there are usually eight or ten people there. They pretty much keep to themselves, so it's likely you'll never see them."

"Will we be staying there in the tents?" Rebecca asked.

"No. We'll be at the Bighorn Mountain Lodge, which is a very nice resort-style lodge about three miles east as the crow flies, about five miles by road. We'll eat dinner and breakfast there and take our lunch to the search area."

"Sees Wolf, how many of your men will be up there with us?" Sam asked.

"It will be me and Joseph, three men to help with the horses and to do any digging, and one young man for general odd jobs. By the way, I don't expect any trouble, but we're going to be a long way from anywhere so I'll have my father's Winchester, and I'm sure the three wranglers will have something."

"Yes, I'll have a rifle, also," Golden Eagle said.

"Sees Wolf, do you think we should carry weapons, or would that be inappropriate?" Sam asked.

"Well, there's an old Indian saying, 'Better safe than sorry'"

"Then I'll have my .45. Steve?"

"Yeah, me too. What about first aid?"

"What about it? I'm a medicine man, what more do you need?" Sees Wolf said with a smile.

"Well, no disrespect," Steve continued, "but we're a long way from where 911 is going to do us any good. I've got a pretty good medical kit, Sam you've got your ski patrol kit, right?"

"Yep"

"And Alicia, you're a doctor."

"No, I'm a pathologist. You have to be dead before I can work on you."

"Very funny. You've got a medical kit, right?"

"Yes, I'll have everything I'll need for anything up to and including minor surgery."

"It sounds like we've got the first aid issue covered from every angle," Sees Wolf said.

Sees Wolf continued, "If there are no other questions, I think it will be best if we wrap this up so you can have an early dinner and get a good night's sleep. We'll be starting our search as soon as we arrive tomorrow so dress accordingly."

Activities Building

St, Stephen's Indian Mission

Wind River Indian Reservation

Tuesday, 12 June

As the group was filing out the front of the building, Eldon White Deer left the shaded spot below one of the windows at the back. He would wait in the church until they were gone, and then he would head to town to report to Jake Cooley what he'd heard. He knew what Cooley wanted to hear, and that's not the story White Deer had to tell, and that worried him. It was never a good idea to disappoint Jake Cooley.

White Deer didn't understand how he'd gotten into this. Cooley had been pressuring him to get on the crew that was going to be helping Old Man Sees Wolf at the Buffalo Wheel, and White Deer had been coming up with reasons why he couldn't do that. His main excuse had been that the old man would never let a druggie be involved in something important like this.

And then old Sees Wolf had shown up at his mother's house and said he wanted to hire him to help with the work up at the Buffalo Wheel. His mother had been glad, it had been a while since he'd done any kind of work or made any honest money. Old Man Sees Wolf had said he wanted him because of the job he'd done when they'd gone up there back in November, but that wasn't it because Sees Wolf hadn't paid any attention to him or any of the others except to tell them what he wanted them to do.

Of course, this had made Cooley happy, and that was usually a good thing. Cooley had given him an extra envelope of meth as a reward. White Deer had come very close to smoking that meth, but, with the help of a few Our Fathers and Hail Marys, had managed to throw it in a dumpster.

But now White Deer was stuck. Cooley had his hooks into him too deep for him to back out. He was going to have to go back up on that damn mountain and be Cooley's spy, and he still didn't know what Cooley was planning to do. Whatever it was, it was going to be bad.

As White Deer sat in the last pew of the church, he felt the familiar calmness come over him. Never a very devout Catholic, and not sure he believed all that he had been taught about the religion, he had nevertheless always enjoyed coming to church. Maybe that's because of the memories of sitting next to his father. Even now, more than ten years after his father had been killed, he could almost feel him, smell him, sitting at his side.

What would he think of me if he saw me now? I don't think he'd be proud. He used to be so proud of me, watching me play ball right out there on St. Stephen's field. I was a good kid then. What has happened? What have I done to myself?

GHOSTS OF THE BUFFALO WHEEL

What about Cooley? How did I let that ..., that ..., that asshole do this to me? No, no, that's not right. It wasn't Cooley, it was me. I'm to blame. But what can I do?

Well for starters I can stop playing his game. He wants to believe there's a treasure up at the Buffalo Wheel, then that's what I'll tell him. Wait 'till he gets up there and sees all those guys carrying guns. That oughtta shut him up.

CHAPTER NINE

Wolf Dreams

"Now this is the Law of the Jungle --
as old and as true as the sky;
And the Wolf that shall keep it may prosper,
but the Wolf that shall break it must die.

As the creeper that girdles the tree-trunk
the Law runneth forward and back --
For the strength of the Pack is the Wolf,
and the strength of the Wolf is the Pack."

"The Law of the Jungle" by Rudyard Kipling

Holiday Inn Express

Lander, Wyoming

Tuesday, 12 June

That Night

IT ALWAYS TOOK GUNNY A WHILE to settle down in one of these little rooms. There were so many new odors—strange people, and strange dogs. The Man always brought Gunny's bed in from the car so he had someplace that smelled right where he could sleep, but it still took time before he felt comfortable, especially on a day like this when he'd just been riding in a car or laying around while the humans talked.

When he'd gotten comfortable in his bed, he started to think back over the things that had happened that day. The two new men were not like any others he had met. The small man had that smell of open, windy places and that other smell like the Dog-not-Dog from his dream. Gunny knew that The Man and The Woman had his scent on them. Did this mean that Dog-not-Dog was part of this man's pack like Gunny was with The Man and The Woman? But Dog-not-Dog was in his dream, and, at some level, Gunny understood that he wasn't real.

He liked the small man. He made Gunny feel very calm and safe. When he blew the strange smoke in his face, it made Gunny think of high mountains with cool breezes.

Gunny liked the other man too, the tall one. He had a different smell, and he didn't smell like Dog-not-Dog, but he still made Gunny feel good. Gunny even liked the water the man threw on him. It had made him feel warm and comfortable, like just before he would go to sleep. Like he felt now.

Gunny began to drift into a dreamless sleep, but then something started to catch his attention, a smell, a smell he knew. He had just recognized the scent of Dog-not-Dog when his image appeared. As Gunny was watching Dog-not-Dog materialize, he caught two other scents on either side. They were also scents he knew. Luke was on his left and the puppy they called Iwo was on his right. Gunny turned to look at Luke and let out a short bark of alarm. Luke didn't look like Luke, he looked like Dog-not-Dog, just a little smaller! Gunny turned and looked at Iwo, and he was the same as Luke. What was happening?

Then Gunny looked down at his own legs, and they weren't his golden color but gray and white like Dog-not-Dog. He looked at Luke and saw that Luke was just as surprised as he was. For a minute the three dogs ignored Dog-not-Dog and sniffed each other all over as if they were strangers. Luke smelled like Luke, and Iwo smelled like Iwo, but there was something else, another scent. They all had the scent of Dog-not Dog, just like the small man.

After a minute Gunny saw that Dog-not-Dog was waiting patiently, watching them discover each other. Finally, all three dogs sat looking at Dog-not-Dog. When he had their attention, he turned and began to slowly trot away, and the three dogs immediately followed him.

They were in a high mountain forest, and there were a lot of trees that smelled like the smoke the small man had blown into his face. Gradually, Dog-not-Dog began to move faster. Gunny found that he was able to keep up even as the pace increased. His legs were longer and felt strong. His muzzle was longer, and he took in more air with each breath. And the smells! Gunny had never been able to smell like this. It was like he was in a new world. He could smell every plant and bush and animal anywhere around him. He could also tell that all of the animals that he could sense were terrified and running away from them.

As Dog-not-Dog's pace continued to increase the three dogs kept up easily. Gunny looked at Luke and Iwo and was amazed at how large their teeth had become, and then he realized that his own teeth were the same, long and sharp and ... ready. But ready for what?

Now they were going up a steep hill and running faster than Gunny had ever imagined, and dodging around and up and over large rocks and boulders. There were no trees here, just rock, and the breeze was crisp and fresh.

They came to the top of a high mountain, and the land fell off steeply all around them. Dog-not-Dog stopped, and the four of them stood panting easily. Above was the largest and brightest moon Gunny had ever seen.

Something was stirring far back in the most primitive part of Gunny's brain. Something that Gunny must do, but he wasn't sure what it was.

And then Dog-not-Dog lifted his muzzle to the sky and began to howl, and Gunny understood. He raised his muzzle, and so did Luke and Iwo, and they howled. It was one of the most joyous things Gunny had ever done. As they howled, Gunny heard a new sound over and over. Gunny began to understand that this new sound was a name.

Their leader was not Dog-not-Dog, he was Wolf, but there was more, and as Gunny howled it became clearer. He was Wolf, too, and so were Luke and Iwo. Wolf wasn't a name, it was what they were. They were all Wolf, and Dog-not-Dog was Alpha, and they were his pack.

◆ ◆ ◆

Holiday Inn Express

Lander, Wyoming

Wednesday, 13 June

Sam, Steve, and Alicia had all been woken by their very anxious dogs at dawn. Now they were standing in a field behind the hotel watching their dogs and trying to figure out what the hell was going on.

"They're acting like they've never seen each other before," Sam said. "They're sniffing each other all over like strangers."

Yes! I can smell it! We all have the Wolf smell! It wasn't a dream, it was real!

"Now what are they doing?" Steve asked.

143

"I dunno," Sam said. "It looks like they're trying to howl."

"Yeah, well, they're not doing a very good job of it. It sounds horrible," Alicia said.

"Yeah, you got that right."

"It's just as well they got us up early, we've got a lot to do today," Sam said. "Let's see if we can convince them to take a poop walk and go get some breakfast and get ready to go."

"Roger that, Major," Steve replied. Alicia just nodded.

CHAPTER TEN

Cooley

"It is a man's own mind, not his enemy or foe, that lures him to evil ways."

Budah

Cowboy Bar

Lander, Wyoming

Tuesday, 12 June

While Gunny Was Having His Dream

JAKE COOLEY WAS A PHYSIOLOGICAL FREAK who could drink all day and get pleasantly high without getting drunk.

At least that's how he thought of himself. The truth was much darker.

Cooley had had his first beer when he was twelve. He liked it and soon progressed on to more serious stuff. On the plus side, the booze was enough for him, and he'd never had any interest in drugs. On the downside, he never figured out that he was no more immune to the effects of chronic alcoholism than anyone else. In his case, those effects were most noticeably manifested by increasingly delusional thinking. Most recently, his primary delusion was that there was a treasure of gold up in the mountains that was going to make him a wealthy man.

Since early afternoon, he'd been chasing beers from the bar with shots of tequila from a flask he kept in his pocket. The bartender pretended not to know about Cooley's flask.

Cooley's mellow mood began to disappear as soon as Eldon White Deer walked in.

I'm getting' tired of dealing with these damn Indians. If it wasn't so easy to get 'em hooked on crank I'd been outta this shithole a long time ago.

"All right, Tonto, what'd you find out."

Maybe because he wasn't half-stoned for the first time in a long time, Eldon White Deer decided that being called 'Tonto' really pissed him off and he wasn't going to put up with it anymore.

But what can I do? He's got me by the balls. If I tell him the truth about what I heard he's liable to beat the shit outta me just 'cause he's pissed, and he don't wanna admit he was wrong. Maybe I can just string him along a little.

"Jake, I couldn't hear a thing. They all sat around in a little circle and talked real quiet. I couldn't get close enough to hear 'em without them seein' me."

Cooley's fist slammed down on the table sloshing most of his beer onto the floor.

"Goddamn it Tonto, I give you one little job to do, and you fuck it up!"

The half dozen or so patrons in the bar looked at Cooley and then quickly looked away again.

"But Jake, you said not to get caught, or that would screw everything up. If I got close enough to hear they'd have found me."

"All right, let me think about this."

After a minute Cooley said, "You're still goin' with 'em, right? What's their plan?"

"I'm ridin' up with the guys with the horse trailers real early, and ever body else is comin' along about seven. They plan to start workin' by about noon."

"What're the horses for?"

"You can't take cars up to the Buffalo Wheel, you gotta walk in a mile or so."

"Yeah, shit. I forgot about that. Let me think. What are the dogs for Tonto?"

"I dunno."

"I do. I bet they're some kind of gold detector dogs or somethin'. You know, like them bomb dogs they use in Iraq or whatever. Yeah, that's it."

"OK, nothin' changes. The only reason they'd be so secret is if they was after the gold. All right, here's what we'll do. I'll drive my camper up about an hour after they leave so they'll be well out ahead of me. I'll haul a trailer with my ATV. There's a campground back up off the main road about a mile or so before you get to the turnoff for the Wheel. That's where I'll set up. Here, take this."

Cooley slid a small, portable radio and a small bag across the table.

147

"That's how we'll stay in touch. You turn it on with this knob here and just push this button on the side to talk."

"I know how to use a radio, Jake."

"Yeah, well you better. There's batteries in the bag. You call me every hour on the hour and make sure nobody hears you. As soon as you think they're on to somethin', you let me know, and I'll head up there on the ATV. I'll be able to get around the gate and get up there quick, and I'll bring plenty of firepower."

"Do you want me to have a gun, Jake?"

"Are you crazy? You think I'm dumb enough to give a gun to an Indian? Now, did they say anything about them havin' guns?"

White Deer looked straight into Cooley's eyes and said, "No, Jake. I heard that part. Old Sees Wolf said they couldn't have no guns at the Buffalo Wheel, so they ain't takin' none."

"Good, this should be easy. We'll let them do all the work, and when they've got the gold, I'll come drivin' in and take it with a little help from my favorite ol' 12-gauge. I'll load the gold on the ATV and get out of there and punch holes in all their tires and get the hell out of Dodge."

"And what about me, Jake?"

"You just pretend like you're as surprised as they are. Just keep your mouth shut and you'll be fine. Soon as I get to California and start turnin' that gold into real money, you'll get a nice little package in the mail full of old, unmarked bills. You'll be the richest little Injun around."

I wonder if he expects me to believe that? I think he does. He thinks we're so stupid that whatever dumbshit plan a smart white man like Cooley comes up will be enough to fool us. I'll be lucky if he doesn't just shoot me.

"But remember," Cooley continued, "You screw this up, and you'll be the deadest little Injun around. And if you think you can get away from me just remember – I know where your mother lives."

I guess that answers my question.

After White Dear left, Cooley ordered another beer and took a long drink of tequila. He was feeling very mellow and very satisfied with the way his life looked to be going.

Eldon White Deer walked away from the bar with his hands stuffed into his pockets and his head down, trying to think. *I don't understand why Cooley is so set on this idea that Sees Wolf is after a stash of gold. It don't make sense. I thought he'd drop the whole thing when I told him I couldn't hear their plans, but he's more stubborn than ever. What the hell happened to make him think like this.*

◆ ◆ ◆

Cowboy Bar

Lander, Wyoming

About Ten Months Earlier

When the old Indian walked up to his table and asked, "You Jake Cooley?", Cooley was almost too astonished to speak. The old man had long, straggling gray hair and a dark brown, wrinkled face. His jeans and shirt looked as old as he was and needed a wash. He looked like any one of a hundred broken-down old Indians Cooley had seen.

"Old man, you better get your sorry ol' Indian ass outta my sight, or they're gonna have to carry you outta here!"

"Mr. Cooley, I think I got somethin' to say that you wanna hear. Something that can make a lot more money for you than sellin' dope."

Cooley just sat and stared. *What could this broke down old Indian know that would be worth a lot of money?*

"I'll give you one minute, and if you ain't told me somethin' I wanna hear I'm gonna throw your skinny ass through that big window."

"Can I sit down?"

"Yeah, just make sure you're downwind, so I don't have to smell you."

"What do you know about the outlaw Butch Cassidy?"

"Butch Cassidy? There was that old movie with what's-his-name – Newman? Redford? They robbed a buncha banks and shit and got themselves killed down in Mexico or someplace."

"What if I told you that I know where the loot from Butch's biggest robbery is hidden? Would that get your attention?"

"How would you know somethin' like that?"

"Buy me a beer, Mr. Cooley?"

Cooley gave the old man his best stare, which scared the shit out of most people, but the Indian looked right back at him. "OK, but you better not be bullshittin' me."

When the beers arrived, the old man continued, "You remember in the movie Butch and Sundance robbed that train and blew up the baggage car 'cause they used too much dynamite to blow the safe?"

"Yeah, that was pretty cool."

"Well, that happened just a little ways south of here down near Tipton. They got over fifty thousand in gold from that, and that'd be worth millions today."

"So what?"

"After Butch and the boys robbed that train, he took his cut and headed for Hole-in-the-Wall. You know where that is?"

"Yeah, somewhere over on the other side of the Bighorns up north of Casper."

"Right. Well, you can check that out in the history books. That was one of the biggest train robberies in the Old West, and there's lots of stuff been written about it."

"Yeah, you got about thirty seconds left."

"What the books don't say, and what nobody else knows is that the gold never made it to Hole-in-the-Wall. The Pinkertons were getting too close, and Butch needed someplace to stash the gold. The other thing the books don't say is that Butch had somebody with him – a young Arapaho. That young Arapaho was my grandfather, and he told Butch he knew the perfect hiding place for that gold."

"Yeah, so where is it?"

"Let me finish."

"My grandfather showed Butch a place where he could stash the gold where it would be easy for him to find when he wanted it, but impossible for anyone else to find."

"How the hell can you have someplace like that? Easy for you to find, but hard for anyone else?"

"It was a landmark, a thing that would always be there. All Butch had to do was find a good place to bury the gold and then measure off the

151

distance and direction from the landmark, and he'd know where it was, but nobody else would."

"If you know where this gold is how come you didn't dig it up for yourself a long time ago?"

"Don't think I haven't tried, and my father before me and my grandfather before him, but there's a little problem."

"What's that?"

"When Butch buried the gold he left my grandfather tied up to a tree so's he wouldn't see where he went. I know where the landmark is, but I don't know where he buried the gold. It can't be too far, 'cause that gold was heavy, and Butch was only gone a couple of hours, but that still leaves a lot of ground to cover."

"How the hell do you expect me to find it?"

"I don't. I expect you to take it."

"What the hell're you talkin' about."

"Are you interested now, or are you gonna throw me through that window?"

"Keep talkin'."

"Here's the deal. I'll tell you how to get the gold – for a price, not much, just a little up-front money. Once you've got it, then I get a cut, just twenty percent and you keep the rest. I'm talkin' millions here Mr. Cooley."

"How do I know you're not bullshittin' me?"

"Look, there's lots of guys here I could sell my story to. I picked you 'cause you're smart, and you're big, and you can handle yourself. Here's what I'll do. You give me five hundred dollars tonight, and I promise I won't tell no one else about the gold. You go check out my story, you read the history books, you'll see I'm tellin' the truth. I'll meet you back here in two days. If you're satisfied I'm tellin' the truth, you give me two thousand dollars, and I'll tell you how to get the gold. If you don't believe my story, I'll give you back the five hundred and go talk to somebody else."

"And how am I supposed to take this gold from somebody?"

"That's what's gonna cost you two thousand bucks."

"What's your name, old man?"

"Folks call me Black Horse."

"If you know about me like you say you do then you know that if you're lyin' to me, you're gonna be one very sorry old Injun."

"I ain't worried. You check it out, you'll see, but get me that five hundred or I'll talk to somebody who wants to listen."

"Wait here. I'll be back in ten minutes."

◆ ◆ ◆

Cowboy Bar

Lander, Wyoming

Two Nights Later

Cooley watched the old Indian enter the bar and thought, *Old man Black Horse must've spent that whole five hundred on booze. He sure as hell didn't spend it on clothes, he's wearing the same stuff he had on the other night, and I bet he smells just as bad.*

"So, Mr. Cooley, did you check out my story?"

153

"Yeah, everything checks out 'cept there's no way of knowin' if your granddad was there."

"Well, the only way to know that is if you get the gold."

"And you want me to pay two thousand dollars to hear the rest of what's probably a bullshit story."

"Yeah, but look, I may look like just a dumb ol' Indian, but I'm smart enough to know that if I piss you off, you can squash me like a bug, and two thousand is a small investment to make millions."

Cooley slid an envelope across the table. Black Horse took a quick look inside and slid it under his shirt.

"You ain't gonna count it?"

"We gotta have some trust, Mr. Cooley if this is gonna work."

"So tell me where the gold is."

"You ever heard of the Buffalo Wheel? You whites call it the Medicine Wheel."

"Yeah, some kinda sacred place where you Indians go and do your dances and stuff."

"That's it. It sits up in the Bighorns a little ways east of Lovell. That's the landmark."

"How do I find the gold?"

"Like I said, you don't. You let somebody else find it for you."

"Who?"

"Old Man Sees Wolf is gonna find it."

"Who the hell is he?"

"He's a medicine man, a big hot shot in the tribe."

"How'd he find out about it?"

"Beats the hell outta me. Maybe I got to talkin' too much one night when I had a few drinks, or maybe he just did some medicine man magic. All I know is that he found out, and now he's gonna go up there and steal that gold."

"How's he gonna do that. You said it would be impossible."

"He's hiring some experts to come look for it. He's gonna pay them a buncha money, and then he's gonna sell the gold and feed all the poor babies on the rez or some shit."

"Sounds like you don't like this old medicine man."

"That old bastard's tryin' to steal my gold! Now you see why I'm makin' you such a good deal, but you gotta be ready to work fast 'cause he's planning to do somethin' soon."

"How come nobody else knows about this?"

"He's got a whatchacallit, a cover story. He's telling people he's going up there to look for a grave and somethin' about an evil spirit that's screwing up the Buffalo Wheel. Ever body on the rez knows about it, they just don't know the real story."

"So what do I do?"

"You just gotta keep an eye on him. He's gonna be goin' up to the Wheel in a few days to check things out then I figure his experts'll come in next spring after the snow melts. You just gotta get somebody who can get close to him and tell you what he's doin' and then when they find it you swoop in and take it from 'em."

"How'm I gonna get someone to keep an eye on him?"

"C'mon Cooley! How many Indians you got who'll do whatever you say for some free dope or to keep from getting' their asses kicked?"

Cooley thought for a long moment, "Yeah, right, that'll work. I can do that."

"See, Mr. Cooley. I knew you were a smart man, and pretty soon you're gonna be a rich man and me too."

"Yeah, you're right. Smart."

♦ ♦ ♦

Cowboy Bar

Lander, Wyoming

Tuesday, 12 June

After White Deer Had Left

James Raven had heard most of what Cooley and Eldon White Deer had said from his seat a couple of tables away. He looked nothing like he had when he had played the role of Black Horse and conned Cooley out of twenty-five hundred dollars. His silver-gray hair was fashionably cut, his face was much smoother, and he was dressed like a successful businessman.

Amazing what a wig, some old clothes, and a little makeup can do.

Raven had been a con man all his life. He had worked cons like the one he had pulled with Cooley hundreds of times. And then he'd discovered that his real talent was gambling. Not only was he smart, but he could turn off his emotions and play with pure logic. He also had an uncanny sense for spotting tells, and he almost always knew when his opponent was bluffing.

Raven had made a fortune in Reno and Vegas and anywhere else men who thought they were smarter than some damn Indian played for high stakes. He didn't have to gamble or con anymore. He just did it for fun, and Cooley had been fun.

Raven was a southern Arapaho from Oklahoma. He was on the rez for his favorite niece's wedding when someone told him about what Old Man Sees Wolf was up to with Butch Cassidy's grave. As soon as he heard the story, he knew that it was custom made for a con. It wasn't any of his business, and he didn't plan to stick around in Wyoming until somebody told him about Jake Cooley.

If anyone ever deserved to be conned, it's that fat, racist bastard, Cooley.

Now he was back in town to see how the con was going. The twenty-five hundred was nothing. He'd given that to the Tribal Council for the food bank. He just wanted to see Cooley be humiliated, but then that damn White Deer told him the wrong story! What the hell was going on? He was looking forward to seeing the look on Cooley's face when White Deer told him what was really happening.

Now I guess I'm gonna have to stick around a little longer to see how this plays out.

Raven was a little worried about what might happen when Cooley went charging up to the Buffalo Wheel to take that fortune in gold away from Sees Wolf, but he knew enough about Sees Wolf to know that the old man could take care of himself. Plus Cooley didn't know that all those boys would be carrying guns.

Wish I could see the look on his face when five Indians and two white men draw down on him.

CHAPTER ELEVEN

Search Day One

"Everything I know I learned from dogs."

Nora Roberts — Author, The Search

US Route 20 North

Between Shoshone and Thermopolis, Wyoming

Wednesday, 13 June

SEES WOLF HAD ASKED SAM TO JOIN HIM and Golden Eagle on the drive so they could ask him some questions. Rebecca was driving their Xterra with Gunny in the back. Alicia and Steve were each in their own rental cars with their dogs and gear.

The drive through the Wind River Canyon north of Lander had been spectacular. Sam had done it several times, but this time he had two Wind River Arapaho as tour guides. They told him stories not just of the old days of the Arapahoe and Shoshone, but also of the remarkable geology of the canyon.

When they had cleared the canyon, Sees Wolf Sam said, "Joseph and I have many questions for you about just how you and your dogs do what you do. There hasn't been time to talk before, so I thought we'd take advantage of the next couple of hours to give you a chance to educate us."

"Is there something, in particular, you want to know?

"Let's start with what we can do to help, and how you want us to act around the dogs, so we don't distract them."

"Well, I doubt that you'll do much to distract the dogs. They're used to having people around, and they're pretty single-minded when they're working. I'm not so sure about the horses, though. They could be a distraction."

"The horses will be out of the search area except when they're taking us from the parking lot to the Wheel," Sees Wolf replied. "Once they drop us off, one of the wranglers will take them back to someplace out of the way."

"That should work. As far as what you can do to help, the first thing would be to help us understand the area you want us to search. Do you have some idea of how far away the grave might be?"

"It's impossible to know for sure, but I don't think it could be more than two or three hundred yards, but that's just a guess."

"Then another thing you could do is think of likely areas where Butch might have wanted to be buried. I agree that he's probably not far since he wanted to be in sacred ground. Also, people who are going to commit suicide often do it someplace that is calm and peaceful or scenic. You could help identify places like that."

"We'll think about that."

"Yeah, when we get there look at the land through Butch's eyes and try to get some idea of what he might have done."

"We can do that."

"I'd like to know a little bit about the science behind what the dogs will do so I can have some idea of what I see," Joseph said.

"If you want to talk science you should ask Alicia."

"I don't think we need to explore Alicia's depth of understanding," Joseph replied.

"Oh, you want the *K9 Cadaver Search for Dummies* version then?"

"Yes," Sees Wolf said, "That should be about right."

"Let me think for a minute."

"All right, I think the first thing we should talk about is odor or scent. What is it that the dogs are smelling?

"When you talk about odor, most people think of some sort of gas, and that's not right. What the dogs are smelling are solid materials, chemical compounds that are unique to their target.

"When a dog is searching for a live person he is looking for the smell of the skin rafts that person is shedding at a rate of about forty-thousand per minute. Those skin rafts are microscopic bits of dead skin along with tiny bacteria that feed on that dead skin. These skin rafts can be deposited on the ground, blown around by the air or suspended in snow or water, and a dog can detect them, sometimes from a long way away."

"Are these skin rafts unique to an individual?" Sees Wolf asked.

"Yes. Race, ethnicity, diet, age, and a lot of other factors can affect the composition and odor of these skin rafts. It's not as unique as, say, fingerprints, but it's unique enough that a scent-discriminating dog, like a tracking bloodhound, can easily find the right track to follow from among many others."

"Are your dogs scent-discriminating?"

"Not the three here, they're area search dogs who look for any human scent. We do have scent-discriminating tracking dogs on our team including a Blab."

"What's a Blab?"

"A bloodhound-lab mix. Her name is Moonshine, and she does a good job."

"That's live-find, I assume cadaver search is something different?" Sees Wolf asked.

"Yes, and that's Alicia's territory—she wrote her Ph.D. thesis on it—but I'll try to give you the highlights."

"Researchers have identified something like five hundred twenty-five different chemical compounds that are produced by different parts of the body at different times during post-mortem decomposition. If you've ever been exposed to a decomposing body, it's a smell you'll never forget, but we smell the mixture of many different chemicals, the dogs can identify and catalog the odor of each chemical in the mix."

"That's amazing!"

"Yes, it is."

"So, you just have to train the dogs to find the scent of certain chemicals?" Sees Wolf asked.

"It's not quite that simple because we have no idea which chemicals the dogs are focusing on. It could be one or two key chemicals, or it could be a whole range of different chemicals. So, we have to try to train our dogs on as many different cadaver sources as possible."

"That must be very difficult."

"It is. That's why Alicia and Iwo went to that cadaver dog seminar in North Carolina a couple of months ago."

"It seems that it would be impossible to train a dog on over five hundred different chemicals," Sees Wolf said.

"Right again."

"What happens if a dog encounters a cadaver that is at a stage of decomposition that the dog has not encountered before, where the chemicals are different?" Golden Eagle asked.

Sam looked at the two men with him. Golden Eagle was driving and Sees Wolf was in the back seat. They were both wearing jeans, cowboy boots and faded flannel shirts. Their black cowboy hats were laid carefully on their crowns in the back seat. *These two look like a couple of aging Arapaho cowboys, and it's easy to underestimate how smart and knowledgeable they are. They'll remember everything I say, so I'd better not screw up.*

"That's where the dog's innate curiosity comes in, and it reminds me of another way you can help with the search."

"A dog will tend to investigate any new or unusual odor whether or not it is something he has been trained to search for. One of the most important things that I do during a search is to watch Gunny for any change in behavior. If he suddenly changes direction or points his nose up into the air, or his nose starts working faster, those are indications that he has some new odor. Even if he doesn't recognize the odor, he'll want to check it out. I need to be alert to these changes and make sure that I support him when he gets some new scent. It may be something completely unrelated to what we're doing, in which case he'll typically check it out, catalog it, and then go on with his search. I need to be able to check it out with him to make sure it's not something important."

"Can you give us an example?" Sees Wolf asked.

"I can give you a couple. Many times Gunny has gone to check out an odor, and it's turned out to be a dead animal. Obviously, many of the decomposition chemicals in animals and humans are the same, but dogs can tell the difference. When he finds a dead animal, he'll usually give it a sniff and then go on with his search without giving me an alert indication. We've been on a few searches along with human searchers who have reported a 'strong odor of decomposition' which Gunny determined to be from a dead rabbit in a bush or some such."

"But that dead rabbit could have been a human at a stage of decomposition that Gunny had not encountered before," Joseph said.

"Exactly," Sam replied, "And that's why I have to be alert to what he's doing and follow up on any new scent he may want to investigate."

"Here's another example. One time we were on a search and Gunny found a pair of jeans. There was no decomposition odor on these jeans, but Gunny was just investigating an odor that was out of place. They weren't what we were looking for, but they were a potential clue to the missing person, so I called it in, marked the location on my GPS and brought the pants to IC."

"What happened?"

"Nothing, they were the wrong size for the missing man, but that's not the kind of thing you want to ignore."

"How can we help with that?" Golden Eagle asked.

"During a search, everyone around should be watching the dogs. Steve, Alicia and I can always be distracted—looking at our GPS, talking on the radio, whatever—and miss a change in behavior. If you see a dog do something unusual or suddenly change what he's doing, let the handler know right away."

"Got it."

163

"But what about a very old body in a grave like we're looking for here? Don't those chemicals degrade over time to the point where the dogs can't detect them?"

"Geez, you guys are askin' all the hard questions. OK, let me try to explain."

"First of all the real answer is, it depends on a lot of things, mostly the environment in which the body has been during decomposition. Remember that the human body is about seventy percent water. After death, as cells in the body die off over time a lot of fluid is released. The chemicals we're talking about get mixed in with these fluids. So, in very broad terms, any environment that allows these fluids to soak in and remain without a lot of evaporation or without being washed away will be good for preserving decomposition odor."

"So, in our case, the chance of success will depend on how he was buried; was he in a casket, or a shroud? And things like the porosity of the soil, how deeply he was buried and so forth."

"Can you hazard a guess?" Sees Wolf asked.

"Well, I've had some experience with pioneer graves that are older than what we'll be looking for, and the dogs are usually able to get scent from those, so I'd say we've got a decent chance."

"I guess that's the best we can hope for," Sees Wolf said.

They drove in silence for a while until Sees Wolf said, "It's the top of the hour, let's see if we can get a weather report."

Joseph turned on the radio but had trouble finding a station with a good signal. Finally, they heard, "… and repeating our top story, we've got a good-sized storm that will hit the western half of the state on Friday. It'll be wind and rain with some thunder for most of us, but the National Weather Service has issued a Winter Storm Watch for western and central Wyoming for areas above eight thousand feet. Boy! Winter Storm in June. That's Wyoming for ya."

Sam turned toward Sees Wolf and said, "That could make things interesting."

◆ ◆ ◆

Medicine Wheel Parking Area

Bighorn Mountains, Wyoming

Wednesday, 13 June

Noon

When they drove into the parking area, there was a Bighorn County Sheriff's patrol car there. When they had parked, a Deputy Sheriff walked over to them.

"Good to see you again, Sees Wolf."

"You too, Deputy Turner. What brings you up here?"

"I'm looking for a Doctor Phillips. Is she with you?"

"Yes. Let me introduce you to everyone, and then you can talk to Doctor Phillips."

When introductions had been made, Alicia asked, "What can I do for you, Deputy?"

"Sheriff Edwards asked me to touch base with you. You're an investigator with the Tennessee State Bureau of Investigation, right.?"

"Yes, I'm a forensic anthropologist, and I do a lot of the CSI work there."

"That's what the Sheriff said. He got a call from the State Attorney General sayin' it was OK for you to look for human remains up here and that we were supposed to give you any help we can. The Sheriff would've been here himself, but … well, it's a big county, and he's pretty busy."

"That's very generous. We appreciate it, and we'll try not to bother you."

"Just let us know if you find anything, and we'll figure out what to do next."

"We will. The medical examiner gave me permission to remove any remains we find unless those remains could be old Native American, in which case we'll leave them in place."

"Yep, that's what the Sheriff told me. Here's my card. You probably won't have any cell reception up here, but you can call from the Bighorn Lodge. I understand that's where you'll be stayin'."

"Yes, that's right. We'll call as soon as we have any information for you."

"Then I'll let you folks get to work. Enjoy your stay in Bighorn County."

"Thank you, Deputy."

When the Deputy had left, Sam walked up to Alicia.

"They don't know anything about Butch Cassidy or ghosts do they?"

With a sharp look and a frown, Alicia replied, "Sam! What do you take me for? Gimme a break."

"Sorry, just checkin'."

166

Turning her back on Sam, Alicia walked to the gate across the road and looked out at the scene before her, "My god, it's beautiful up here. What a view! And the air is so fresh! This sure puts Tennessee to shame."

"Enjoy it while you can," Sam said, "Did you hear the weather report?"

"No, what's up?"

"Possible winter storm for Friday."

"Winter storm? I know you said we could get some snow, but an actual storm?"

"That's what it sounds like."

"What does that mean for us?"

"For one thing, it means that we don't have a lot of time to stand around and enjoy the view. We need to get moving."

"Aye, aye, Sir!" Steve said, "Let's saddle up and get movin'."

While the others were getting organized, Sam ignored his own advice and took a minute to look around.

Just beyond the parking area to the southwest, the summit knob of Medicine Mountain with the radar dome on top rose up several hundred feet. To the west, a dirt road ran along the top of a very narrow ridge and then angled to the northwest toward the Buffalo Wheel, which was out of sight a mile or more away. Along the right-hand side of this ridge, the ground sloped steeply to pine forests. On the left side, there was no slope, just a sharp-edged cliff that dropped two hundred or more feet down to a high alpine bowl.

A temporary horse corral had been built alongside the road about fifty yards from the parking area. Twelve horses, ten of them saddled, were in the coral calmly munching hay scattered on the ground.

Once he had gotten himself oriented, Sam started getting his gear out of the Xterra. He let Gunny out for a short potty break while he and Rebecca got organized.

Sees Wolf brought over the three wranglers and the young man who would be helping them during the search and introduced them. All four were dressed alike in jeans, boots, cowboy hats and flannel shirts and looked alike with the same dark skin, sharply hooked noses, and long, black hair. But Sam was reminded of the old children's game, "Which of these is different?"

The three wranglers were lean and hard-looking men who obviously spent their time outdoors doing physical labor. Sam had a sudden image of them with their faces painted and eagle feathers in their hair and wondered what it must have been like for Captain Fetterman and his men to have had this image as the last thing they would ever see. None of them spoke or did more than nod when Sees Wolf named them. Sam didn't sense any hostility, just disinterest. He was so focused on examining them that he never did catch their names.

The fourth Arapaho was the odd man out. He was younger and softer looking. His posture was less erect, and his overall air was less confident. He smiled ingratiatingly when he was introduced, but never met anyone's eyes. Sees Wolf explained that this young man's role would be general help around the camp or search area. For some reason, this was the only one of the four whose name Sam remembered—Eldon White Deer.

Sam was surprised to see that Gunny had no problem loading into the cart behind one of the pack horses. Then Sam remembered that Gunny liked to ride in almost anything from helicopters to snowmobiles. *He probably thinks it's a really slow ATV with a funny smelling engine.*

The other two dogs followed Gunny's lead, and more quickly than Sam had expected they were all on their very gentle trail horses and heading toward the Buffalo Wheel. Both pack horses were loaded down with tents, stoves and other gear for the search camp they would establish.

As they moved slowly along the road, Sam and the others had a good chance to get a feel for the area they would be searching. It was very open ground with only patches of trees here and there. The ground vegetation was low, wiry buffalo grass interspersed with some sagebrush and other hardy shrubs. Sam checked the altimeter on his watch and found that they were right at ninety-six hundred feet. There were significant patches of snow on the northern flank of the ridge. It also looked like there was scattered snow in among the trees. Some of the snow drifts looked like they could be pretty deep.

Sam turned to Steve, and Alicia, who were riding nearby on his left side, "Does this remind you guys of anything?"

They both replied, "Yes!" immediately and Steve continued, "If anything there's even less cover here than there was in the Amphitheater on Iwo. Of course, we didn't have to deal with snow on Iwo."

"Yes, Sam, do you think that could be a problem?" Alicia asked.

"I don't know, we'll have to see. If some places look like possible grave sites that are snow covered, we may have to do some shoveling."

"I saw some shovels on the pack horses," Steve said,

"Those are for diggin' if we find somethin' buried — not sure how useful they'll be if we have to move a lot of snow. Remind me to check to see if they've got snow shovels we can borrow at the lodge."

"Roger that."

◆ ◆ ◆

Buffalo Wheel

Bighorn Mountains, Wyoming

169

Wednesday, 13 June

One PM

When they arrived at the Wheel and let the dogs out of the cart, the first thing Gunny did was to walk over to one of the rock cairns, lift his leg, and take a piss on the ancient, sacred monument.

"Gunny! Knock it off!" Sam yelled.

"Sam, it's all right," Sees Wolf said, "Coyotes, wolves, mountain lions, and god knows what else have been pissing on these rocks for thousands of years. A little dog piss isn't going to hurt anything."

"I'm sorry," Sam said, "We don't want to do anything disrespectful."

"I understand, but don't worry. Yes, we think of this as sacred ground, but we also think of it as a part of nature. Without the wind, sun, snow, and occasional deposits of fecal material it wouldn't be as sacred."

"Thanks," Sam said, "But if any of the dogs decide to deposit any fecal material, we'll pick it up."

"Fair enough."

Rebecca accompanied Sam, Steve, and Alicia while they walked with their dogs around the outside of the Wheel to get a feel for the area. The four Arapaho men took the pack horses about seventy-five yards to the northeast and began to set up a couple of army surplus tents near a Forest Service pit toilet. These tents would provide some shelter from the sun and weather, both of which could be brutal at this altitude, and give everyone a place to relax and eat a meal or snack. A table would be set up in one of the tents for what Alicia referred to as her, "high-altitude CSI kit," a set of basic tools that would allow her to do a quick assessment of any remains they might find.

When Sam and the others got around to the western side of the Wheel, they were only twenty yards or so from the cliff edge. Sam noticed that Alicia had put Iwo on leash.

"Are you worried about Iwo near this cliff?" Sam asked.

"Yes," Alicia replied, "He's never been around something like this before. I don't know how he'll react."

"Then it's a good idea to keep him leashed until you can give him a chance to figure it out. If he knows it's there, he won't do anything stupid. On the other hand, we'll want to make sure that none of the dogs, or us, get anywhere near that cliff if it's dark or the weather is bad."

"Do we expect to be out here at dark?" Steve asked.

"No, but you never know, and we do have that storm coming in. I've been up on mountains when the visibility has gone from good to zero in less than a minute. If it looks like that storm is gonna materialize, we'll want to talk about some safety measures, and don't let me forget to talk about lightning."

"Fine with me," Alicia said, "I'm basically a flatlander myself."

"Lightning?" Steve said, "I hate lightning."

"You'll really hate it if you get caught out here in the open in a thunderstorm."

"The main thing right now," Sam continued, "is to remember that we're at ninety-six hundred feet and that altitude is going to affect the dogs and us. Take it slow and stay hydrated, and make sure the dogs stay hydrated. Steve, you've done this before up in the mountains of Afghanistan, right?"

"Yes, Sir."

"How much water are you planning to carry?"

"About three and a half liters."

"Alicia?"

"Uh … I've got two liters."

"Get another liter."

"Sure."

"So," Sam continued, "Do you two have any ideas about our search plan?"

"You're the boss," Steve said, "You've done more of this than we have, you tell us."

"Well, let's look at what we've got to work with. Behind us, back toward the parking area, the ridge is narrow, and that cliff is definitely a concern. In front of us, this plateau widens out in a vee shape, and the ground rises slightly toward those woods out there."

Sam let everyone get a good look at the area before continuing. "I think we should divide the search into three areas. Let's focus up here on top of the plateau first. If we don't get anything here, then we'll look at going down that slope to the north."

"Since I think that Gunny and I have the most experience working around cliffs, I'll take the area behind us on both sides of the road. Rebecca, do you want to come with me?"

"Sure, I can use the exercise after sitting in the car all morning."

"Steve you and Alicia figure out some landmark you can use to divide that area in front of us in half. Steve you take the left half near the cliff, Alicia you take the right half."

"We're looking for an old grave, and there won't be a lot of scent, so we'll work slowly and keep our grids tight, maybe ten yards or less, depending on how thick the vegetation is."

"Since we think the grave will be fairly close, we don't have to hurry. Let's see how long it takes you two to work out a hundred yards from the center of the Wheel. That'll give us a good idea of how long it will take to cover this area. My area along that narrow ridge is smaller, so I should get a little farther than you do."

"Make sure your GPS and your dog's GPS collar are on and tracking. Let's get a radio check before we leave and make sure we stay in contact. Alicia, I'll ask Sees Wolf to go with you to point out any areas of particular interest. Steve you take Golden Eagle."

"Any questions?"

"What about the Wheel itself?" Alicia asked as Sees Wolf and Golden Eagle walked up.

"Damn, Alicia, good point. We'll divide that into three sectors, and we'll each search a sector now, and then we'll search a different sector tomorrow and Friday."

"Sam, we've searched the Wheel a lot, you shouldn't have to worry about that," Sees Wolf said.

"If it ain't been searched by a dog," Sam began, and then the other three joined in, "**it ain't been searched**."

Seeing the look on Sees Wolf's face, Sam said, "Sorry, no offense, but that's just the way we do things."

"Fine with me," Sees Wolf replied, "You're the experts."

It took a lot longer than Sam had expected to search the Buffalo Wheel. Sees Wolf had been right about there being thousands of years of animal piss on the rocks. All three dogs were fascinated by the new odors, and the handlers had to keep giving them commands to get them back to work. There was one rock cairn in particular that all three of them sniffed repeatedly.

Wolf, Gunny thought, *this is Wolf. He has been here, and not long ago.*

The dogs showed no other interest in the Wheel itself, so the three teams split up to search their areas.

Sam decided to work back and forth across the ridge toward the parking lot for a couple of hundred yards to give Gunny a chance to familiarized himself with the area. Coming back, they would work more slowly with tighter grids. Since his area was smaller than the other two, he figured he could do all that in the same time that Steve and Alicia covered a hundred yards.

When Sam commanded, "Gunny! Look close! Adios!" Gunny headed straight for the cliff edge, as Sam had expected. Gunny was a curious dog, and that cliff was the most interesting thing around. Even though Gunny had worked around cliffs before, it always made Sam nervous when he went right up to the edge and looked over, but Sam knew he had to trust his dog and let him do his job. Besides, that cliff edge was what is called in search theory an "attractant," and it would have to be searched. The view out over the cliff across the mountains and down to the Bighorn Basin was spectacular, which made it just the sort of place that someone about to die might choose for their burial plot.

Sam and Steve had talked about this before they split up and Sam knew that Luke was probably doing the same thing as Gunny.

Sam let Gunny explore the cliff for a while and then called him to start walking a loose grid. Rebecca followed, keeping an eye on Gunny. On the north side of the ridge where the ground sloped down to pine forests, Gunny spent a lot of time sniffing, but he didn't show any particular interest.

As Sam looked down the slope, he thought, *This'd be a pretty sweet ski run. Nice and steep, maybe forty degrees. A couple of those snow drifts are big enough to make some good turns on. I hope we don't have to search that, though. That'd be a bitch.*

Sam and Gunny settled into a routine with Sam setting the grid and Gunny working back and forth to check new odors or get his nose into the wind. The air was just brisk enough to offset the heat of the sun, and it was nice to be out with Gunny and Rebecca exploring a new place. He was enjoying himself so much that he was surprised when he checked his GPS to find that they had covered two hundred yards.

"Steve, this is Sam, over."

"Go ahead, Sam."

"Gunny and I have covered two hundred yards in a loose grid, and I'm ready to head back and hit it again a little tighter. How are you and Alicia doing?"

"We're at just about a hundred yards out. We're taking a break and watering the dogs now and then we'll work our way back toward the wheel. You getting any interest where you are?"

"Nah, we're pretty much just out for a walk. Anything on your side?"

"Nope, same over here."

"Sam this is Alicia."

"Go ahead."

"Sees Wolf says that we should try to be back at the Wheel by five-thirty so we can get back to the cars before it starts to get dark."

"Good. It's a little after four now. That gives us an hour and a half to work our way back to the Wheel. That should be just about right."

"See you then."

♦ ♦ ♦

Buffalo Wheel

Bighorn Mountains, Wyoming

Wednesday, 13 June

Four PM

After the tents had been set up, the wranglers took the horses and moved them up along the widening plateau for a half mile or so to a spot where they could graze until it was time to make the trip back to the cars. For the first time that day Eldon White Deer was alone, and he breathed a sigh of relief.

Those cowboys sure don't like me much, and they didn't try to hide it. Guess I can't blame 'em, I'm pretty much of a loser. Now I gotta call that asshole Cooley. Guess I better get it over with.

Eldon's brain was clearing a little more with each day he didn't use meth. He was beginning to understand his situation more clearly.

I should'a told Cooley the truth about what Sees Wolf is doin' up here, but I don't think he'd believe me. He's got it set in his thick skull that he's gonna get rich off Butch Cassidy's treasure, and he probably would'a just kicked my ass for lyin' to him. Now I gotta play along until I figure a way outta this.

White Deer turned on the radio and made his call.

"Cooley, this is White Deer. Cooley this is White Deer."

No answer.

"Cooley, this is White Deer, over."

"Goddamn it, Tonto don't use my name on the radio! You're Tonto, I'm Moore."

Moore? What the hell ... oh damn! Clayton Moore – the Lone Ranger. What an asshole.

"Tonto, what's goin' on?"

"Well, we're all set up here at the Wheel, and the three dog teams have been out searchin' for a couple hours."

"They find anything yet?"

"Nah, they're just out all around the Wheel, and the dogs are sniffing at everything, but no one's getting' excited or anything."

"Are they usin' metal detectors?"

"I ain't seen anything like that. Just the dogs."

"Ok, you keep a good eye out and call me every hour until I tell you to stop."

"I don't know if I can get away and use the radio every hour."

"You'll find a way. If you know what's good for you."

♦ ♦ ♦

Bighorn Mountain Lodge

Wednesday, 13 June

After Dinner That Evening

It had been a long day, and everyone was glad to get to the lodge at around six. The Bighorn Mountain Lodge was old and rustic, but very comfortable. Sam and Rebecca had a room as did Sees Wolf and Golden Eagle. Steve and Alicia each had a small room to themselves and the four young Arapaho were in a bunkhouse cabin.

Dinner had been a delicious venison stew with homebaked bread and a salad. Even though it was the middle of June, the hearty stew was a perfect meal because the temperature dropped sharply with the setting sun.

Now the three dog handlers along with Sees Wolf and Golden Eagle were sitting in comfortable rockers on the porch, bundled up in warm coats and having a glass of wine or beer. The three dogs were curled up sleeping at their human's feet. The young men were off on their own.

Rebecca stood by the porch rail, looked out into the evening sky, and took a deep breath of the fresh, pine-scented air. Turning to the others, she said, "It's been a long day, but standing here like this makes it all worth it. This is beautiful."

"Wouldn't it be fantastic if we could find evidence to change the whole story about Butch and Sundance? To prove that they didn't die in Bolivia, to show how they gave up the outlaw way at the end of their lives?"

"Sounds like you're getting' into this search," Sam said.

"Yeah, bein' up here all by ourselves with just the dogs is pretty special. I can see why you guys do this stuff."

"It's not always like this," Alicia said, "Sometimes I can still smell the sulfur from Iwo Jima. You didn't spend a lot of time thinking about the beauty of nature there."

The group was lost in their own thoughts for a couple of minutes until Sees Wolf brought them back to the present.

"So, none of the dogs showed any interest today?"

"No," Sam replied, "They were interested in all the new smells up here and did a lot of sniffing around, but no sign that they had gotten any cadaver odor. Does that sound right to you two?"

"Yeah," Steve said, "Luke was pretty much just out for a walk. I mean he was searching, but nothing caught his interest."

"Same with Iwo. I did get a chance to get him over to the cliff on a long leash. It scared the hell out of me, but it didn't seem to bother him. He was curious, not nervous."

"Yeah, it always scares me when Gunny gets close to something like that, but these guys ain't stupid. They know to be careful, and, now that they know it's there, they won't just go running up to it."

"This is a bit different from your search on Iwo Jima," Golden Eagle said, "Gunny found a bone in the first hour you were searching there."

Sam looked around to make sure that they were alone and then replied, "Yeah, but remember, we think that Gunny had help from Robby Durance's ghost that day."

"Maybe, we need some spiritual help ourselves," Sees Wolf said.

"You're the medicine man," Sam said, "I think that's your department."

"Yes, it is. Let me think about that. In the meantime, what is our plan for tomorrow?"

"You all heard the weather report," Sam said, "They sound pretty positive about that storm on Friday so tomorrow may be the last full day of good weather. We'll want to hit it early and hard."

"What do you propose?"

"I think we should do two things in the morning. Steve and Alicia, I'd like you to work on expanding your search out another hundred yards. While you're doing that, Gunny, Rebecca, and I will go with Sees Wolf and Joseph to investigate any places that they think might be potential burial sites."

"What about the ridge back toward the parking area?" Steve asked.

"I think that's a low priority. We went about two hundred yards that way, and from there you can't see the Wheel. My feeling is that Butch would want to be buried somewhere in sight of the Wheel and that means out on the side where you and Alicia were searching today."

"What about the afternoon?" Alicia asked.

"We'll make an afternoon plan at lunch based on what happens in the morning. Does that sound OK to everyone?"

"Yep, … sure, … got it."

"Good," Sam said, "I think I'm gonna have another beer and then toddle off to bed. Long day tomorrow."

CHAPTER TWELVE

Search Day Two

*"Most discoveries ... are a combination of
serendipity and of searching."*

Siddhartha Mukherjee

Bighorn Mountain Lodge

Thursday, 14 June

Six Thirty AM

WHEN THEY HAD ALL GATHERED FOR BREAKFAST, Alicia asked
Golden Eagle, "Where's Sees Wolf?"

"He spent the night at the Buffalo Wheel."

"What??"

"Yes, he took Sam's comment last night about getting some spiritual help to heart, and decided he needed to go to the Wheel to pray and, I think, to see his wolf."

"How did he get there?" Sam asked.

"He walked."

"He walked? That's five miles!"

"It's five miles by road, but there's a trail through the woods that's only about three miles."

"But he's an old man, well, he's my age. Old men don't walk three miles on a mountain trail in the dark carrying a pack."

"No pack, Sam, just a Navajo blanket."

"He spent the night out at ninety-six hundred feet with no food, no water, just a Navajo blanket?"

"Yes, as you pointed out, Sam, he's a medicine man, and that's the sort of thing they do."

"But I didn't mean …"

"Sam, it's all right, don't worry. Sees Wolf knows what he's doing and knows how to take care of himself. He's been doing this sort of thing for a long time."

"Let's eat quick and get going I want to make sure he's OK. Should we bring him some food and hot coffee?"

"I'm sure he would appreciate that, Sam."

Even moving as quickly as they could, it was over an hour before they got to the parking area. The horses had been left in the corral overnight, with feed and water.

Once everyone was mounted, Golden Eagle sent the wranglers ahead at a fast trot to check on Sees Wolf and to bring him food and coffee.

By the time the search team got to the Wheel, the four young Arapaho and Sees Wolf were sitting in one of the tents with a small stove going. They were drinking coffee and joking.

Sees Wolf looked up as Sam walked over to him, "Thank you for the coffee and food, I needed it. It used to be that I could do this sort of thing for days at a time, but now that I'm an old man one night is about my limit."

"You and I are about the same age. I would have frozen to death out there, and that's assuming I didn't kill myself hiking three miles in the dark. I'm impressed. Was it successful? Did you get some help?"

"I think so. *Hooxei* was there. He helped keep me warm. It seems like the older I get, the more real he becomes. Or, maybe I'm turning into a spirit myself."

"Do you think your wolf knows where the grave is?"

"I'm sure he does. The question is whether he will show me. In all these years he hasn't shown me yet."

"Why is that?"

"I don't know. You have to understand that *hooxei* is almost as big a mystery to me as he is to you. We have become like brothers, but he is not only a spirit but the spirit of a different species. I think that he understands what I want and that he will help me, but he will do it in his own way."

Sam noticed that all four of the young Arapaho were looking at him with much more interest than they had shown yesterday.

Probably the first time they've heard a white man talking to one of the medicine men about spirit wolves. I wonder if that's good or bad.

183

"Ok, we've got cool temps and a little breeze, perfect for searching so we'd better take advantage of it. I'll go out with Joseph first. Why don't you stay here until you're warmed up and then maybe see if you can figure out how your wolf is gonna help us."

"All right, Sam. One more cup of coffee and then I think I'll go back over to the Wheel and see if I get any inspiration."

♦ ♦ ♦

Buffalo Wheel Search Area

Thursday 14 June

Ten AM

"Uh ... Moore, this is Tonto, over."

"Goddamn it, Tonto, where the hell you been? You shoulda called me hours ago!"

"This is the first time I could get away. They got me bustin' my ass helping with the horses and gear. Besides, there ain't nothin' to report."

The three wranglers had been surprised to learn that White Deer knew his way around horses. That had meant a lot more work for him, but it had brought him a feeling something like pride for the first time in a long while.

Dad taught me about horses from before I could walk. Mom, too, a little, after he died. I remember how to take care of a horse. I wonder if I can remember how to act like a man?

"Whatta ya mean nothin' to report?"

"Well, I mean they're out there searchin' like yesterday, but it don't look like they're findin' anything."

"Shit! You better call me as soon as you think they got somethin'. Them dogs must not be much good."

"OK, Cool … Moore. I'll let you know."

♦ ♦ ♦

Buffalo Wheel Search Area

Thursday 14 June

Ten Thirty AM

The day had warmed quickly once the sun was well up. The three dog teams had been working for an hour and a half and were all taking a break.

Steve and Alicia had extended their search area by about seventy yards. Since the plateau widened as they got farther from the Wheel the area to be searched increased with each sweep, but it looked like they'd be able to finish the hundred yard extension Sam had asked for by lunchtime.

Sam and Gunny had worked with Golden Eagle to search likely burial spots, mostly along the edges of the plateau. Golden Eagle had picked places that were in sight of the Wheel and were either unusually peaceful or that had an even more spectacular view than the rest of the area. Places, he thought, that a dying man might choose for his eternal rest.

Gunny had shown no interest in any of these places.

Sees Wolf joined Sam and Golden Eagle. "No luck, I take it?"

185

"No," Sam replied, "Do you have any ideas?"

"What about those trees out there?"

Sam and Golden Eagle looked where Sees Wolf was pointing toward a large stand of old pine trees over a quarter of a mile away.

"Well, it's scenic, and it looks peaceful and, since the ground is rising in that direction you should be able to see the Wheel, but it's pretty far away," Sam said.

"Yes," Sees wolf said, "But there's something …"

Gunny, who had been lying quietly, sprang to his feet. At the same time, Luke and Iwo jumped up and broke away and ran toward Gunny with Steve and Alicia chasing after them.

When Luke and Iwo came alongside Gunny, they stopped. As Steve and Alicia caught up, they saw that the three dogs and Sees Wolf were all staring intently toward the trees in the distance.

Sam said, "I don't know what's going on, but I think we need to get these dogs on leash."

At that moment a high, bone-chilling howl sounded across the plateau.

Before anyone could react, all three dogs started running.

"Holy shit! Was that a wolf?"

"Yes, Sam, that was *hooxei,* my brother. It appears that he has decided to help."

Gunny had smelled him first and knew immediately that it was Wolf. He heard the other dogs behind him and knew that they had smelled him too. Then he saw Wolf coming calmly toward them. Wolf stopped a short distance away, lifted his muzzle and howled, then turned and started trotting away.

Gunny and the others had no decision to make, there was no choice. They would follow the pack leader.

Luke and Iwo surged ahead as Gunny lagged. He was too old to do all this running, but he wouldn't stop. By the time they got to the trees Gunny was ten or fifteen yards behind and was glad to see the others slow to a walk. When he got into the trees, he could no longer see Wolf, but Luke and Iwo were just ahead of him. He followed them for about twenty yards into a small clearing, and he saw Wolf again sitting patiently. And, next to Wolf was something else. It was hazy and strange looking, and Gunny was confused, but then he got the scent— Old Bone. For the first time since they had been searching here, Gunny smelled Old Bone.

As he came closer to Wolf, the hazy image became clearer. It was a man, but it wasn't any man that Gunny knew, and Gunny didn't recognize his Old Bone scent. He had the same kind of hat and clothes that the brown men with them wore, but Gunny didn't think he was a brown man. The man was saying something that Gunny could barely hear. The man sounded very tired.

The man was saying, "Help me, help me."

◆ ◆ ◆

Buffalo Wheel Search Area

Thursday 14 June

Ten Forty-Five AM

By the time they had caught up to the dogs, everyone was breathing hard, especially Sam.

Been a while since I ran a quarter mile dash— uphill, through sagebrush, Sam thought.

At first, they couldn't see the dogs, but they could hear them nearby. When they broke into the clearing, all three dogs were working back and forth in the same area with their noses to the ground and sniffing rapidly.

As Sam and the others watched, the area the dogs were searching became smaller and smaller until they were almost bumping noses. And then, as if on command, all three dogs sat and gave one emphatic bark.

"Sees Wolf," Sam said, "I don't know if this is Butch Cassidy's grave, but I'll bet my next Social Security check there's a body under there."

"Guys, let's reward our dogs."

In the next moment, all three dogs were happily playing tug with their favorite toy.

Once the dogs had played and been given treats and lots of praise they were put in the shade of the nearest tree and told to "Down" and "Stay." The humans gathered in the clearing to discuss what had happened and what to do next.

"Sees Wolf, can you explain what we just saw?" Alicia asked.

"I can't explain anything, but I can tell you what I think."

"Go ahead."

"You all heard *hooxei*, right?"

When everyone had nodded, he continued, "He was here, and your dogs knew him and followed him to these woods."

"How would our dogs know your wolf?"

"I don't know, Alicia, but didn't you say something about your dogs trying to howl before we left Lander yesterday?"

"Yes, that's right."

"Did it seem that they were trying to howl like wolves?"

"I've never seen wolves howl except on TV documentaries, but, now that you mention it, yes, it did seem that way. Sam? Steve?"

Sam and Steve both nodded.

"My guess is that *hooxei* visited them in their dreams the night before."

"Has he done that with you?"

"Yes, many times. I often dream of him, but sometimes it's more than a dream. It's like he and I are together somewhere and actually doing something."

"Oh my god. Sam, Steve, isn't that like ..."

"Yes, Alicia," Sam replied, "That sounds very much like the dreams we had of Robby Durance on Iwo Jima, with one difference."

"What's that?"

"We didn't just dream of Robby, we were Robby, and we experienced everything from his point of view. Right, Steve?"

"Yes, Sir. And it was scary as hell."

"I don't experience things through the eyes of *hooxei*," Sees Wolf said, "But he often leads me to places that I later find have some meaning or significance."

"So, you think our dogs knew him because he was in their dreams?"

"More than that. They all made the decision to run toward these trees at the same time. I think that they were following *hooxei*, which means that they have accepted him as their leader."

189

"Could they have run here because they got the scent of this grave?" Golden Eagle asked.

"No, I don't think so," Sam replied, "Gunny got help from Robby's ghost on Iwo to find that first bone, but that was much closer. I would say that Sees Wolf's explanation is more logical, except that logic has nothing to do with this."

"We can try to figure this out later, but I think the more pressing issue is what do we do now? Alicia, you're the crime scene investigator, what do you want us to do?"

"Sam, I'm as confident as you are that there's a body down there, but is it possible that there is more than one grave here? Do we need to keep searching?"

"Let me answer that, please," Sees Wolf said, "There may be other graves around here, but I am confident that this is the grave that we have been looking for. Usually, when I am at the Wheel, I can only feel the spiritual disturbance if it is very quiet and my mind is peaceful and open—something like a meditative state. Even then the disturbance is very slight. But here, I can feel it now, even as we are talking. Also, look back toward the Wheel. You can see it clearly through that gap in the trees. Then look to the south and west. The view out across the forests may be the best of anywhere up here. This spot fits all the requirements we have discussed for a place that someone who believed he needed to be in sacred ground might pick for his grave."

"Like Sam, I don't know if this is Butch Cassidy's grave, but I am sure that this is the source of the problem we are trying to solve."

"I guess that answers my question. We don't need to do any more searching."

"I don't think so, Alicia, but Sam is in charge of the search."

"No, I agree, Sees Wolf. If you say that this is the place, then this is the place. So, back to you Alicia, what's your plan?."

"I'll want to get a good look at the area before I make any sort of plan, and I may need some more help from the dogs while I'm doing that. But right now, we need to get my CSI kit and all of our digging tools over here. Also, I don't know how long it might take to recover whatever we have here, and I'm worried about that storm tomorrow. Do you think we can move those tents over here?"

"That's a good idea," Golden Eagle replied, "I can go over and get our men working on tearing down those tents, and, in the meantime, I'll have one of them bring all the digging tools over."

"Make sure they bring those metal rods and sledgehammer with the first load."

"Sure, what are they for?"

"The dogs have indicated on the point where the scent is strongest on the surface. That isn't necessarily directly above where the body is. I'll want to sink some holes around that point and let the dogs check to see if there is a place where the scent is stronger before we go digging in the wrong place."

"Did I get that right, Sam?"

"Yeah. Sounds like you didn't sleep through all your classes at Western Carolina."

"Anything else?"

"Yeah, Joseph, maybe they could bring us some lunch?"

"You got it, Sam."

Buffalo Wheel Search Area

Thursday 14 June

Eleven Forty-Five AM

Eldon White Deer had a decision to make. It was almost time for his noon call to Cooley, and he had to decide what to say. When Joseph Golden Eagle had walked into the tent area, it was clear that search teams had found something in the trees on the other side of the plateau.

What do I tell that asshole? If I tell him they found somethin', he'll figure that it's the treasure and come charging in here to steal it. If I don't tell him, then what? Well, nothin' terrible – at least not right away.

After they'd gotten the first horse and rider on the way with all the digging tools, White Deer said he had to go to the toilet.

"Get right back," Golden Eagle said, "We're burnin' daylight."

When he was out of sight behind the pit toilet, he took out the radio.

"Moore, this is Tonto, over."

"About time, Tonto. What's goin' on?"

"Uh … nothin' that I can see. Looks like they're still searchin' around."

"Damn it! What the hells the problem?"

"I dunno. I guess it's pretty hard to find somethin' buried in a place this big."

"All right, you let me know the minute somethin' changes, you hear?"

"Sure, sure. I'll do that."

"You better Tonto."

◆ ◆ ◆

Buffalo Wheel Search Area

Thursday 14 June

One PM

Steve and one of the young Arapaho had used the sledgehammer and metal rods to put "scent holes" two to three feet deep in the places that Alicia indicated. When they had finished, each handler worked their dog independently to see where they had the keenest interest. That point turned out to be about a yard away from where the dogs had indicated initially. Alicia then outlined a dig area about six feet square around these two points.

They finished just as Golden Eagle and the other men rode up with the tents and other equipment.

"Joseph, do you think that the smaller tent will fit in that clearing?" Alicia asked.

"I think so, no problem."

"OK, we'll put that up over the dig area to protect it, and we can put the other tent just outside the trees."

"Do you want to dig first, or put tents up first?"

"Let's dig. We've got good weather now. We'll put the tents up last before we leave."

"How do you want to do this?"

"C'mon over here, I'll show you."

The soil in the dig area was very rocky, and even with four young Arapaho men working it took an hour to clear the dig area down to a foot deep. Alicia wanted to go slowly to minimize the chance of damaging or missing any remains. After each foot, the diggers would stop, and the dogs would be brought in to confirm that they were still in the right spot.

"What do you think Alicia?" Sam asked after they had all run their dogs across the dig.

"Looks to me like they're interested in the entire hole now. I'd say we're right on track. What do you guys think?"

"Yeah," Sam and Steve said together.

"Gentlemen, another foot deep, please."

Two and a half hours later they found the first piece of the shroud.

Alicia crawled into the hole wearing a headlamp attached to a pair of magnifying glasses.

With her face inches from the dirty, gray piece of cloth sticking up at the bottom of the hole she said, "This looks like linen. Probably a tablecloth or something like that. Since we're not finding any wood, I'm pretty sure this is what he was buried in. That means the easy part's over. Now we've gotta get to work."

For the next hour, Alicia alternated digging with White Deer, whom she had determined to be the most careful worker. White Deer would carefully scrape a thin layer of dirt out, and Alicia would go in the hole to see if anything had been uncovered. If she found something, she would use a hand trowel to recover it. So far all she had was small bits of cloth.

It was tedious work, and it was killing his back, but Eldon was glad that he had been the one selected help the white doctor. *It's been a while since anyone chose me to do anything.*

He was scraping his shovel across the bottom of the dig when it struck something that didn't feel like a rock.

"Doctor, I think you should come look at this."

Alicia jumped into the hole and examined what looked like a thin, brown rock.

"Very good, Eldon. We have our first piece of bone, a rib if I'm not mistaken. Excellent work. That would have been easy to miss. You should be a CSI tech."

"What are you thinking Alicia?" Sam asked.

"The bad news is that it's gonna be pretty much trowel work from here on out. The good news is that now we're at the body there shouldn't be much more rock so it'll go faster."

"Yeah, but it's five o'clock, and Sees Wolf says that we need to be starting back by six if we don't want to get caught out here at dark."

"What about the tents?"

"The larger one is up just outside the trees. They're waiting on you to put the one up here."

Alicia came up out of the grave dusting off her hands. "Here's what I can do in an hour. I'm gonna excavate enough to confirm that that's a rib. That'll give me a landmark. Once I have that, I'll try to locate the skull. If I can get the skull exposed enough for some good photos, I can take those back to the lodge and get a pretty good idea of what we're dealing with."

"Can those guys put that tent up here while I'm working?"

"I don't see why not. Golden Eagle?"

"Sure, we'll just have to be careful not to kick any dirt down on you."

"Sounds like a plan to me. Eldon, I'm gonna want you down there with me to hold the light and hand me tools and things. You OK with that?"

"Yes, Doctor."

That settles it! I'm not telling that son-of-a-bitch Cooley nothin'. These people have treated me a hell of a lot better than he ever did. I'll keep their secret.

"OK, let's get to work."

◆ ◆ ◆

Buffalo Wheel Parking Area

Thursday 14 June

Two PM

While the team was working at the grave site, Jake Cooley was making a reconnaissance.

He drove his four-seater ATV slowly up to the parking area and made a slow circuit to see if anyone was there. With no one in sight, he parked and got out.

He hadn't been up here for several years, and he wanted to refresh his memory. The place hadn't changed much. There was still just the one way in and out, and that was the key. He had no idea where Sees Wolf and the others might be searching, but he knew they'd have to come past here on their way out. This is where he would wait when the time came.

Looking off to the north he saw the low hill he remembered. It was a couple of hundred yards away, and he started walking to it. He had to duck under the gate across the road. He wouldn't be able to get his ATV through there, but he saw that he could easily get it around the fence that extended a short distance on each side of the gate.

A service road branched off from the main road, and he walked along that up the hill. The two small maintenance sheds he remembered were still there, tucked back into the pines that covered the top of the hill.

The sheds had sliding doors secured with sturdy-looking padlocks. The hasps the locks attached to weren't as sturdy, and Cooley knew he could get them off quickly with a crowbar.

The higher shed sat near the top of the hill and had a view down to the parking area. There was even a convenient window.

That's the plan, then. When Tonto tells me they've got the gold, I'll scoot up here and wait for 'em. I'll get the drop on 'em and march 'em up here and into the shed. I'll get 'em tied up inside, block the door on the outside, and I'm gone. It could be days before anyone thinks to look for 'em in here. By that time I'll be a whole new man in LA.

♦ ♦ ♦

Big Horn Mountain Lodge

Thursday 14 June

Seven Thirty PM

Dinner that night was buffalo burgers cooked to order with steak fries and salad.

"What do they feed vegetarians around here?" Rebecca asked.

Golden Eagle replied, "Wyoming's not the best place to be if you're a vegetarian. I'm sure they could put something together, but it wouldn't be great. You're not a vegetarian, are you?"

"No, not at all. I'm enjoying this. Venison one night, then buffalo. This is great! I was just curious."

"Where's Alicia?" Sees Wolf asked.

"She said she'd be eating in her room. She's got her laptop with her forensic identification software, and she's working on her pictures of that skull," Sam said.

"She certainly was excited to be able to find that skull."

"Yeah, she thinks she'll be able to tell a lot about who our mystery person is."

"Steve, what about you? How're you doin'," Sam asked.

"Me?" I'm fine, no problem."

Sam had noticed that as soon as they had gotten back to the lodge, Steve had changed to a bathing suit and headed for the spa tub. He had taken off his prosthesis and given a long sigh of relief as he eased into the hot water.

It's been a tough couple of days working at this altitude. I feel like I've been shot at and missed and shit at and hit. I can't imagine what it's been like doing all this with only one good leg. That's an amazing kid.

"If you say so."

An hour later, Sam was struggling to stay awake when Alicia joined them on the porch.

"So, Alicia, what have you got?"

"I have—we have—a male, human skull with about half of the teeth still in place. Everything I've seen so far is consistent with remains that have been in the ground since the mid-1930's. I also have a very likely cause of death."

"What's that?" Sam asked.

"There's a hole in the right temple that will probably match a .22 caliber bullet. There is no exit wound on the opposite side of the skull, so it's a typical soft-nosed bullet. If I'm not wrong, I should find the actual bullet when I get the skull out and can examine it."

"Is a .22 a common weapon that people use for suicide?" Steve asked, "I would think they would use something larger to make sure they died quickly."

"You're right that a lot of suicides use a larger caliber weapon, but something like a .22 works better. A soft-nosed .22 will expand quickly, and because it doesn't have enough power to blow out the opposite side of the skull, it tends to bounce around inside and do a lot of damage. It has the added advantage of being a lot less messy."

"Whoever did this knew something about guns and what they can do."

"So, is it Butch?" Sam asked.

"There's no way to tell without doing a lot more analysis. If we can recover some artifacts, clothing, a locket, an engraved watch, I'll be able to say something definitive. Barring that, we'll just have to wait until we can get him to the lab where I can learn a lot more than I can out here."

"Is there any chance he is an Arapaho or Shoshone? Can you tell if he's white or Indian?" Sees Wolf asked.

"He's almost certainly Caucasian. I called the Sheriff's Office and notified them. They expect to be pretty busy tomorrow if this storm comes in so they won't send anyone up before Saturday. I told them I'll have photographs of the body *in situ* and that I'll document every step of my recovery. They were happy with that."

"Speaking of the storm, have you heard the latest?"

"No," Alicia said, "I've been too busy."

"We've got a ninety percent chance of a winter storm hitting late morning or early afternoon. They're talking high winds and anywhere from a couple of inches to a foot of snow up here. There's probably going to be some lightning too."

"Wow! It's a good thing we've got the grave under cover with that tent. We should be able to work through it."

"Yeah, I just wanted to make sure you knew about it. Are you going back to work?"

"Yeah, I want to make sure all my documentation is in order."

"While you're doing that, the rest of us will put together the plan for tomorrow."

"OK, Sam, thanks."

"So, what sort of planning do we have to do?" Steve asked.

"Not much, I guess, other than getting back up there as early as we can in the morning. Joseph, can you get your guys to make sure those tents are tied down tight in case we get a lot of wind?"

"Sure, we'll get the stoves set up in there too for when it gets cold."

200

"Can anyone else think of something we need to do?"

When he got no answer, Sam continued, "Let's get some sleep so we can be back at the grave at first light."

♦ ♦ ♦

Five Springs Campground

Near Medicine Mountain

Thursday 14 June

That Same Evening

Cooley watched the man walking toward him from the RV that had just parked in the campsite across from his. He was about to tell this idiot to go the hell away and leave him alone when the man spoke.

"Hey, neighbor. Did those Indians chase you away from the Medicine Wheel too?"

Huh? What's he talkin' about?

"No, I ain't been up there. What's goin' on?"

"Me and the wife went up there a little while ago to take some pictures. They had this sign that said the place was closed, but we figured it wouldn't do no harm if we just walked up and took a few shots. I'm a pretty good photographer, ya know?"

"Yeah, sure. So, what happened?"

"Well, we walked all the hell the way out to the Medicine Wheel, and I'm startin' to take some shots, and these two Indians come trotting up on horses. Told us the place was closed to the public and we had to leave."

"Yeah, well that's too bad. They say why you had to leave?"

"They said it was somethin' to do with some ceremony next week, but I don't know."

"Yeah. Whatta you think's goin' on?"

"I dunno, but there was some more Indians and some white folks doin' somethin' in the trees up the hill a ways. They had a tent set up, and it looked like they were getting' ready to do some diggin'. They had some shovels and stuff."

"Oh, yeah? So what happened? Did they chase ya off?"

"Nah, they were pretty polite. Said I could take some shots, but then I'd have to leave. Wanna see what I got?"

"You take any pictures of what was goin' on up in them trees?"

"Yeah, I snuck in a couple when they wasn't looking. I got a good telephoto lens. Shots came out good, but there's nothin' interesting."

"Well sure, I'd like to look at what you got. How about I come over to your camp and bring a couple beers."

"Sounds like a plan, partner."

An hour later, Cooley knew that Eldon White Deer had been holding out on him.

They found the gold and that goddamn Tonto didn't tell me! He musta figured he could get a better deal from Sees Wolf than he could from me. Well, he got that part right, 'cause I wasn't gonna give him shit, but now he's gonna find out what happens when you cross Jake Cooley.

GHOSTS OF THE BUFFALO WHEEL

CHAPTER THIRTEEN

Search Day Three Part One

"Anyone who has spent a few nights in a tent during a storm can tell you: The world doesn't care all that much if you live or die."

Anthony Doerr, Author, "All the Light We Cannot See."

Bighorn Mountain Lodge

Friday, 15 June

Five Fifteen AM

"Is this really necessary?" Alicia asked.

Rebecca put her tea mug down, "Is what necessary?

"Getting up in the middle of the night to go back to the grave. It's obvious they got the forecast wrong. It's forty degrees out. We're not getting a snow storm today."

"Actually, this is pretty common in this part of the country. I was just outside. The reason it got warm last night is that we've got a wind out of the south that's bringing up warm air. That means we've got low pressure to the north. That's where the storm is. It's comin' all right."

"Where's the rest of the group? How come we're the first ones in for breakfast?"

"Uh … you're the last one in. Everybody else already ate. Sam and Steve are out walking dogs, and all the others are getting stuff packed up."

"Damn!"

"Relax, take your time and eat a good breakfast. You may need it. Besides, nothin's happening today without you. You're the star of the show."

"But I'm always the first one up!"

"Evidently not when you're working with Marines and Arapaho."

"All right. Let me get some food in me, and I'll get Iwo out for a quick walk. We'll be ready in fifteen or twenty minutes."

"Don't forget your cold weather gear."

Five Springs Campground

Near Medicine Mountain

Friday, 15 June

Five Forty-Five AM

"Tonto this is Moore, over."

Cooley was surprised when White Deer answered almost immediately.

"This is … me, over."

"What's goin' on."

"We're just getting' ready to start out."

"Why so early?"

"They wanna get as much done as they can before the storm hits."

"What storm?"

"Ain't you been listnin' to the radio? There's a big storm comin' today."

"So what? A little rain won't hurt ya."

"No, they're talkin' snow – a buncha snow – and a lot of wind."

Cooley walked to the door of his RV and stepped outside.

It's the middle of June, and it's warm. There ain't no snow storm comin'. That little bastard White Deer is up to somethin'.

"So everybody's gonna be workin' out past the Wheel then, right?"

"Yeah."

"There won't be nobody down by the parking area?"

"No, we'll all up where they're searchin'. Why?"

"You don't need to know. You just keep feeding me info on what's happenin'. Got it?"

"Yeah, sure."

"And don't even think about fuckin' with me Tonto."

When White Deer didn't reply Cooley went on.

"What's their plan?"

"They're gonna try to get a few hours of searchin' in and when the storm hits they're gonna hunker down and see what happens, but this may be the end cause some of them dog team's gotta go home soon."

"What time are they gonna get up there?"

"We're leavin' in a few minutes. They want to start workin' at first light."

"Tonto, you call me as soon as you see anything. Got it?"

"Sure, yeah, sure."

That lyin' goddamn Indian! They found the gold and they're gonna take it out today while I sit on my ass back here. Well, they'll find out it don't pay to fuck with Jake Cooley.

◆ ◆ ◆

Buffalo Wheel Parking Lot

Friday, 15 June

A Little After Six AM

The sun had come over the horizon just before six. The Arapaho wranglers with White Deer helping were getting the horses saddled and loaded. By the time they finished there would be plenty of light for the ride to the grave site.

Alicia was finishing the last of her coffee when Sam walked up.

"I'm sorry I was late this morning. You guys were up early."

"No problem. If we had gotten here much earlier, it would still be too dark to do anything."

"Rebecca said that storm is on track. That's hard to believe. It's still so warm.'

"Have you noticed anything that's changed in the last few minutes?"

"No, not really."

"Pay attention to the wind direction. It's starting to shift around to the northwest. That's a typical storm pattern."

"But I just can't get over how warm it is. Is that bad?"

"Yeah, my experience from workin' with the ski patrol is the warmer it is before the storm, the worse the storm's gonna be."

"Then we'd better get to work."

"Yeah. Sees Wolf and Golden Eagle are ready. Why don't you go ahead with them and decide what you need to do? The rest of us will come along when we've got everything loaded."

"OK."

"And look, you're the boss today. This is your show. You need somethin' done, you tell Joseph or me or Sees Wolf, and we'll get it done."

"Thanks."

GHOSTS OF THE BUFFALO WHEEL

Buffalo Wheel Grave Site

Friday, 15 June

Seven AM

During the ride out to the grave site the wind had been shifting around toward the north and had started to develop a cold bite.

Just like Sam said, Alicia thought. *Maybe this storm is for real after all.*

Golden Eagle and his four Arapaho had gone ahead and were already busy tying down the tent over the grave with extra ropes. Inside, Alicia was happy to see that the small propane stove had been lit.

That'll make working in here a lot nicer if the temperature keeps dropping.

Looking down into the grave, Alicia started planning her recovery.

The only parts of the body immediately visible were the portion of the upper chest where Alicia had dug to examine the rib that White Deer had found and the skull. That first rib had been sticking up, but it looked like the rest of the rib cage had collapsed forming a shallow concavity. This was pretty typical as the organs within the chest, and the ligaments connecting the ribs to the spine and the sternum decomposed allowing the rib cage to collapse under its own weight.

Alicia saw that below the ribs the dirt appeared to be looser and less compacted than the soil around the body. She knew this meant that there was another concavity where the abdomen and pelvic girdle had collapsed.

"Eldon, come here, please."

209

When Eldon came in from outside and stood next to her, Alicia continued, "You did such a good job yesterday I'd like you to work with me again today. First though, I need to ask you something I should have asked yesterday. I know that the Arapaho and other tribes have many beliefs about evil spirits who may linger near the bodies of the dead. Are you uncomfortable working here with me?"

"Oh, no. I don't think so. I mean it's a little ... creepy, but it's interesting too. I never thought too much about spirits, and I reckon if there was anything bad here Old Sees Wolf wouldn't let us get too close. So, no. I'm OK."

"Good. Here's what I'd like to do. You see the skull?"

"Yes, Doctor."

"You see that shallow hole just below the skull, and the place below that where the dirt is looser?"

"Yes, Doctor."

"That's the chest and abdominal cavity, and that's where I'm going to be working. I'm going to put some marks in the dirt to outline the area where the legs and feet should be. I'd like you to start scrapping away the dirt there to see if you can find those bones. You'll need to work slowly and carefully. Can you do that?"

"Yes, Doctor."

Alicia looked closely at Eldon White Deer. *This young man has changed in just the past two days. He's alert and focused and seems interested in what we're doing. He's just like one of our dogs. He's smart, and he's got a lot of energy, but if he doesn't have something to do with that energy he gets bored or gets in trouble. He just needed a job.*

"Let's get started."

GHOSTS OF THE BUFFALO WHEEL

◆ ◆ ◆

Medicine Wheel Parking Area

Bighorn Mountains, Wyoming

Friday, 15 June

Eight AM

When Cooley rode into the parking area, he saw seven vehicles he recognized from the day before. There was no one around.

Looks like the gang's all here and all the little gold diggers are out diggin' up my fortune. Wish I'd brought a heavier coat, though. It's gettin' cold, and I don't like the looks a them clouds. Oh well, I can stand a little cold to get rich.

He drove the ATV to the south along the fence. It was a little tricky going around the fence on the side of the hill, but he managed. He then headed over to the maintenance shed he'd picked out and drove the ATV around to the back out of sight. Thirty seconds work with his crowbar, and he was inside with all the gear he thought he'd need.

His primary tool was a Remington Model 870 Tactical shotgun with a magazine that was illegally modified to hold seven rounds of twelve-gauge double-ought buck. This was backed up with a Glock G41 .45 caliber pistol in a quick-draw tactical holster on his right hip, a wicked looking K-Bar knife on his left hip, and a .32 caliber Saturday night special in a holster on his left ankle.

Jake Cooley was literally loaded for bear.

He also had a hundred feet of five-millimeter nylon rope and a roll of duct tape.

211

He checked the view out the window and, just as he thought, he would be able to see anyone heading to the parking long well before they got there.

Jake was not a planner. He had always gotten by on his size and meanness and figured he would today. He had a vague idea of charging down on his ATV, blowing a couple of rounds over everybody's head, and slapping a couple of 'em around to get everyone in the right frame of mind.

Then he'd march 'em up to the shed and have Tonto tie 'em all up, and then he'd beat the holy shit outta that goddamn lyin' Indian.

Then it would *hasta la vista, baby* and off to his new life as a rich man.

◆ ◆ ◆

Buffalo Wheel Grave Site

Friday, 15 June

Nine Fifteen AM

After two hours of painstaking effort, Alicia decided that she and White Deer needed a break. They headed over to the larger tent about fifty yards away.

When they walked inside they saw Rebecca, Sees Wolf and Golden Eagle sitting next to each other and talking, and two of the Arapaho wranglers in a corner playing cards.

"Hi Joseph, Sees Wolf. Where's everyone else?"

"The other wranglers are checking on the horses. Sam and Steve are out doing some training with the dogs," Golden Eagle replied, "Sam took Iwo so he could learn to work with other dogs."

"Good. We have any coffee?"

"Sure, over there. Help yourself."

"Eldon, what do you take in your coffee?" Alicia asked.

The white Doctor is getting me coffee??

"Uh ... black's fine."

When everyone was seated with coffee in hand, Sees Wolf asked, "How are things going with the recovery?"

"We're making good progress. You're welcome to come watch."

"Thank you, but I think I'll just look at the photographs later. Joseph and I are a bit old-fashioned about being around bodies. It's just the way we were brought up."

"Sure, I understand."

"How's Eldon doin'?" Sees Wolf asked.

"Eldon is a big help. I wouldn't be half as far along without him. He's an excellent worker."

With a long look at White Deer, Sees Wolf said, "That's good. I'm glad to hear that. Maybe he's ready to become a real Arapaho."

White Deer hung his head so he wouldn't have to meet Sees Wolf's eyes.

Turning back to Alicia, Sees Wolf continued, "The wind is picking up, and it's getting colder. I'm starting to worry about this storm."

"Yeah, we know. It's getting a little chilly in that tent. Do you think it will be a problem?"

"Possibly. If we have to leave in a hurry, will that be OK?"

"Well, I can pack up some critical bits – the skull and a couple of long bones – and that way I'll have something I can work with back at the lodge."

"I think that would be a good idea."

"When we've finished our coffee and warmed up a bit, we'll go back and do that. I'll use the smaller crate I have. It's about three feet long and a foot and a half wide. Will we be able to carry that back with us?"

Joseph turned and spoke to the two wranglers in Arapaho. When they had finished, he asked Alicia, "Can the dogs walk back? They don't need to ride in the cart do they?"

"No, they should be fine since they're finished searching."

"Then we'll put the crate in the dog cart."

"Works for me."

Maintenance Shed Near the Parking Area

Bighorn Mountains, Wyoming

Friday, 15 June

Ten AM

As a gust of wind rattled the steel sides of the shed, Cooley thought, *Damn, it's getting' cold. Maybe we are gonna have a snow storm. How's that gonna change things?*

After a few minutes of thought, Cooley had a new plan.

214

He loaded all his gear back into the ATV and drove it down toward the parking area. Again he carefully maneuvered it around the fence and over to the east side of the car park. About twenty yards away from the graveled parking area he found a small copse of scrub oak just large enough to hide the ATV behind. Just past this, the ridge sloped sharply off at about a thirty-degree angle down toward the pine forests below. This was one of the places where the snow drifts had not melted, and the ground was snow covered most of the way down.

Then he went around checking the doors on the vehicles parked there. As he expected, a couple of them were unlocked, and he found the one that had the best view of the approach from the Medicine Wheel and settled himself in out of the cold.

He had been ready to smash a window to get in, but this way he wouldn't have a bunch of wind blowing in on him.

Of course, this means I'm gonna have to tie those people up outside instead of in a nice warm shed, but that's just too bad for them.

◆ ◆ ◆

Buffalo Wheel Grave Site

Friday, 15 June

Eleven AM

It had been snowing for forty minutes when Sees Wolf decided it was time to leave.

"Do you agree, Sam?"

"Yeah, this is gonna be a bad storm. Let's get the hell outta here. I'll tell Alicia to pack up."

Just then Alicia and Eldon came through the tent flap carrying a large crate between them.

"No need, Sam. Even a flatlander like me knows when it's time to get off the mountain."

It was another twenty minutes before everyone was ready and the wranglers, with help from Golden Eagle and White Deer, had brought the horses around. They loaded the crate with the carefully padded bones into the dog cart.

All three dog handlers attached twenty-foot lengths of rope to their dog's harness and tied them off to their horse's saddles. That way they wouldn't have to worry about their dogs if the visibility got bad.

"Steve, you got your compass with you?" Sam asked.

"Yeah"

"I'd like you to ride up front with Sees Wolf. I know he's an Indian, and he's got a great sense of direction, but if we get caught in a white-out, I wanna make sure we don't go off in the wrong direction and head toward that cliff face. Alicia and I will keep our GPS out, and we'll be a double-check. Make sure you got your radio where you can hear it."

"Sam you're starting to scare me," Alicia said.

"Good! 'Cause this storm is startin' to scare me."

As the team started back toward their cars, the snow started falling faster.

CHAPTER FOURTEEN

Search Day Three Part Two

"Cry Havoc! and let slip the dogs of war."

Mark Antony in Julius Caesar, Act 3, Scene 1

Medicine Wheel Parking Area

Bighorn Mountains, Wyoming

Friday, 15 June

Twelve Ten PM

EVEN INSIDE THE CAR, COOLEY WAS GETTING COLD. He'd had to get out and clear off the windshield a couple of times to be able to see. Despite that, the visibility was sometimes limited to less than twenty yards with the blowing snow. There were at least four inches of snow on the ground already.

You'd have to be crazy to stay out in a storm like this even if you was in a tent. But you can't ever tell with them Indians. They do some crazy shit.

Just then the wind died so that the snow was falling straight down and Cooley saw them. They were about forty yards from him and moving slowly. They had so much snow covering them that they blended into the snow falling around them. As they got closer, he could see that at least some of the horses had scabbards with rifles in them, and it looked like a couple of the men might be carrying pistols.

That goddamn Tonto lied to me again. He is gonna be one sorry little Indian. That's OK. Long as I know they got guns, I can deal with it.

OK, boys and girls. Showtime!

Medicine Wheel Parking Area

Bighorn Mountains, Wyoming

Friday, 15 June

Twelve Fifteen PM

Rebecca had been skiing on a lot of stormy days, and this wasn't the coldest she'd ever been, but it was getting close. It seemed like she could feel the temperature getting lower every minute. The wind, which had been steady out of the north had begun to swirl, coming from every direction. That not only killed visibility, but the cold wind and snow found every tiny opening in her clothes.

Rebecca got down off her horse and handed the reins to one of the young Arapaho. He and the others would put them in the corral until everyone got settled in the cars and then load them into the horse trailers. They wouldn't be leaving them out today.

Rebecca found Joseph Golden Eagle and asked, "What do you need me to do?"

"Nothing," he shouted over the noise of the wind, "Get in your car and get warm."

"Sam?"

"Yeah, do what Joseph said. We'll all be along in a minute."

Rebecca felt guilty at leaving everyone else out in the storm, but she realized that it didn't make sense for her to stay out there with nothing to do so she headed to her car.

She had her hand on the door handle when she stopped and thought, *Why is my windshield the only one that doesn't have snow on it?*

Before she could answer her own question, her mouth and nose were covered by a huge, gloved hand and the muzzle of a large pistol was jammed painfully into the side of her face.

"Hello there, little lady. Today is your lucky day. You and me are gonna go for a ride."

◆ ◆ ◆

Medicine Wheel Parking Area

Bighorn Mountains, Wyoming

Friday, 15 June

Twelve Twenty PM

Sam took a quick head count and saw that everyone was with him except Rebecca. Then he helped one of the wranglers get the saddle off his horse, and move the horse into the corral.

When he had finished that he walked over to Golden Eagle. "Joseph, do you think those horses will be OK for a little while until we get the cars started and warm up a bit?"

"Yeah, they're pretty sturdy, but we don't want to leave 'em for too long

"Naw, just a few minutes. When we're a little warmer, Steve and I'll be happy to help your guys move 'em into the trailers."

Before Joseph could reply, they were all startled by a loud explosion just behind them, and Sam heard the *vrruupp* of a sub-sonic, large-caliber bullet passing inches over his head.

"Good afternoon, friends and neighbors! Do I have your attention now? I want everyone to turn around real slow and careful so you can see me and my new friend here. If any of you try anything stupid, you'll hear her scream a mile away."

Sam turned and saw his wife being held with a pistol to her head by a man at least twice her size. The muzzle of a shotgun was just visible over his right shoulder. The man had crazy eyes and a broad grin on his face.

This son of a bitch is stoned, or crazy, or both. This is bad.

"The first thing I want is all you boys with guns on your hips to take 'em out real slow and careful and then throw them off as far as you can. If you don't throw 'em far enough, the lady screams.

Sam and Steve slowly and carefully did what the big man had said.

"Now, if any of you other boys are hiding something from me, you and the lady here are both gonna be real sorry.

"No? Nothin' else? OK, now you folks with the dogs make sure you got a tight hold on 'em. They don't look too happy, and I got no problem with shootin' a dog.

"Now who can I get to help me? You there, yeah you, Tonto. C'mon out here.

Eldon White Deer walked slowly out toward the big man holding Rebecca with his head low so he wouldn't have to meet the eyes of the others.

"Grab that bag there, Tonto, and do what I tell ya.

"Now ever body start moving over to the other side of the corral there. Anybody tries anythin' stupid and the lady's gonna scream and then I'll shoot one a yer dogs.

When everyone was in place on the far side of the corral, the big man said, "Tie them dogs up over there at the end. I want 'em far enough away they can't come chew on yer ropes.

"Now Tonto, there's rope in that bag. Start getting' all these folks tied up to this corral. And tie tight, Tonto, or you and this lady both will be screamin'."

When White Deer got to Sam, there was a gust of wind that made the big man duck his head for a second. White Deer quickly whispered to Sam, "I'm tyin' you real loose. I know you got a knife. You'll be able to get everyone free fast."

When Sam realized what White Deer was saying, he yelled out, "Damn it! That's too tight! You'll cut off my circulation."

"Shut up!" the big man yelled, "Yer lucky I don't just shoot the bunch a ya."

When White Deer was finished Cooley called him over.

"OK, Tonto, the plan stays the same. We're goin' over to my ATV. You get that cart with the box of gold in it and follow me."

"Jake, I don't want no more of this. Somebody's gonna get hurt. You can tie me up with the rest of 'em."

"It don't matter what you want you lyin' little sack of shit. I know you made a deal with Old Sees Wolf. You ain't fooling me. You're gonna do what I tell you, or it's gonna be real bad."

Cooley started levering Rebecca's arm up behind her back until her shoulder was on the verge of dislocating. Rebecca whimpered, and White Deer could see the pain on her face.

"Right little lady? The boys gonna do what I say, or I'll rip your damn arm off."

"OK, OK, don't hurt her. I'll do what you say."

"Now you're bein' a smart little Injun. All right, now get that cart and follow me.

Near the Medicine Wheel Parking Area

Bighorn Mountains, Wyoming

Friday, 15 June

Twelve Thirty-Five PM

The storm was nearing its peak as White Deer struggled to keep up with Cooley and Rebecca. The snow was at least an inch deeper, and the wind was almost in his face. The cart's wheels were caked with snow and were sliding more than rolling. Even though Cooley was only a few yards in front of him, he couldn't see the big man half the time through the blowing snow. He had lost all sense of direction and had no idea where they were heading.

White Deer's head was down trying to bull through the storm, and he almost ran into Cooley when he stopped next to the ATV. He was gasping for breath, and he could barely hear what Cooley was telling him over the roar of the wind.

"Listen up Tonto. The first thing you're gonna do is load that box of gold into the back here."

God, what an idiot. If that box was full of gold, there's no way I could have dragged it over here. How did I let this evil man get control of me like this? I've got to stop him, but what can I do?

"Then you're gonna get in and drive. The key's in the ignition. I'll be in back with the old lady."

The keys in the ignition! Can I do this? If I don't, I'm afraid he's gonna kill Rebecca. All I gotta do is stall him long enough so Sam can get everyone loose and then we can stop him. I've got, I've got to.

"Cooley look at that box. I can't lift that much gold into this thing."

When Cooley turned to look at the box with the remains from the grave, White Deer lunged into the ATV and snatched the keys from the ignition.

Cooley turned back to White Deer and yelled, "You better figure out how to do it, Tonto. Now snap outta your shit. Let 's get movin'."

White Deer held up the ATV keys in his hand where Cooley could see them and then turned and threw them as far out into the snow as he could.

"Fuck you, Cooley. And my name ain't …"

Cooly raised his pistol and pointed it White Deer's face less than three feet away, but just as he pulled the trigger, Rebecca pushed back and jarred him just enough that the shot went inches wide.

White Deer ducked behind the ATV and started back toward the corral. He was gone from sight in the blowing snow before Cooley could recover.

"You stupid bitch!" Cooley screamed as he leveled the pistol at Rebecca's face.

The dumb bitch deserves to have her head blowed off, but she's my last ticket off this goddamn mountain.

Cooley spun Rebecca around and hit her with a vicious backhand across the face that knocked her into the snow. If he hadn't been wearing a bulky glove, it would have dislocated her jaw.

"That's just a taste, darlin' of what you'll get if you try to fuck with me again. Now get on your feet, we're movin'."

As Rebecca staggered to her feet, Cooley roughly grabbed her by the collar of her jacket and began to drag her toward where the cars were parked.

I know one a them cars has got the keys in it. I just need a couple minutes. They won't mess with me as long as I've got the woman. I need to figure out how I'm gonna bargain – her life for my gold.

As Cooley started walking, he didn't realize that he had become disoriented in the swirling, blinding snow and he was heading away from the cars instead of toward them.

After only a few steps he came to the edge of the snow-covered slope that ran down toward the pine forest. When he put his next foot down, there was nothing there. In an instant, he and Rebecca were sliding and tumbling out of control.

224

◆ ◆ ◆

Horse Corral

Medicine Wheel Parking Area

Bighorn Mountains, Wyoming

Friday, 15 June

Twelve Forty-Two PM

The knot tying Sam's wrist was loose as White Deer had said, but he was having trouble getting free. His hands were numb after the forty-five-minute ride in from the grave site, and he couldn't make his fingers do what he wanted.

After what seemed like an hour, he could finally feel the rope slipping, and a few seconds later his hands were free. He slapped his palms together a half dozen times to get some circulation going and then pulled his multi-tool out of its holster. It was another struggle to get it opened and get the knife blade out. As he struggled, the storm seemed to be getting stronger.

Just as he got the knife freed there was the *boom* of a large caliber pistol being fired somewhere on the other side of the parking area.

"Shit! Sees Wolf, can you hear me?"

"Yes, Sam. Are you free?"

"Yeah. Look, I'm gonna get Steve and Alicia loose first so we can get the dogs movin'. Then I'll get you, and we'll get the dogs started after Rebecca while you're gettin' everyone else cut free."

Sam had to yell to be heard above the wind. While he talked to Sees Wolf, he quickly cut Steve and Alicia's ropes.

"Are you going to send the dogs alone?" Sees Wolf asked as Sam was cutting his ropes.

"Yeah, I think we got to. You get the rest of the Arapaho nation loose, and get your horses and guns and follow as soon as you can."

"Good luck."

By the time Sees Wolf was free Steve and Alicia had all three dogs untied and were holding onto them for dear life as they lunged in the direction the shot had been fired barking and growling.

Looking at his two friends Sam leaned in closely to be heard, "Guys, I've gotta go after Rebecca. It's gonna be dangerous, you don't have to come with me."

"Nice try Sam," Steve said, "We're in this together."

Alicia just nodded.

"OK, here's what we'll do. Gunny's the only live-find dog, so I'll put him on search. I'll be able to track him on my GPS. I'll follow Gunny, you guys follow me. You good with that?"

Steve and Alicia nodded.

"Let's go.

Sam moved quickly to the other side of the corral holding tight to Gunny's harness. When he got close to the parking area, he stopped and gave Gunny a quick "Sit."

"Gunny, you know somethin' bad's happened. Mom's in trouble. You gotta find Mom. Ready?"

"Gunny! Go find Mom!"

◆ ◆ ◆

Medicine Wheel Parking Area

Bighorn Mountains, Wyoming

Friday, 15 June

Twelve Forty-Five PM

Gunny knew the sound, Mom. Knew that this was The Woman, and he already had her scent. It was faint and being blown around by the wind, but he knew he could find her.

He also had the scent of the Bad Man, but he ignored that.

Gunny had known immediately that the big man was bad. His scent was sour, and smelling him had made Gunny think of dark places and crawling things. He knew that the Bad Man was hurting Mom, and Gunny had to make him stop.

As soon as The Man said Go Find and released his harness, Gunny was off. He started quartering across the wind to find the direction Mom's scent was coming from. As he moved past the cars there were places where her scent was strong, and he slowed to check these, but only for a second. The scent kept coming from in front of him, and he kept moving in that direction.

◆ ◆ ◆

Near the Medicine Wheel Parking Area

Bighorn Mountains, Wyoming

Friday, 15 June

Twelve Forty-Five PM

Rebecca had had the wind knocked out of her and was disoriented by her tumble down the snowy slope. When she regained her senses and understood what had happened. She knew she would have to act quickly.

I don't know where that son of a bitch is. I hope he's dead, but I gotta get some help.

Her fingers fumbled with the small object attached to a loop in the front of her jacket.

Sam's always sayin' the best piece of survival gear you can carry is a whistle. I hope he's right.

She almost had the whistle to her mouth when a huge fist knocked it away into the snow and bloodied her nose.

"Nice try, bitch, but you ain't getting help that easy. There's no way they're gonna find us down here. I'm still in charge."

Oh yeah? You think they won't find us? You don't know my dog Gunny.

In the next second Rebecca was lifted to her feet and half-dragged, half-carried by the big man with his left arm tight across her chest.

After a few minutes, she began to see the outline of trees through the blowing snow.

"Don't worry old lady. We're gonna get in those trees outta this wind and settle in 'til this storm blows over. It can't last forever. That'll give me time to figure out my bargainin' position."

♦ ♦ ♦

Near the Medicine Wheel Parking Area

Bighorn Mountains, Wyoming

Friday, 15 June

Twelve Forty-Eight PM

Gunny stood at the edge of the slope and lifted his nose into the wind.

Mom is still ahead. Her scent is coming from down this hill.

He dropped his nose to the ground.

Yes! Her scent is here too. I can follow her.

Gunny ran down the slope alternately sniffing at the ground and up into the air. As he got to the bottom, a different scent stopped him in his tracks. He pawed at the snow, and it came away red.

That's from Mom! She's hurt! The Bad Man hurt her.

Gunny charged ahead, pushing his old body to go as fast as he could. It was hard running in the snow that came almost to his chest, but he wouldn't slow down.

In a minute he was into a stand of pine trees.

Mom's scent was getting stronger with every stride. The wind was blowing harder and seemed to come from all directions at once, but that didn't matter, Mom's scent was on the ground and Gunny was running as fast as he could with his nose down low.

He broke into a small clearing in the trees and there she was! Gunny wanted to run to her but the Bad Man had his arm around her neck, and he was pointing the little boomstick at her head. Gunny wasn't sure what to do, and then Mom yelled at him.

"Gunny, go back!"

Gunny knew Go Back. That's what Mom would say when he was first learning to Go Find, and he still needed some help to know what to do next. Gunny spun around as fast as he could to go tell The Man that he had found Mom. As he turned, he heard the loud bang of the boomstick, and he felt a hot, burning pain in his back leg. He almost fell, but he pushed hard with his front legs and got into the trees before the Bad Man could use the boomstick again.

Sam and the others had just reached the bottom of the slope when he heard the shot and looked down at his GPS screen.

"Gunny's found them. They're about 150 yards straight ahead, and Gunny's coming back on a recall."

"What are you gonna do, Sam?" Alicia yelled.

"I'm gonna send him back and follow as fast as I can."

"You're not sending a golden retriever back against an armed perp by himself. Luke's goin' with him." Steve said.

"I'm not sure how much good he can do, but I don't think I can hold Iwo back."

Sam looked at his friends and saw the dogs straining against their leashes, and he knew that somehow the dogs understood that Rebecca and Gunny needed help. They were going to go, with or without a command.

"OK guys. Gunny's almost back. Get ready."

Just then Gunny appeared out of the blowing snow about ten yards away. Sam could see that he was bleeding badly from his right hip and running with a slight limp, but running just as hard as he could.

When he got to Sam Gunny jumped up and put his paws in the middle of Sam's chest—a perfect final indication—and Sam knew beyond any doubt that he had found Rebecca.

"Gunny! Good boy! Show me!"

As Gunny turned to go back to Mom, the big gray Alpha Wolf appeared in front of him. For the first time, the Alpha's hackles were raised, and his tail stood erect like a flag, and he snarled as he looked at Gunny, but Gunny did not feel any threat – the Alpha was there to help. As Gunny started to run the big wolf pivoted to run in front of him.

Sam watched as Gunny spun around and ... *Holy Shit! What the hell ...??? That's a goddamn wolf!!!*

Sam watched as Gunny and the wolf were joined by Luke and Iwo, and the four of them began to run into the woods.

Gunny, Luke, and Iwo know this wolf. It's like they're a pack. Just like Sees Wolf said. What the hell is going on???

Just before they disappeared into the trees and snow, Sam saw the big wolf lift his muzzle into the air and make a sound that Sam had never heard up close before. A second later the dogs joined in.

The three dogs and the big wolf were howling a high, keening ululation that caused the hair on the back of men's necks to stand erect and from which every wild creature instinctively ran. It was a sound that dogs hadn't made for fifteen thousand years, but the memory of that sound was buried deep in the oldest parts of their brain.

It was the sound of a wolf pack on the hunt.

For a long moment Sam, Steve, and Alicia were too shocked to move. Then they took off running trying to follow the dogs who had disappeared into the snow-covered woods.

Sam ran as fast as he could, and he did pretty well for the first fifty yards or so, but then he started feeling every one of his seventy-plus years. Steve and Alicia pulled away from him. As Sam pushed his way through some thick brush, he heard behind him the sound of horses running at a gallop. He turned to look just as two riders charged past him expertly guiding their horses through the thick trees.

As the riders passed, Sam recognized Sees Wolf and Golden Eagle, but they didn't look like anything he had ever seen before outside of a museum. Their horses had no saddles, and the men were naked from the waist up. Their faces were painted in red and black patterns, and they each wore two eagle feathers on their heads. They were both carrying Winchester Model 94's, and they were screaming a high-pitched yell that was almost as frightening as the howl the dogs had made.

Jake Cooley heard the howling of wolves and the savage screaming of Arapaho warriors, and it was all he could do not to piss on himself.

"What the fuck have they got out there???"

The sounds came closer, and Cooley knew that he was trapped. Then, as suddenly as they had begun, they stopped. As Cooley stared ahead, he saw four gray-white shapes moving fast through the blowing snow.

Cooley took the gun away from Rebecca's head and started to point it at whatever it was coming at him.

I don't know where that goddam noise came from, but I sure as hell know how to shoot a dog.

As Cooley was about to pull the trigger, the figures coming at him materialized into four large, gray wolves.

Cooley's hand went slack, the gun dropped into the snow, and his bladder and bowels let go.

A second later the Alpha's teeth closed on Cooley's arm with enough force to break the femur of a full-grown bull elk. The effect on Cooley was devastating. His arm was nearly torn in half. His scream reverberated through the woods and he fell to the ground and curled into a ball to try to protect himself.

Rebecca pulled herself away from Cooley's grasp and fell hard onto the snow-covered ground. She couldn't believe that she was watching a huge wolf tear Cooley's arm off just feet away. Then three more wolves ran out of the woods and tensed to pounce on Cooley. She knew that they would rip him apart. She had to stop them, but how?

"No! No! Don't! Stop!"

Amazingly, the four wolves stopped and looked at her. The largest one had the wildest, fiercest eyes she had ever seen. She tore her eyes away from him and looked at the nearest wolf who was injured and bleeding from one hip. When this wolf met her eyes, she recognized him immediately.

"Gunny???"

When she spoke, the other two wolves looked at her.

"Luke? Iwo??"

The largest wolf was about to finish off Cooley when two half-naked men with painted faces carrying rifles rode out of the woods on barebacked horses.

Rebecca stared at them in disbelief. *My god! That's Sees Wolf and Golden Eagle, but how ..., what ...?*

Sees Wolf spoke calmly in Arapaho to the large wolf. The wolf turned to look at him with an expression something like disappointment. Then he stepped away from Cooley and walked to Rebecca.

Rebecca stifled a scream as the wolf came closer and she could see Cooley's blood dripping from both sides of its massive jaws, but she saw no menace in its eyes, and she relaxed. The wolf walked right up to her and looked her calmly in the face.

This is the most magnificent animal I have ever seen.

After a moment, the wolf turned and trotted away toward the woods and disappeared into the snow.

Rebecca closed her eyes and shook her head to try to clear her mind. When she looked again, Cooley was laying still in the snow bleeding badly, and all the wolves were gone. Luke and Iwo were standing over Cooley snarling, and Gunny was limping toward her, barely able to walk. Sees Wolf and Golden Eagle were still on their horses pointing their rifles at Cooley, but now they were dressed as she had last seen them and there was no paint on their faces. A minute later Steve and Alicia ran into the small clearing.

By the time Sam caught up, Alicia was holding both Luke and Iwo, and Steve was getting a tourniquet out of his first aid kit to try to stop Cooley's bleeding. Sees Wolf and Golden Eagle were just dismounting to help.

Sam ignored all that because he saw his wife kneeling in the snow cradling a bloodied and very still dog as she rocked back and forth crying.

Gunny was very tired, but he could smell Mom, and she was holding him and telling him that he was a Good Dog. Then he felt The Man put his hand gently on his head. Gunny knew that they were sad, and wanted to show them that it would be all right, but he didn't know how. He didn't feel the pain anymore, and he wasn't tired, but he felt sleepy and warm, and everything around him was getting darker. He thought he knew what was happening. He wasn't afraid, just a little sad.

Then he smelled something, two smells he recognized. He was having trouble remembering, but ... Yes! It was the Old Bone smells of the Good Man, Robby, and his dog, Rusty. Then he saw them walking to him. Rusty came forward and gently licked his muzzle, and the Good Man squatted down in front of him and stroked his head and started talking to him. Gunny didn't know the words the Good Man was saying, but, somehow, he understood.

Robby Durance, who had died on the island of Iwo Jima on March 1st, 1945, was saying, "Not yet, Gunny. Not yet."

Steve came over carrying his first aid kit.

"Is Cooley gonna live?" Sam asked.

"Don't know, don't care. I got a tourniquet on his arm. As soon as Alicia gets Luke and Iwo tied up, she'll take over with him. Let's focus on Gunny."

"I think we're losin' him."

"Naw, Luke was hurt worse than this in Afghanistan. Let me get some Quick Clot in that wound and stop the bleeding, and then we'll need to get some fluids into him, preferably some warm fluids."

"Hey, Joseph, can you guys get a fire started?"

"Yes, Steve. We're Indians."

"Yeah, sorry. As fast as you can, please, we need some hot water. Where'd the other guys go?"

"Sees Wolf sent one of them back to the lodge to call for help. The others are heading here with blankets and food and stuff."

In a couple of minutes, Steve had gotten Gunny's bleeding slowed to a trickle and bandaged the wound.

"Sam, as far as I can tell that bullet didn't do any major damage. Gunny's only problem's gonna be blood loss."

"So, what's your plan?"

"I've got an IV kit. As soon as we get some hot water, I'm gonna warm up the saline and get him started on an IV. For now, let's just keep him as warm and comfortable as possible. Rebecca, how about you? You OK?"

"Yeah, my jaw's awful sore, but I'm OK. I'm just worried about Gunny."

"Just keep holdin' him and keep him warm. Sam, you got a space blanket?"

"Yeah, right here."

"Good there's one in my pack, too. Let's get those around Rebecca and Gunny. And then you should probably check Rebecca's eyes."

"I already did. Her right pupil's a little dilated. She may have a concussion."

"All we can do right now is keep her warm and hydrated. Rebecca, you let us know if you start getting a headache or feel sick or anything. OK?"

"Yeah, sure, but let's focus on Gunny."

◆ ◆

200 Yards Northeast of the Medicine Wheel Parking Area

GHOSTS OF THE BUFFALO WHEEL

Bighorn Mountains, Wyoming

Friday, 15 June

One Fifty-Three PM

By the time the first highway patrol officer arrived about an hour later things had settled down a lot. The storm had blown itself out, and the sun was putting in more and more frequent appearances between the clouds. Two lean-tos had been set up alongside a good, hot fire. Gunny and Rebecca were in one and Cooley in the other. Both of Steve's IV bags had gone, one into Gunny and one into Cooley. Gunny was sound asleep, but his breathing and pulse were regular, and his gums were beginning to pink up.

Cooley was in rough shape. He was in a lot of pain and going into shock. He needed more fluids, but the first time Joseph Golden Eagle tried to give him some water he lashed out and tried to grab Joseph's throat with his good hand. Sees Wolf kicked him in his injured arm just below the tourniquet. That quieted him down quickly. Since then, they'd left him alone, and someone with a weapon kept an eye on him all the time.

Officer Turner explained that a rescue squad ambulance was on its way and would be at the parking area in about twenty minutes. Once he got a good look at Cooley, he got on his satellite phone and called for a Life Flight helo out of Casper, and then went to work figuring out how best to restrain the big man so he could be moved to the parking area where the helo would land.

"What the hell happened to his arm?" Turner asked.

"Luke, the Black Lab, nailed him just before he was about to shoot my wife," Sam said.

I just hope that none of the docs who work on Cooley know the difference between a dog bite and a wolf bite.

"Wow! I had no idea that a Lab could do that much damage."

"Yeah. I guess he was pretty angry."

Rebecca had told Sam and the others what had happened to Cooley, and, based on what everyone had seen and heard for themselves, they had no trouble believing her. The team hadn't had much time to make up a story, but they decided the only plausible thing was to make Luke the hero and give him credit for taking down an armed kidnapper three times his size.

The weird shit just seems to follow us around, Sam thought.

Sees Wolf, Golden Eagle and the two wranglers set to work fashioning two travoises, one for Cooley and one for Rebecca and Gunny. Cooley's good hand was firmly zip-tied to his belt, and his feet were zip-tied together before his injured arm was splinted and put in a sling, and he was dragged into a travois. The four Arapaho made a bed for Rebecca and Gunny with blankets and loaded them much more gently than they had loaded Cooley.

Two paramedics, one from the rescue squad and one from Life Flight, met them when they were about halfway to the parking area. They refreshed both Cooley's and Gunny's IVs and got Cooley started on O2. They examined Rebecca and agreed that she probably had a concussion, but that she could go to the smaller hospital in Sheridan, which was much closer.

As soon as they got to the parking area, Cooley was loaded onto a gurney, firmly strapped down, and loaded into the helo, which took off for the hospital in Casper where he would be met by a trauma team and an armed deputy.

The rescue squad had no problem with taking Gunny in the squad truck with Rebecca, and they promised to monitor him and deliver him to the twenty-four-hour veterinary hospital in Sheridan.

Sam would follow them as soon as he had given his statement to Officer Turner.

Turner suggested that they go to the Bighorn Mountain Lodge where they could warm up, and he would take their statements there. Everyone agreed that was a good idea.

CHAPTER FIFTEEN

After The Storm

*There are some things you learn best in calm, and
some in storm.*

Willa Cather

Bighorn Mountain Lodge

Saturday, 16 June

AFTER THE STORM HAD BLOWN ITSELF OUT the weather turned beautiful. At breakfast, Alicia asked if anyone would be willing to go with her and finish the recovery job at the grave site. Steve volunteered, and Sees Wolf sent two of the wranglers along to help.

On the way out to the grave site, Luke found the pistols that Sam and Steve had thrown away.

After he had given his statement, Sam had driven to Sheridan and spent the night at the hospital with Rebecca. He made frequent calls to the vet to check on Gunny's condition.

Sees Wolf and Golden Eagle worked with the remaining Arapaho wrangler to take care of the horses and collect up all the gear that had been blown around by the storm.

It was warm and sunny, and despite their concern about Rebecca and Gunny, everyone seemed to enjoy it after their experiences in the storm. By unspoken agreement, no one talked about what had happened. They would wait until Sam, Rebecca and Gunny were back.

Around noon Sam called the Lodge and said that Rebecca and Gunny would both be released that afternoon and he would drive them back. He hoped to be there in time for dinner.

Everyone was back from the grave site by three with the rest of the remains carefully boxed up.

Steve and Alicia had changed their travel plans. There was no way they could leave without talking through with everyone what had happened. After they got back to the Lodge, they spent the rest of the day on the phone rearranging flight schedules.

The Lodge had extended everyone's stay for an additional day. The only change in the lodging arrangements was that Eldon White Deer was now sleeping on a cot in the room with Sees Wolf and Golden Eagle. When they weren't working, the three of them had spent hours talking, either in the Lodge or out on one of the hiking trails.

Sam drove in just before dinner. He helped Rebecca to a chair in the dining room, and then he and Steve went back for Gunny and carried him to his bed near Rebecca.

One side of Rebecca's face was swollen and turning blue and black, but nothing was broken. She was a little unsteady on her feet, but the doctors

241

had put her through the same concussion protocol the NFL uses and said she was cleared for anything short of full-contact scrimmages.

Rebecca hadn't thought that was funny.

Between the sedatives from his surgery and the pain medication he'd been given, Gunny was pretty well out of it, but he still managed to wag his tail each time one of his friends came up to stroke his head. The area around his right hip had been shaved, and he had about twenty sutures holding an eight-inch-long wound together.

As Steve scratched Gunny behind the ears, he said, "You and Luke make a real pair now – a couple of heroes with the scars to prove it."

As the meal was served, everyone was quiet not knowing what to say. Finally, Alicia asked,"So, how's Gunny going to be?"

"He'll be OK, but his search days may be through. There was some damage to the muscle, and that leg is always going to be stiff. He'll be able to get around all right, but the docs say he'll either have a limp or, if it's really stiff, maybe he'll just tripod."

"Tripod?" Alicia asked.

"Yeah, walk on three legs," Sam replied, "Dogs that have lost a limb typically learn to get along without it pretty well. We'll just have to see what he decides to do. There's a good vet in Park City who's certified in canine sports medicine. She's worked on Gunny before, and we'll get him in to see her and get some therapy and exercises."

"What are you gonna do to keep him active?" Alicia asked, "Just 'cause he's only got three good legs doesn't mean that he'll have any less drive."

"Nosework," Sam replied

"Nosework, what's that?" Steve asked.

"It's something fairly new that's pretty similar to search and rescue except you don't have to climb mountains or run through the snow. It's a dog sport where dogs compete to see which one can find the most hidden scent sources the fastest. All I should have to do is teach Gunny some new target odors. Sharon runs a Nosework class as part of her dog training business. I sent her a couple of e-mails about what happened, and she's already putting together a training schedule for him."

"Typical Sharon," Alicia chuckled, "How's she doing in … what? … Germany?"

"Yeah, they're in Germany, and Rascal has identified a couple of possible places where there might be some old remains, and they're getting ready to do some digging. She said to say, 'Congratulations,' to everyone for doing such a good job on finding Butch's grave."

"Wait a minute," Alicia said, "We don't know for sure who was buried in that grave."

"Yeah, well, I'm gonna call it Butch's grave until somebody proves me wrong."

After a minute of silence, Golden Eagle said, "So, what are we going to talk about now?"

"Nothing!" Sam replied, "Let's finish dinner in peace, and then get ourselves something to drink – a big whiskey for me – and go sit by the fire – I don't know about the rest of you, but I've still got a chill – and then we can talk."

When everyone had replied or nodded they all focused on dinner.

Twenty minutes later they were all seated around the fire in the main room of the Lodge with a variety of drinks. Gunny was on his bed just a couple of feet from the fire and Luke and Iwo were lying on either side as if they were protecting him.

"Rebecca, do you think you should be drinking that wine with your concussion?" Alicia asked.

"Yes, Doctor Phillips, I do, Thanks for your concern, but I'm gonna need something to get me through what we're gonna talk about, and a little wine probably won't kill me."

"Before we go over what happened yesterday let me bring everyone up to speed on Cooley. You all know that was Jake Cooley, a meth dealer, who grabbed Rebecca, right?"

'Yes," Sees Wolf replied, "I recognized him immediately, and I told the others about him. He has been a scourge for the Shoshone and us for several years now. Is he gone for good?"

"Yeah, Officer Turner came by the hospital just before we left. Those Wyoming Highway Patrol boys cover a lot of territory. They amputated Cooley's arm. Evidently, the Docs were surprised that a dog could do that much damage, but Cooley was being such a problem that no one was too concerned about what actually happened."

"What kind of problems was he causing?" Steve asked.

"According to Turner, the arm wasn't his biggest problem. Before they even got him into surgery, he started showing all the symptoms of acute alcohol withdrawal syndrome. D.T.'s, hallucinations, cold sweats, the whole nine yards. He's a sick puppy."

"That explains a lot," Sees Wolf said.

"What do you mean?"

"I talked with White Deer and made some phone calls, and I think I know how Cooley got the idea that we had found a treasure up here."

"That should be interesting. How?" Sam asked.

"He was conned by a southern Arapaho I know named James Raven. Raven has made a very good living as gambler and con man. Seems he heard about Cooley and decided to teach him a lesson. He convinced Cooley that he had information about where Butch Cassidy had buried some loot from one of his train robberies. He used the fact that we would be searching up here to make the con more realistic. He got a couple thousand dollars off Cooley that he donated to the Tribal Council. He figured Cooley would realize eventually that he'd been conned by an Indian and that would piss him off which is all Raven wanted to do."

"I talked to Raven a little while ago. He couldn't understand why Cooley never figured out that he'd been conned. He also said he was sorry for the way things turned out. He never imagined that anything like that would happen."

"Why didn't Cooley figure out what was going on?" Sam asked.

"I'll bet Dr. Phillips can answer that question."

"Sure. He was delusional. It's a common symptom of chronic alcoholism, and the worse of a drunk you are, the more you can fixate on your delusion."

The room was quiet for a minute while everyone tried to absorb what they'd just heard.

Finally, Sam spoke up, "All right, that answers one question, but we've got a lot more stuff to try to figure out."

"Why don't we start by each of us telling the story of what happened from their own perspective, and maybe that will help us to understand things a little better. I'll go first."

Forty-five minutes later when everyone had finished, Sam said, "This is pretty amazing. None of us saw everything, but we all saw some of the same things. Tell me if I've got this right."

"There was a wolf, a big wolf, that Sees Wolf says was his spirit wolf in the flesh. Right?"

"Yes," Sees Wolf replied, "I would know him anywhere. I thought that I had seen him in the flesh before, but this is the first time that I am sure of it."

"And our dogs seemed to know this wolf, and they had no problem following him."

"Yes," Steve and Alicia said together.

"And when the four of them ran off after Rebecca and Cooley they started howling like a wolf pack on the hunt. I've heard that sound at a distance in Yellowstone, and it's not something you forget."

"Yes," Alicia said, "And remember the morning we left Lander the dogs were trying to howl, and we all laughed because it sounded so horrible?"

Steve and Sam nodded.

"Well, it sure didn't sound horrible yesterday. It was scary as hell, but it was beautiful, too."

"Right, and then sometime between when they left us, and before they got to Rebecca, our three dogs changed into wolves. Sees Wolf, how in the hell is that possible?"

Sees Wolf closed his eyes and gazed upward. In the firelight reflecting off his face, he could have been an Arapaho medicine man from centuries before.

"I am thinking about how a Buddist would explain this."

"A Buddist? Really?"

"Yes, and the more I think about it, the more sense it makes. Would you like to hear what I think?"

"Go ahead, please," Sam said. *I've gotta learn not to underestimate Sees Wolf, he's probably the smartest one here.*

"Cooley is a truly evil man, and he was threatening not only Rebecca, who was here to try to help the Arapaho people, but also the people themselves by disturbing the peace of the Buffalo Wheel. That's not to mention what he had already done by selling his drugs. I believe that sometimes, when the balance between good and evil shifts too much toward evil, *Hichaba Nihancan,* the Creator, steps in to restore the balance. I think that this is what a Buddist would call 'karma,' which is a way of saying, 'He got what was coming to him.'"

"As for the dogs, a Buddist would explain that as reincarnation."

"You mean the dogs died and came back as wolves and then the wolves died and came back as dogs?" Alicia asked.

"No. I think it was more like the dogs became the wolves they had been fifteen thousand or so years ago."

"So," Steve asked, "Would that also explain how you and Joseph became ancient Arapaho warriors?"

"Yes, perhaps in another life that's exactly what we were."

"Yes," Alicia said, "What about that? Can you describe what that was like? Maybe that would help us understand what happened."

"I must admit that I took that whole experience for granted. It was not the first time that something like that has happened to me."

When he saw the quizzical looks on everyone's face, he continued, "That is something we can talk about at another time. Perhaps Joseph can describe what he saw and felt."

"Yes," Golden Eagle replied, "I've been thinking about this a lot. It was an amazing experience."

After closing his eyes to collect his thoughts, he continued, "When Uncle and I got to the horses, they were tethered in the corral, and their saddles were nearby, so the part about us riding bare-backed was real. Our rifles were in their scabbards on the saddles. As soon as I grabbed my rifle, I ran and jumped up on my horse."

"Now I'm a decent horseman, but it's been a long time since I'd ridden anything bare-backed and even longer since I've done it at anything but a slow walk. But I was able to jump right up on that horse like a movie stuntman, and when we got the horses turned Uncle and I both took off at a gallop."

"How did you feel?" Alicia asked.

"I felt some mild surprise that I was able to ride this horse so well, but I probably just rationalized it to be the effects of adrenaline and wanting to get to where we could help as quickly as possible. Nothing registered until I looked at Uncle, and saw what he had become."

"And what was that?"

"Just as you and Rebecca described, Sam. He wore buckskin pants and was naked above the waist. His face was painted, and he wore feathers in his hair. He also looked a lot younger, and ... well, ..."

"What?" Rebecca asked.

"He looked like he was having a lot of fun."

"Yes," Sees Wolf said, "I was. Men my age don't get many chances to ride into battle as an Arapaho warrior to save a fair maiden in distress."

"Thank you, Sees Wolf," Rebecca said with a sharp look at Sam, "No one's called me a 'fair maiden' in a long time."

"Yes, dear," Sam replied, "Drink more wine."

Joseph continued, "Then I looked down at my arms and saw that I looked much like my Uncle. The next thing I knew it was like we were flying through the air and we went down that steep slope at a full run. I've never done anything like that in my life, but that was just the beginning. I saw the trees ahead of us, and I knew we were going much too fast. There was no way I could ride a horse through there at that speed, but Uncle wasn't slowing down, so I kept going."

"Riding through those woods was the most exciting thing I've ever done, and it all felt perfectly natural. All I had to do was nudge the horse with my knees and lean a bit to one side or another, and we weaved through the trees at full gallop. Then Uncle began the war cry. I had never heard that before, but I knew exactly what it was and joined in as loudly as I could. I couldn't make that same sound now if my life depended on it."

"You scared the hell out of Cooley, I can tell you that," Rebecca said.

"I think that was mostly the dogs, I mean the wolves."

"It sounds to me like you were having a lot of fun yourself."

Golden Eagle paused and thought, "Yes, Steve. Yes, I was."

"By the way," Sees Wolf said, "All this talk reminds me of something I should have mentioned. Those weren't any saddle-broken, trail horses we were riding. No way we could have done what we did on those horses. No, we were riding Arapaho war ponies."

"OK," Sam said, "We're in agreement that our dogs turned into wolves, and Sees Wolf and Golden Eagle turned into Arapaho warriors riding war ponies. This wasn't some sort of group hallucination."

Sam looked at each person, and they all nodded.

"And I guess it goes without saying that it was Sees Wolf's spirit wolf made flesh who almost tore Cooley's arm off."

Again, everyone nodded.

"Any questions?" Sam asked.

"Yes," Alicia said, "What Sees Wolf has said sounds reasonable—if that word even applies here— but we're talking about some incredible transformations— dogs into wolves, spirit wolf into real wolf, men into ancient warriors. If these sorts of things are actually possible, why don't we see them all the time?"

"I think these things could only happen in a place like the Buffalo Wheel," Sees Wolf replied, "The Buffalo Wheel has been the focus for spiritual events for thousands of years. Like Stonehenge and other circles, I think that places like the Buffalo Wheel were centers for spiritual or extra-normal energy long before they were discovered by men. I think that Iwo Jima today is like that too because of all the suffering and violent death that occurred on that tiny island. I doubt that anything like what happened here or on Iwo Jima could happen anywhere else."

Everyone was quiet and lost in thought for several minutes before Sam continued, "So, I guess there's just one more thing to talk about. What, if anything, are we going to do about White Deer? And speaking of White Deer, where the hell is he?"

Sees Wolf replied immediately, "Eldon is in our room. I told him to stay and have his dinner there and that we would call for him when it was time. Before we do that, I'd like to say thanks to all of you for … obfuscating his role in what Cooley did in your official statements."

"I'm not sure how I feel about that," Sam replied, "I know he did the right thing at the end, and if he hadn't tied me up so loosely and then thrown those keys away Cooley might have made it off with Rebecca. On the other hand, it would have been nice if he could have warned us about what Cooley planned to do."

"Yes," Sees Wolf replied, "And I take some of the blame for what happened. As you know, Joseph and I have been talking with White Deer since last night. May I tell you what we've learned?"

"Of course."

"White Deer is one of the young men that I have been watching for some time. Many of our young men have trouble with drugs and alcohol, but his case was particularly disturbing to me."

"I knew his father and mother well. They were good people. Young and still learning about life, but they had good hearts. I am certain that if his father had lived even a year or two longer Eldon would have become a different person."

"When did he die?" Rebecca asked.

"He was killed in an accident on an oil rig when Eldon was ten. He was making decent money then, and they had a small ranch with some horses and a few cows. His Dad was teaching Eldon how to be a cowboy. There was an insurance payment after his death, but it wasn't enough to keep the ranch. They had to move into town, and his Mom had to find work. She'd never been anything but a wife and mother, so there wasn't much she could do."

"Eldon's story is the same as many of our young men. He was drifting, and he was fair game for any predator like Cooley. Cooley was a master at manipulation through intimidation and guilt."

"But there was something different about Eldon. He had something decent at his core. That's what Father Smithers told me, and that's why I picked him to come up here with us. I thought that this could be a good experience that might help him get straightened out."

251

"Turns out I was right. He told us over and over how much it meant to him that all of you treated him decently and included him in the group. He feels very badly that he put us in danger."

"What do you think we should do?"

"I think for a start we should bring him in here so he can apologize to everyone. That would help a lot."

A half an hour later Sam and the others were convinced that White Deer was genuinely sorry for what he had done.

"Sam," Sees Wolf said, "I think that all Eldon needs is to learn some pride, discipline, and self-respect."

"Is that true, Eldon,"

"I don't know, but if that's what Sees Wolf thinks then he's probably right."

"How hard are you willing to work?"

For the first time, White Deer met Sam's eyes directly, "I swear I will do whatever it takes to become the kind of Arapaho my father would be proud of."

"Steve, can you think of anyplace a young man like Eldon could go to learn about pride, discipline, and self-respect?"

Steve's face split into a broad grin, "Why yes, Sam, I think I do."

CHAPTER SIXTEEN

Eagle, Globe, and Anchor

"We don't promise you a rose garden."

Marine Corps Recruiting Slogan, 1971 - 1984

Marine Corps Base

Camp Pendleton, California

Friday, 9 November

Just Before Dawn

FITY-THREE HOURS AGO Eldon White Deer and the rest of the recruits in Fox Company had been rousted out of their bunks in the middle of the night by their Drill Instructors. That had been the beginning of the Marine Corps' rite of passage known as "The Crucible."

Since then, they had been continuously on the move. They marched for mile after mile with sixty-five-pound packs plus their rifles and combat gear. They ran obstacle courses, and did fire and maneuver drills and casualty evacuation drills. Then they did more marching. They crawled under barbed wire through mud and water at night with temperatures in the forties. Later, soaking wet and freezing, they worked in teams to solve tactical problems when they were so tired they could barely think.

During these fifty-three hours Recruit White Deer, as he had called himself for the last twelve weeks, had gotten about five hours of sleep and three MRE meals to sustain him. He was tired, cold, hungry, and every muscle in his body hurt. Of course, the goddamn Marine Corps had saved the worst for last

As the sun started to lighten the eastern horizon, White Deer approached the bottom of "The Reaper," a series of steep ridges that towered into the sky above him. Somewhere up there, an impossible distance away, was the finish line. Make it, and for the rest of your life you would be a United States Marine. Fall out, and you just wasted twelve tough weeks.

White Deer was marching at the front of his recruit platoon as the guidon bearer, a position of honor he had earned by his performance so far. When he had been told that he would carry the guidon it had made him proud, but now all he could think of was how heavy the damn thing was and the way the small flag kept trying to pull him off balance whenever it caught a gust of wind.

The Reaper was the Marine Corps' official name for this last heart-breaking obstacle the recruits had to endure, but for as long as anyone could remember, all the way back to World War II, the Marines who had to climb it have had their own name for it.

They call it Mount Motherfucker.

White Deer's platoon, number 375, had won the Honor Platoon competition and was the first in the line of march, so White Deer was the first of three hundred or so recruits to start the climb. This didn't mean that White Deer got to set the pace. A Drill Instructor was walking alongside him to see that he and the rest of the Company kept going at a rate that was enough to exhaust them, but not quite enough to kill them.

There were three false summits on the ridgeline. Looking up, it would appear that the top was coming tantalizing close only to find that there was just a short level stretch before the next, even-steeper climb began.

White Deer had never experienced pain and exhaustion this complete before. His body's natural reaction was to close in on itself. White Deer didn't know how long he had been just plodding with no awareness of what was going on around him until suddenly there was a harsh whisper in his ear, and he jerked back into consciousness to find the lead Drill Instructor alongside him.

"Tired Recruit? Can't hack it? You're supposed to be keepin' up with me, and you're fallin' back. Want me to take that guidon away from you and let some other Recruit carry it?"

White Deer felt as if he'd been slapped in the face.

God! What am I doin'? This is my chance to make my father proud. I just gotta keep goin'.

"Sir! You want this guidon you're gonna have to fight me for it!"

Oh my god! Did I say that out loud?

"That's a pretty gutsy thing for a Recruit to say, White Deer. Let's see if you mean it. I'm stepping up the pace. You fall back one stride, and you lose that guidon. Let's move it!"

"Sir! Aye, aye, Sir!"

The DI surged ahead.

White Deer leaned forward and pushed up with everything he had. In two strides he moved up abreast of the DI.

As long as I can still breath, I'm not fallin' back one inch. They can kill me, but they can't make me quit.

The agony was interminable. Each step revealed some new pain, and White Deer had no way to know how much farther he had to go. His whole world resolved into a single goal.

One more step, one more step.

White Deer was so focused on pushing himself farther and farther upward that he almost fell over when the trail suddenly flattened out.

He looked up into a blaze of floodlights and saw nothing but level ground in front of him. As the rest of Platoon 375 staggered to the top of the ridge, loudspeakers began to blare out John Phillip Sousa's "Semper Fidelis March."

White Deer looked back and saw that the platoon formation was ragged and many of his fellow recruits were bent over almost double and just stumbling along.

That's not the way we're supposed to do this.

Turning so that he was walking backward, he yelled,

"Platoon 375, get that goddamn formation squared away! Dress right and cover down. March at the position of attention. We're gonna be Marines in a few minutes. Let's start actin' like it!"

If he had looked behind, he would have seen a satisfied grin on the Drill Instructor's face.

♦ ♦ ♦

Atop Mount Motherfucker

GHOSTS OF THE BUFFALO WHEEL

Marine Corps Base

Camp Pendleton, California

Friday, 9 November

The recruits of Fox Company were aligned in formation in front of a small reviewing stand. Their packs and gear were staged just behind them. They kept their rifles with them.

In a few minutes, the Company Commander would administer the oath of enlistment. Then the Drill Instructors would present each of them with the Marine Corps' emblem, the Eagle, Globe, and Anchor, and would address them as 'Marine' for the first time.

White Deer was still trying to get his breathing under control when he heard his name called.

"Recruit White Deer fall out and report to the Company Gunnery Sergeant."

"Sir! Aye, aye, Sir!"

The Company Gunnery Sergeant? Oh shit, what now?

White Deer knew that the Company Gunny had just completed the same march he had, but when he found him the man looked like he'd just stepped out of the shower and put on a fresh uniform.

"Sir! Recruit White Deer reporting to the Company Gunnery Sergeant as ordered, Sir!"

"At Ease, White Deer."

White Deer snapped to a rigid position of Parade Rest.

"No, White Deer, At Ease. Relax."

White Deer allowed his posture to sag slightly.

"I understand you know a Marine Sergeant by the name of Steve Haney."

"Sir! Yes, Sir. Sergeant Haney and I were on a search together back home."

"So you know Luke? And you can knock off the 'Sir, yes Sir' stuff. You're not a recruit anymore.

"Sir ..., uh ... I mean, yes Sir. Luke is Steve's dog. I mean Sergeant Haney's dog."

"I was a Force Recon Platoon Sergeant back a few years ago in Afghanistan. Steve and Luke were on a few of my patrols. They saved my ass a couple of times."

"Steve got in touch with me when Fox Company formed up. He told me a bit about you. Said he thought you might make a good Marine."

"Sir, I ... I don't know what to say."

"He told me about your Dad and how you wanted to make him proud of you."

"Yes, Sir"

"Well, I got some news for you. You're gonna be your platoon's Honor Graduate. Number one man in the number one platoon in the Company. I know your Dad's lookin' down on you right now, and he's as proud as he can be. Good job, Marine."

Gunnery Sergeant Tom Farnan looked on as Private White Deer struggled and failed to hold back his tears.

Bein' a Drill Instructor's a hard goddamn job. But sometimes it's worth it.

GHOSTS OF THE BUFFALO WHEEL

◆ ◆ ◆

Marine Corps Recruit Depot

San Diego, California

Tuesday, 13 November

Parents, grandparents, sisters, brothers, and friends, over five hundred of them, had come for Fox Company's graduation parade. They all understood that the young men standing in ranks before them had done something special. Most of them had not realized the extent of the transformation until they had seen their Marine for the first time in twelve weeks the day before.

Eldon White Deer's mother had been as surprised as anyone. She had stood in shock as the erect, confident young man with the flashing black eyes in an immaculate green uniform had walked up and wrapped her in a hug.

Later when she was with Sam, Rebecca and Sees Wolf in the stands alongside the parade deck, she asked, "What happened? I don't understand. I sent them a broken boy. They sent me back an Arapaho warrior."

"Yes, ma'am," Sam replied, "That's what they do here."

CHAPTER SEVENTEEN

Butch?

"Who are you?

Who, who, who, who?.
——"Who Are You" The Who, 1978

Ogden Valley, Utah

Friday, 16 November

"This is Jim, checking in."

"Welcome Jim," Sam said, "We've got everyone online now. Rebecca and I are here in Utah, Sees Wolf and Joseph are up in Wind River, Alicia's in Knoxville, and Steve's in Charlottesville."

"Alicia, you called this conference, so I'm guessing you have some info on our mystery man."

"Yes, Sam, I do. But before I get started, how about bringing all of us up to date on Rebecca, Gunny, and White Deer."

"I'm fine," Rebecca replied, "My jaw was sore for a week or so, and I couldn't chew very well, but no lasting damage."

"Gunny's OK, too," Sam said, "We've done a lot of therapy with him, and he can get around pretty well. He only has a little bit of a limp when he's walking. He can't run very well, and he has a hard time going up anything steep. He can make it up the stairs, but he goes slow."

"I guess his searching days are over?" Steve asked.

"I still take him out to training and just work him in small areas on mostly flat ground. He could still do an HRD search like he did on that guy's patio last year, and he still likes training, so I'll keep him going for a while."

"Sam, I have a question for you and Steve."

"Sure, Alicia, go ahead."

"Have your dogs been doing anything ... strange lately?"

"You mean like howling at the full moon?" Sam said.

"Yeah, what about you, Steve."

"I wasn't gonna say anything, but, yeah, Luke's been doing that. Iwo too?"

"Yeah, and it doesn't sound like it did that time in Lander it sounds like ... well, a real wolf. What does Gunny sound like?"

"Gunny sounds enough like a wolf to scare the hell out of the local coyote pack."

"Is this something that they're going to do from now on?"

"Beats me. What do you think Sees Wolf?"

"I think you'd better figure out a way to explain to your neighbors why you have a wolf in your backyard."

261

Everyone had a good chuckle, and then Steve said, "I've said it before, and I'll say it again, the weird stuff just seems to follow us around."

"Yep," Sam said, "Let's move on. Sees Wolf you want to tell 'em about Private First Class White Deer?"

"I'll be happy to. Eldon is back home on leave now, and everyone is very impressed with him. Most people can't believe that this is the same person who left here three months ago. He has already been to speak at the high school. I watched him on stage in front of the whole school, and I couldn't believe how confident he was or how well he spoke."

"I think he's going to be a great asset to our tribe."

"That's wonderful," Alicia said, "Sam and Steve that was a great idea you two had. I was skeptical at first, but you knew what you were doing."

"Well, it wasn't a sure thing," Steve said, "You should have seen the look on his face when we started tellin' him about boot camp. But Sees Wolf was right, the kid has something in him. He said he'd do whatever it took, and he did."

"What will he do now?"

"When he finishes his boot camp leave he'll go back to Camp Pendleton for eight more weeks of training at the School of Infantry, and then he'll most likely be assigned to a Marine infantry battalion somewhere in the world," Sam replied.

"By the way," Sees Wolf said, "Did you know that Cooley died?"

"No!" Alicia said, "What happened?"

"I don't know, but I think the combination of the alcohol withdrawal and getting' his arm chewed off by a wolf was more than he could recover from. One Doc I talked to said that Cooley was so miserable he couldn't stand it, and he just stopped livin'."

"Yeah," Rebecca said, "The impression I got during our brief but intense encounter was that despite his physical strength he was really a weak person."

"I hate to speak ill of the dead," Sam said, "But I think the world is a little better place with Jake Cooley gone."

"Yep" ... "Yeah" ... "You got that right" ... "For sure"

After a short pause, Sam said, "We're all up to speed, so tell us what you've got, Alicia. Is our mystery man Butch Cassidy?"

"Maybe"

"I was afraid you were gonna say that."

"I know. Let me explain."

"First, I apologize for taking so long with this. A lot of it was out of my control. The first thing I had to do was convince the Bureau of Indian Affairs that our remains were not from an ancient native American. I was able to convince the Bureau's anthropologists in about five minutes. Then it took three weeks to convince all the lawyers."

"Then I had to get permission from Wyoming to bring the remains to Tennessee. There wasn't any problem, it just took a while."

"When I finally got to take a good look at the remains in the lab I knew this was gonna be tricky."

"Why was that?" Jim asked.

"Those remains had been in the ground with only a shroud for protection for over eighty years. They were pretty badly degraded, which was gonna make DNA analysis difficult. Before I spent a lot of time on DNA, I decided to make sure we had at least a possibility of a match.

"I did all the usual measurements and compared them to the descriptions we have of Butch, and there was nothing there that would rule out a possible match.

"Since the skull was whole, the next step was to do a computer reconstruction of the face for comparison to pictures of Butch.

"That went pretty well. The reconstruction definitely looks like it could be Butch to the naked eye. I'll send you all some images so you can see.

"The problem was the only image of Butch that was good enough quality was from the Ft. Worth photo that Jim showed us. Even though that's a good likeness, we have no information about lighting, angles, scale, or anything else.

"The bottom line of the facial analysis was that, yes, this definitely could be Butch Cassidy, but not certainly.

"So, once I knew that this could be Butch, I started looking for DNA.

"As I expected, the genomic or nuclear DNA I was able to find was too degraded for analysis."

"You're gonna have to explain that," Sam said.

"It'd take the rest of the day to tell you the whole story. Let me give you the two cent version.

"There are two types of DNA. Genomic is found in the cell nucleus, so it's also called nuclear DNA. This is the stuff that looks like a spiral staircase that holds all of our genetic information. Mitochondrial DNA lives outside the cell nucleus, and it has nothing to do with our genetics.

"Genomic DNA is what we use when we have blood, fluid, or semen samples from a crime scene. If we can match genomic DNA from a crime scene to a sample from a suspect, we can make a positive ID that will stand up in court.

"Mitochondrial DNA is what is used by all of those programs that tell you what your ancestry is. There's a lot more of it than the genomic so it's more likely that we'll find usable samples. The downside is that it is only passed down the maternal line, and it can seldom be used to make a positive match.

"Even over the phone I can see everyone's eyes glazing over, so I'll skip to the bottom line.

"I was able to extract usable mitochondrial DNA from our remains, and I found a distant cousin of Butch's on the maternal side who was willing to give me a sample of her DNA. I ran the tests to compare the samples, and I found a ninety-three percent match."

"That sounds like a pretty positive match to me," Sam said.

"No, not even close. At ninety-three percent there are tens of thousands of other possibilities."

"The thing that was strange was that it was ninety-three percent. It's usually either ninety-nine point something or much lower. I had to do some research, and the only thing I can find to explain it is that, if this was, in fact, Butch Cassidy, he must have had some sort of genetic mutation that affected his mitochondrial DNA. That modified it just enough that it didn't match."

"So, your conclusion is …?"

"Sam, my conclusion is that I think there's a high likelihood that we have the remains of Butch Cassidy, but there's no way I can say for sure."

"So, what will happen to those remains now?" Sees Wolf asked, "If that poor soul is going to be allowed to move on he must be re-buried."

"Yes, I'd thought of that. I didn't get a lot of cooperation from the family when I was trying to get DNA samples. I think they preferred to let sleeping dogs lie, as it were. But when I explained about the need to reinter the remains they offered to put them in the old cemetery in Circleville, Utah, Butch's hometown. He'll be buried with a stone that says, 'Unknown.'"

"Then he should be able to move on. That's what's important."

"Yes, I agree."

The friends chatted about other things for a while, and then it was time to say goodbye. Before everyone hung up, Steve spoke, "Sam, one last thing."

"Sure, what?"

"The next time you set up a search for us, could we do it without any ghosts?"

"Without ghosts??? Where would be the fun in that?"

CHAPTER EIGHTEEN

Epilogue: Notoniheihii Renewed

*I come into the peace of wild things who do not tax
their lives with forethought of grief...*

Wendell Berry

Buffalo Wheel

A Couple of days later

Three Thirty AM

WINTER WAS SLOW IN COMING THIS YEAR, and the Buffalo Wheel was almost free of snow. Sees Wolf had planned to make a vision quest to the Wheel to see if he could gain some understanding of what had happened there. He thought he would have to wait for spring, but the mild weather allowed him to make a quick trip on the spur of the moment.

This trip would also let him visit with *hooxei* one last time before winter. He believed that he would see *hooxei* in his dreams, but coming here was more real.

267

He was by himself, so he'd had to make some compromises. He had driven to the Bighorn Mountain Lodge and walked to the Wheel from there carrying his Navajo blanket. He arrived at the Wheel just before sundown. It had then taken him a long time to settle his mind.

It may not be snowin', but it's sure cold enough. How can I concentrate when I feel like I'm freezin' to death?

Hooxei waited until it was completely dark before he came and sat next to Sees Wolf. As always, his calm presence and the warmth of his body had helped Sees Wolf to quiet and open his mind.

After almost eight hours of quiet meditation Sees Wolf came to realize that, as it had often been before, he was seeking the wrong vision. He now knew that he was not meant to understand. He must become more like *hooxei* or the dogs and simply learn to accept what had happened and be grateful for the experience.

Once he had come to this acceptance, he began to feel a presence. It was the same presence he had felt here before, but it had changed. With this presence he felt peace, not anguish, and calmness instead of turmoil.

Soon after Sees Wolf had begun to feel the presence *hooxei* stood up and the hairs along his back came erect, and a low rumbling growl started in his chest.

Sees Wolf looked into the darkness and saw a cowboy walking toward him from outside the Wheel. As the vision came closer, he recognized it as the spirit he had seen in the trees where they had found the body. He had not told the others about seeing this spirit. They already had too many strange things to deal with.

Hooxei's nose was working rapidly, and, when he got the cowboy's scent, he relaxed and sat calmly again next to Sees Wolf.

The cowboy stopped a few feet away.

"Mornin'"

"Good morning to you, sir."

"I'm glad you're here. I come to say thanks."

"From where did you come?"

The cowboy looked lost in thought. "I don't know. Somewhere else. Somewhere good. Maybe not the best place, but a good place. I seen your father and grandfather, but just for a short while. I think they're usually someplace else. Maybe a better place. They said they're real proud of you, and they'll see you soon."

"How soon?"

"Didn't say."

"So you're free now?"

"Yep and I don't expect I'll be back again messing up your ceremonies. I'm sorry about that."

"It's all right. You made an honest mistake. You meant well."

"Has it helped?" Me bein' gone, I mean."

"Yes, I think it has. We had more people at the solstice ceremony this year than we've had in a long time, and everyone seemed to go away feelin' good about it. James Raven was there and the next thing we know we got an anonymous gift that's let us put some of our most troubled young people into treatment programs. I think that was Raven's way of sayin' he was sorry for causing all that trouble with his story about the gold."

"Did you know Cooley died?"

"Yeah. I don't know much about Cooley 'cept you don't wanta ever go where he is."

"The police were able to get enough evidence from his home and trailer to put three or four other dealers in jail. That's helped a lot. So, yeah, it looks like things might be getting' a little better."

The cowboy was quiet for a long time. "That's a damn fine lookin' wolf you got there."

"Thank you. He is my brother, and he seems to know you."

"Yeah, I seen him a lot when I was here all them years. The worst part was the loneliness. He'd come and visit me from time to time and then I'd feel good for a little while. Seems like he always showed up when I was feelin' the worst."

"So it was tough for you?"

"Yeah, but I don't think I'd be where I am now if it weren't for that. I did a lot of thinkin' in all those years and maybe I figured some things out. Anyway, I've mostly forgot about it now."

"You think you would have gone to a different place if you hadn't spent those years here?"

"Yeah. I think you can go to a better place if you've learned your lesson so to speak. But I ain't sure. This is all pretty new for me."

"I wonder why *hooxei* took so long to show me where you were?"

"I don't know, but I think it had somethin' to do with the dogs. The dogs could see me too, you know, like you could. But it was different with the dogs and your wolf. It was like they understood. One thing I've learned is that animals understand a lot more than we do about the stuff that really matters."

"Are there animals where you are?"

"Sure, all kinds of animals, but they mostly keep to themselves. 'Cept for the dogs, of course. There's dogs ev'ry where. All the dogs you ever knew and a million more besides. I don't think the dogs have a place. I think they can go to all the places 'cept maybe the bad places."

"What will happen now?"

"I'll be sayin' Adios' here soon and goin' away for good. I don't expect you'll be bothered by no more spirits for a while."

"I hope I'll still have *hooxei*."

"Oh yeah. Your wolf is somethin' … special. He ain't exactly a spirit. He's somethin' more. That's all I know about it."

"I'm glad that you're in a good place, and I'm glad you came to talk to me. Thank you."

"Yeah, I'm glad, too.'

"So long, Sees Wolf."

"Goodbye, Butch."

Joe Jennings

AUTHOR Q AND A

Q: Is the Buffalo Wheel real? Did Butch Cassidy and the Sundance Kid really come back from South America? How much of the book is factual?

A: The Buffalo Wheel is known to non-native people as the Medicine Wheel. It is a National Historic Landmark located on Medicine Mountain off of route 14A in Big Horn County, Wyoming. The discussion in the book of the Buffalo Wheel is as factual as I could make it — except for the ghost. There is strong evidence that Butch did come back and visited his family in Utah as described in the book. Less is known about Sundance. As Jim did in my story, I would recommend Bill Bentenson's, *Butch Cassidy, My Uncle*, for anyone who wants to know more about Butch and the Wild Bunch. I hope that reading *Ghosts of the Buffalo Wheel* has inspired you to learn more about this period in American history. Then you can go back and decide for your self which parts are real and which parts are fiction.

The *Hoofprints of the Past Museum* in Kaycee, Wyoming that is mentioned in the book is also real and is well worth a visit for anyone who wants to learn about the old West in the heyday of the cowboy.

As for the dogs, pretty much everything I have the dogs do in the story are things that trained search and rescue dogs can do.

Q: Do you believe in ghosts and the afterlife?

A: Let's say that I don't not believe. I tend to agree with Hamlet that there are more things in heaven and earth than are dreamt of in our philosophies (or sciences). I take Hamlet to mean that we know a lot less about our world and the universe than we think we do. This turns out to be a very convenient philosophy for a novelist to have.

Q: What's next? Will Gunny be back?

A: As you know, Gunny's getting kinda old. I don't think he'll be back as a search dog unless I decide to do prequel. My next project is a young adult book tentatively titled *The Very First Dog*. There's a good chance that Gunny will be the narrator.

Thanks for reading *Ghosts of the Buffalo Wheel*. I hope you found it to be both entertaining and educational. If you haven't read *Ghosts of Iwo Jima* — well, why the heck not?

Joe

Joe Jennings

80672060R00171

Made in the USA
San Bernardino, CA
29 June 2018